LOST IN DREAMS

LOST IN DREAMS

DESTINED FOR DREAMS, BOOK 1

by

GINNA MORAN

SUNNY PALMS PRESS

For those who believed in my dreams.

1

A TERRIBLE HOST

NADIA

THE ROOM SPINS, sending my stomach lurching. I feel so sick from hunger I can barely stand. Gripping the small wooden table in the hallway, I blink until my vision restores.

My chest tightens, and I drag my feet forward. The lobby to the dormitory is empty this time of night, and the only light in the room glows from a flat screen TV that was accidentally left on.

I keep my feet moving. If I stay out here any longer, I won't make it back to my room at all. I cross through the lobby, and a glass door slides open into another hallway. The low ceiling does nothing for the air flow in the stuffy corridor.

"Twenty more feet," I say out loud. "Keep walking. You can make it. You're not hungry. You're not hungry. You're not hungry." I chant the words over and over like an anthem, but it doesn't help.

I'm starving.

I stop at my closed door and touch my hand to the doorknob. I don't twist to open it but instead turn to face the closed door behind me. A small whiteboard is nailed to the wooden door with a red heart and the name Alyssa written across the heart in black block letters. *Just go in quietly. Alyssa said you could use her anytime you needed.*

I wish Alyssa never made the offer in the first place. She doesn't understand what I'll do to her. She's going to despise me for it. I hate I let my hunger get so out of control that I'm outside my best friend's dorm, dying to give her nightmares. Creating nightmares is my sustenance.

I run my finger along the door, staring at my plaster-white fingers, and count to myself. Dark purple veins pulse on my wrist, nearly the same shade as the color of my long nails. I haven't been outside in the daylight in weeks, and it shows. I'm bound to the night the longer I resist. But it's okay—I love the night. *You're lying.*

The door swings open.

A small nightlight shines from below Alyssa's desk and casts shadows across the wall and her bed. She doesn't stir when I click the door shut.

I swallow hard. Alyssa hides under her dark brown comforter. A stack of books climbs toward the ceiling next to a small reading lamp on her night table. Hundreds of sketches hang from her walls, making it an art piece in itself. The sketches are so full of detail and accuracy that the drawings could be mistaken for black and white photos.

I glide across the room, my feet above the threadbare carpet without actually touching the floor, and run my fingers over a drawing of a moon setting on water. Below the glittering path of moonlight, a body lies in the sand and a giant fishtail cuts through the waves. It's surreal and magical, and I'm not sure if it was a vision or her imagination.

I plant my boots on the carpet. I'd give anything to leave the Creature Council's compound. If my father didn't work here, I'd go somewhere else far from this place. But, he'd never let me leave. It's his way of protecting me. He doesn't want to lose me like he lost my mother. The images Alyssa sketches will always be of faraway places to enjoy on paper. Places I'll only ever see in dreams.

I look away from the wall. I can't torture myself anymore with ideas of the outside world. This, standing in Alyssa's room while she sleeps, is my world. I just wish I didn't hate it so much.

Kneeling next to Alyssa's bed, I tuck my white hair behind my ears. It's lost all its pigmentation during my failed attempt at a hunger strike. When I don't create nightmares, it reveals me as the monster I am. I'm frightening enough at the moment that everyone in the compound is uneasy around me. Once I eat, I'll look more human again.

I pull back the dark brown comforter just enough to see Alyssa's gorgeous red hair sprawling over her pillow. She looks as beautiful asleep as she does awake, so alive and full of life compared to me, with my withered, stringy hair and gaunt figure. *You'll look less like a nightmare inflictor soon.*

But I am a nightmare inflictor—just like my father.

I run my hands over Alyssa's hair and press my thumbs to her temples and rest my fingers on her scalp. My vision fades despite my open eyes. My whole body trembles as I force my way into her head.

I manifest myself into Alyssa's dream world, ignoring the sudden falling sensation from sneaking into her dream. Gray fog swirls around me, and I wave my hand, blowing it away. As it clears, my eyes widen in wonder. Dreams are always so magnificent and breathtaking. I wish I could dream on my own.

I stand in the center of a vibrant valley speckled with red, yellow, and orange poppies. A crystalline waterfall rushes over a black rock cliff and into a translucent lake. I glide to the pebbly shoreline and peer at glittering silver fish swimming with a gracefulness I wish I had.

Stop messing around.

I pull my hands from my pockets. This is the part I love and hate the most. It's why I'm called a nightmare inflictor—because I ruin the best dreams. I destroy them and devour them to survive on like a human eats food.

I shift and force my feet to touch the ground. I'm no longer an observer to Alyssa's dream but a participant, and by the time I'm through, she'll regret her offer. Even the toughest people can be frightened by their dreams.

My cracked lips curve into a smile. I taste the sweet chocolate flavor dripping onto my tongue just from breathing the air. Every dream tastes differently, but they're all mouthwatering and fulfilling. The deep, insatiable hunger starts to subside the moment I run my hand over the crystal clear lake.

The water churns and darkens and the fish pop up to the surface. Their dead bodies smell rancid, and I turn away toward the field of poppies.

Each step I take leaves an oily footprint that seeps into the vibrant green grass, killing it. I bend over and tap the blossoming flowers and they shrivel up and disintegrate. Everything I touch rots and decays, turning this beautiful paradise into a hellish place fit for monsters like me.

Laughter echoes through the air, and I jerk my head in its direction. I crave the very noise I'm hearing and it cuts short, leaving me in deafening silence. I stomp up the hillside and smile at the plant life dying around me. The azure sky darkens as gray clouds roll in and thunder booms. I lick my lips, sensing a tinge of fear coursing through the air. I breathe deeply, sucking it into my soul.

"We have to run for cover, love," a deep, masculine voice says.

Reaching the top of the hill, I peer into a forest of tall redwood trees. The trees reach higher than the hill I'm standing on and yet I didn't see them from the valley. *Stop getting distracted. Find the dreamer and leave.*

I follow the voices deep into the forest. My boots crunch

on dried leaves, turning them to mush. My hands smack against every reddish-brown tree trunk I pass, and they dry and crack. Dead leaves rain down like I'm standing amid a raging storm.

Pausing, I lean against a dying tree trunk wider than a car and stare through the thick greenery at a couple sitting on a red blanket. Between them lies a wooden picnic basket with a baguette protruding from it. The boy drops a green glass bottle, and it clatters to the ground, shattering into a million sparkling green pieces. His mouth gapes open, but he doesn't scream. Instead, he reaches over and picks up the neck of the broken bottle and points it at me.

I can't help smiling at his bravery.

He jumps to his feet and steps in front of Alyssa, who doesn't move. She stares at me without emotion. In this dream world, I'm not Nadia Petrov. I'm Alyssa's worst nightmare.

I stop ten feet away and cock my head to the side.

Alyssa's dream boy is perfect. His dark brown hair, cut short on the sides and styled neatly with hair gel, matches his almond shaped, coffee brown eyes. He glares at me, his jaw twitching, twisting his mouth into a scowl. He's tall, over six feet, and tan from hours outside.

The veins in his muscular arms swell as he squeezes the broken bottle, and he rolls his shoulders, preparing for a fight he can't win. Alyssa stares between us and reaches out to touch the boy's leg. He turns his head to glance over his shoulder and then shifts back to me.

I don't move.

Alyssa clears her throat. "You should leave, Lucas." She

stands and grabs his shoulder.

He tenses. "I'm not leaving you. Can't you see you're in danger?"

She smiles softly. "You're mistaken, babe. It's not me he's after."

Alyssa is afraid of someone—a man. Without mirrors to see myself in the dream world, I don't know who I appear to be, but since they didn't run away screaming, I'm guessing I'm not a hideous monster. Alyssa isn't afraid of monsters—she's terrified of a man. *I wonder who...*

Before he can question her, I glide over the dried leaves and cup his face in my hands. He explodes into a cloud of black dust, and I suck in breath after breath of his essence.

My hunger dissipates, leaving me facing Alyssa. She doesn't run but just stands there with tears gleaming in her green eyes. Her red hair blows in a breeze, and she stares at the ground where remnants of her dream boy lie mixed with rotting leaves.

She covers her mouth with her hand. "You killed him."

My mouth drops open. Things shine clearly now that I'm not starving, and a horrible pit settles in my stomach. I can't believe I'm standing here, destroying Alyssa's dream. I need to leave, and the only way out is to finish off the dreamer and consume the nightmare.

I cup her face.

Tears spill from her vibrant eyes, and her mouth hangs open in a silent scream. She drops to her knees and falls over, pressing her face to the muddy ground. Shining light radiates from her, and I inhale the rest of her nightmare as the dream world around me crumbles.

My eyes snap open, my stomach heaving. I'm back in Alyssa's room away from the nightmare. She tosses and turns under her comforter, thrashing from the terror I instilled in her mind. I'm already gone and opening the door to my room before she wakes up.

I feel alive, full, and normal again. I stare at my hands. The color returns and my skin glows with flush. Sitting on the edge of my bed, I resist looking in the mirror on my vanity table because I don't know how long I'll look like myself. I don't know when I'll create another nightmare.

Soon. I never want to starve myself again.

HUNTER

"You're a terrible host," I say. *"The least you can do is take me somewhere fun or hold something more interesting than your diary in front of your face."*

"Shut up," Jacqueline thinks. She wouldn't dare speak out loud. Not to me. It would make her look as crazy as she really is, and she wouldn't stand for it.

"Oh, wouldn't you love it if I shut up and went away? Well, Jackie, guess what? You're stuck with me until you release me back into my body."

"Don't call me Jackie. And Hunter, you know what the deal was. I took you as collateral to make sure Dr. Sullivan holds up her end of the bargain. I want my freedom as much as you do. You're lucky I let them keep your body at all."

My mom agreed to spare this monster her life if she would conspire against her own kind and obtain information about a legendary council made up of supernatural creatures the Human Preservation Agency's board members want to destroy. To prove to Jacqueline she wouldn't harm her, my mom let her take my soul as collateral so Jacqueline would trust her. Funny, though. I'd never trust a woman who traded her own son for some stupid information that may not even be helpful to her.

"Why did you, anyway?" I ask. I'm as good as dead without a body. Jacqueline could've just taken me whole as her prisoner. Instead, we're forced to share space in her head.

Jacqueline stares at her pink fingernails. "It's complicated. I expected you to be different, more like your mother. I didn't expect you to be so...pure."

If I had a body, I'd frown. *"I'm insulted. What makes you think I'm pure?"*

"Enough with the questions."

I sigh. *"I wouldn't have so many if you'd tell me what you're going to do with me."*

Jacqueline throws her journal at the wall, and it clatters to the floor. "Hunter Sullivan! If you don't shut up right now, I will make you." Jacqueline's melodious voice echoes through the small room.

Standing up, she strolls across the dirty carpet to a dusty mirror on the wall. She wipes it with the sleeve of her shirt and stares at herself. Her light purple eyes glow against the golden brown of her skin. The color of her irises shift for a split second, and it's like I can see myself in her eyes. They're not the windows to her soul but mine.

"Please, don't send me away," I say.

I regret aggravating her. When she doesn't want me around, she shoves me into a dark void in her mind. It's awful not knowing which way is up and being blind and deaf. I feel like I'm dying every time she does it and then it's like I don't exist at all.

Someone knocks on the door and she turns toward it. "I'm sorry, Hunter. You know the rules."

"Please, I'll be quiet."

"The answer is no."

"Jackie, don't—"

She closes her eyes, and I'm blind to the world again, alone, and in pitch blackness. I want to die.

2

THE OUTSIDE WORLD

HUNTER

"COME BACK, HUNTER."

I've lost track of time after counting to three thousand, six hundred and two seconds. Sometimes, I shut my mind down and envision being somewhere else. I may not have a body, but I can still imagine things. It's all I have left

"Just release me. Death would be better than this," I say.

"Oh, Hunter, you don't mean it. If you did, you would've died already."

"What do you mean?"

"I've anchored you to life through me. You're not a prisoner. You can leave whenever you want."

Really? She is delusional if she doesn't think I'm her captive. And the choices I have? They're crap. Die or hang out in her head with no control over anything. It's like I'm watching TV through her eyes, stuck on a channel I hate. Torture.

"Where would I go? I don't see my body anywhere." My sharp tone makes her sigh. *"You know you're a dead girl if I ever get out of here."*

"I would've been dead if I didn't take you, so what's the difference? I had nothing to lose."

Bad things happen when someone feels they're out of options. I know this because I remember how fragile Jacqueline looked at the termination facility. She was hunkered in a corner, surrounded by two agents, both from the Special Abilities Task Force, and she was about to die. Fortunately for her, my mom had other plans. Unfortunately for me, I was with her and Jacqueline wanted someone my mom would want to see alive again.

"Do you even feel slightly guilty?"

"Not really."

"No wonder the board wants to eradicate the world of supers. You are all really monsters."

"I feel the same about you, Hunter."

NADIA

I sit in the pale morning sunlight. The emerald grass grows greener than I remember, vibrant against the azure sky full of puffy white clouds. A forest nymph, dressed in a silky green gown, tends to the large garden. Her sunflower yellow hair is pulled into a ponytail and tied with a vine, and I wonder if she'd help me manage my hair. Nymphs are some of the most beautiful creatures I've ever seen, and they're good at what they do. This one manipulates nature and can encourage any plant to grow at any time. Our gardens always flourish in her care. *Why couldn't I have been born a nymph?*

"Nadia," a musical voice calls. It's the last person I want to see.

I don't turn or acknowledge Alyssa. I'm embarrassed by my actions and wish I could crawl into a hole and hide—maybe a grave would be more suitable. A shadow blocks the sun, and I stiffen. Alyssa isn't going to leave me alone. She never has. Besides my father, she's the only other person in the world I'd call family.

"Why are you ignoring me?" she asks.

I tilt my head up and stare at her upside down. "Oh, hey, Lys. I didn't hear you. What's up?"

She plops down next to me. "You're a terrible liar."

I blush. Nothing gets by a seer. "Why are you even asking me? You know why."

She blows her blazing red hair out of her face. "Because you're my best friend, and I'm not all knowing. Things can be interpreted wrong."

My gaze shifts to the forest nymph. She kneels in the dirt and lowers her head until it's an inch from the ground and whispers something. I press my lips together and try to gather my thoughts. I hate talking about this. I *hate* it.

"I—I'm sorry." It's the best I can do.

Alyssa arches her brows. Her green eyes shine in the sunlight, like two glittering gemstones, and she smiles. "Don't ever apologize to me. I was worried about you."

"Don't be. I know what I'm doing." It's always like Alyssa to check in on me and see how I'm doing, especially when my father is out on business. She's been this way since she found my father, and he brought her here over a year ago. She's my age, seventeen, but you'd think she was going on thirty.

She rests her hand on my knee. "You were starving yourself."

I meet her gaze. "I was not." *Please, let it go.* "I'm fine, really. I was just experimenting."

I reach out and rest my hand on hers. She twists her lips to the side, and I expect her to argue some more, but instead she nods. She turns away and stares at the forest nymph for a few seconds before saying, "There are a lot worse things you could be."

I crinkle my nose. "I live on terrorizing people in their sleep. How can I be any worse? You know it's going to be hard for me to resist you now, right? Your dream was amazing." I swallow, my mouth watering at the memory. My cheeks flush, and I shift uncomfortably. *Control yourself.*

Alyssa smirks. "It really was terrifying. Maybe next time try not killing Lucas."

I cringe. If I didn't know her, I'd think she was unaffected by the situation, but the way she stiffened when I touched her assures me that she really is bothered by the nightmare I created for her. I don't blame her, though. If I continue, she'll hate me for it. A person can only go so long, dreaming about the death of someone they care about, before it affects them in real life.

"You knew what to expect, Lys." I push my blond hair from my eyes.

She stares at the sky. "I was kidding. It's not that big of a deal. I see a lot more horrible things in my visions. Lighten up, Nadia. You're not a monster."

She'll never understand. Now that I fed from her dreams, I won't be able to stop unless I move on to someone else. Her dreams will call to me. They awakened the monster within me and its hunger will consume me until I let it have what it wants. It's how nightmare inflictors choose their victims. It's easiest to prey on the people closest to us; the people that allow us in.

"How can you say that after last night?" I ask. "Who did I appear as anyway?"

"My Uncle Drew."

I don't ask why her uncle would be her worst nightmare, and she doesn't explain either. Alyssa doesn't talk about what her life was like before coming here. All I know is she ran away from home and convinced my father to bring her here. She knew everything—who the council was, what it did— everything. My father asked the council to let her stay and the compound has been her sanctuary since.

I push to my feet and offer Alyssa my hand. I can't sit here and pretend what we experienced together was okay. "Want to get out of here?" I ask after a minute. It's been a while since I've been able to stand the sun. I need to take advantage of it while it lasts.

Alyssa beams a smile. "Are you serious? You never want to

leave.”

I shrug. “I guess not being confined inside during the day does something to you. Think we can make it?”

She takes my hand. “Of course. You know I always see everything coming.”

HUNTER

“Where are we going?” I ask.

“None of your business. You’ll find out soon enough.”

Being stuck in Jacqueline’s head is pure torture. I miss doing simple things like blinking and glaring. I imagine I’m doing them, but it’s not the same. I never get over the disappointment when Jacqueline doesn’t move her arm when I imagine I’m moving mine.

“A little hint?”

“Somewhere far enough that I have to take a train. Now, be quiet. I’ll let you stay around if you behave.”

I’m surprised she’s not pushing me into the void. I’m relieved, too. For once I’ll get to see and hear real people instead of only being let out when we’re alone in the abandoned apartment.

“You have a deal. You won’t even know I’m here.”

“I doubt it.”

NADIA

We sneak out the back gate of the compound. It’s mostly used by the forest nymphs going back to the forest. A spelled talisman opens the gate, and since there’s always one available, we don’t have a problem getting out.

“I hid my car not far from here,” Alyssa says.

I scrunch my brows. "You drive?"

"I can teach you. Maybe your father will let you get your license since you'll be eighteen in a few months."

Nine months and two days to be exact.

I laugh. The thought of getting a license is ridiculous. The outside world isn't safe for people like me. The council created the compound to keep us safe from the Human Preservation Agency. The HPA would do anything to destroy us. My father brought me to the compound because an agent from the HPA murdered my mother. Plus, I'd never choose to leave the compound alone even though I'd love to. I imagine I may be braver when I'm a legal adult. I hope I am.

When we reach the car, Alyssa removes a camouflaged car cover, revealing a silver Corolla. Its paint looks brand new, and it's well taken care of. Even the tires gleam like they're coated in tire shine.

"Where did you get a car anyway?" I run my fingers along the smooth paint.

"I've had it. Your father suggested I hide it if I didn't want to turn it in as communal property. It's my most expensive possession."

I knit my brows. This is the kind of thing best friends tell you about. "You know you can trust me with your secrets."

Alyssa unlocks the doors. "You're mad I didn't tell you."

I open the door and get in. "A little."

"I'm sorry. It just never came up. You've never wanted to sneak out before. I didn't think it mattered."

I sigh. It doesn't really matter. We don't talk about a lot of things, especially things from our past, and I get it. I was just taken by surprise. "It doesn't. I'm overreacting."

Alyssa smiles and starts the engine. "I'll make it up to you. I know this great little place in the city to go to. It's safe. You'll love it."

3

A STRANGE FEELING

NADIA

MY ARM HAIRS rise when we pass a small cemetery. I've only ever seen them in movies because the council cremates the bodies that don't take care of themselves. Any evidence of a creature's existence can't be left behind.

I almost ask Alyssa to stop but bite my tongue because visiting a graveyard is a strange request. I stare out the window at the different shapes and sizes of the headstones and turn away when I meet the eyes of a woman standing at the fence with a bouquet of white lilies. I wonder if my mother is buried somewhere since she was human. It'd be nice to have a place to visit her.

Tears rim my eyes. It's been too long since I've thought about my mother. It's an unspoken rule between my father and I that we don't bring up the past. We can't change it, so we just have to keep going forward.

"We can stop there on the way back if you like." Alyssa messes with the dial on the radio until a rock band blasts through the speakers. She turns the volume down a notch and cracks her window to let in fresh air.

I smile gratefully at her, then turn away. "Where are we going?" I tap my fingers on the arm rest.

Alyssa smiles. "It's a surprise, but there are lots of people. Hot boys, too. Don't worry. You'll fit in."

My chest tightens from excitement and anxiety. I don't have any other friends at the compound, and I've never been on a date either—not that my father would allow me to go on one anyway. Now that I have some freedom, I don't know how to feel. What if my nightmare inflicting side starts to show? How can anyone like a monster?

"Maybe we should go back," I say after a minute. I don't really want to, but meeting new people is scary, especially with how unsafe it is outside the compound. It's dangerous not knowing people's intentions, and I'll have to be even more guarded.

Alyssa changes lanes as we drive into the city. "You don't really want to go back."

"What if something bad happens?"

"It won't. I can see things coming, remember?" Alyssa has a point. While her visions aren't always concrete, they can show her how things play out. She can keep us safe.

I glance out the window. Alyssa slows down because of heavy traffic and then merges into the right lane and turns onto a narrow one way street.

I grip the dashboard, afraid of getting trapped on this street with nowhere to go, but then the street connects to a wide alley that turns into a small, private residential parking structure. A security guard hands Alyssa a permit, and she tosses it on the dashboard and maneuvers through the parking structure until we reach the middle level.

I follow Alyssa out of the car. She loops her arm through mine, pulling me to a stairwell in the corner, ignoring the elevator to our left. She tugs the door open, and I step in behind her. Our footsteps echo off the concrete walls as we climb up two flights of stairs and through another door that leads into a spacious lobby.

Plush black couches sit around a coffee table on a large red and gold area rug. Modern, black-framed portraits of people I don't recognize line the walls, and on the opposite side is a set of opaque double doors.

Alyssa guides me across the lobby and waves at the camera stationed in the corner of the ceiling. The door clicks and automatically swings open into a narrow hallway with dark wooden floors.

At the end of the corridor, a troll leans against the wall with a built-in touch-screen computer. His short, brown hair is styled to the side and blue-framed glasses sit low on his thin nose as he reads a magazine. The sleeves of his green dress shirt are rolled up to his elbows and his dark-washed jeans hang a little too long on his short stature.

He looks up and tucks the magazine under his arm. His brown eyes reflect green in the dim lighting, and he offers his hand out to Alyssa. "You've brought a friend, doll face," the troll says, looking me up and down.

She kisses the man's cheek. "This is Nadia, Cian. I've told you about her, remember?"

He studies my face for a moment. "You're lovelier than I imagined."

I offer my hand, and he takes it. He kisses my knuckles, his lips lingering, and I gently tug my hand away. Trolls can be possessive if you give them the chance.

"It's nice to meet you." I step back to put distance between us. "This is my first time away from—"

Alyssa bumps my shoulder. "Home," she says, finishing my sentence. "Nadia has never been to the city before."

I was going to say that it was my first time away from the compound in a long time, but I'm glad Alyssa intervened. I almost blew our cover. No one needs to know where we came from. It'd get back to the council one way or another.

Cian raises his eyebrows. "You're going to enjoy it here. All members are welcome."

I nod, and he opens the door.

Alyssa touches Cian's arm before leading me into a dimly lit club. Without windows to allow in sunlight, the club is the perfect place for me. Music pulses through the air, making it hard to hear anything, and colorful lights dance across the walls.

Black leather booths line the perimeter and a few tables scatter around a small dance floor.

A million scents thicken the air, and a door behind an impressive bar swings open, revealing a brightly lit kitchen. The room is packed with patrons, and it's hard to tell what everyone is. People laugh and sway to the music, and some talk in small clusters, enjoying their time. No one even turns to stare at me. My ability makes a lot of people at the compound uncomfortable, because it doesn't discriminate. All dreams are the same to me so anyone is susceptible.

Alyssa leans into me. "I see an open booth in the corner," she says, nearly pressing her lips to my ear.

I trail behind her to get through the throng of people dancing. Alyssa slides in before me, and I scoot in on the other side. A candle flickers in a blue crystal jar in the middle of the table, reflecting cool light over everything.

A girl in a tight black dress appears at our table. Her short, black hair shines blue in the candlelight. Her amber eyes crinkle at the corners, and her nose twitches when she beams a perfectly straight smile before setting two goblets filled with a red elixir on the table.

Alyssa raises her eyebrows. "I hope these are from Lucas, Maddie."

I shift in my seat and peer around the room to see if there's a boy staring in our direction, but I don't notice anyone. "*The* Lucas?" I ask, smiling at Alyssa.

Maddie rests her elbows on the table. "He's near the door. Styled brown hair, brooding dark eyes, hot. He's the one in the blue hoodie and jeans." Lucas is identical to his dream persona, and I blink a few times to hide my surprise. Maddie winks before sauntering away.

I reach out and grab Alyssa's hand. "I think we should dance."

Alyssa smirks and slides from the booth, offering me her hand. I laugh when she dances around me as we make our way onto the crowded dance floor. We sway to the upbeat tempo, and I giggle when she twirls me around.

I peer toward the door to see if Alyssa's dream boy is watching and notice a girl with dark, curly hair and the most dazzling lavender eyes staring at me. A chill runs up my spine, though she turns away when my gaze meets hers.

Alyssa grabs my arm, startling me. "We have to leave. Now."

I don't hesitate and take Alyssa's hand. She pushes through the crowd and instead of guiding me to the front entrance, she pulls me behind the bar and toward the kitchen.

"Someone's coming through the front," she says. "This is a better way out."

HUNTER

If I wasn't trapped in Jacqueline's head, I'd be terrified to be in this club. I don't recognize half the supers, and it freaks me out. The room is too dark and the music is too loud to even hear someone scream. I almost want to be in the void instead of watching everything through Jacqueline's eyes, but I'd never tell her that.

We sit in a booth near the entrance with our back to the

dark red painted wall. It gives me a view of the entire club. I watch through Jacqueline's eyes as a pretty girl struts onto the dance floor. Her pale blond hair absorbs the colors shining around her, and she sways her hips to the beat of the music.

Jacqueline doesn't take her eyes off the girl. A flash of light from the kitchen shines over the girl, and I notice her indigo eyes shift to a much paler blue, like the color drains from them. Her pale pink lips pout when she doesn't smile. I can't stop myself from wanting to talk to her. But, that's impossible considering the Jacqueline situation and because she's a super. For all I know, she could be a man-eater.

"Are you sure it won't be any trouble?" Jacqueline asks.

A man I recognize as a leshy—a tree spirit embodied in human form—sits across from us. His thick, gray hair is tied with a tree branch, and he hasn't done a good job at hiding his bark-like skin. Only half of one of his arms looks like human flesh instead of the bark-like texture of his true form. While you'd think a tree spirit would be friendly, leshies are not, and after a few fatal incidents at the lab, the board made sure we all knew about these monsters.

"I can get you in right away if everything checks out. A member from the Creature Council will meet us here to fill out the paperwork."

"*What is that girl?*" I ask, despite Jacqueline's directions to stay quiet.

"Not now," she thinks.

Jacqueline glances where the girl was dancing. Disappointment washes over me as I watch her run into the kitchen with a red-haired girl. It's a strange feeling. I know better than to be attracted to a super, but I can't stop myself. I hope she'll come back so I can convince Jacqueline to talk to her, but I doubt it. It's not like she'll ever know I exist. I'm nobody inside Jacqueline's body. I'll probably never be somebody again.

NADIA

My heart races as I speed after Alyssa. I'm starting to feel sluggish since I'm still recuperating from my hunger strike and exerting myself isn't helping much. She thrusts her arm out near the exit and stops me in my tracks.

I clutch the wall and gasp. "What did you see?"

"A council member entering the club. If we get caught here, we'll lose all privileges for a year," she says.

I frown. I hate how the council runs things. They have pretty harsh punishments for stupid little things. They're even harder on younger people. I'm guessing so we learn from the start to respect their authority, which I have no choice to because my father works for the council. I'm stuck. I can't really avoid punishment for breaking the rules, no matter how lame I think they are.

"You saw us getting caught?"

"That's why we're standing in the kitchen. I played the different scenarios in my head, and if we try to leave now, we'll get caught in the parking garage. If we stay in the club, we'll get caught there."

"But we don't get caught in the kitchen?"

She shakes her head. "Don't worry. I know what I'm doing."

It's easy for her to say since she's the one who predicts the future. I, on the other hand, can see a hundred things going wrong because the future is never set in stone and a single decision can mess it all up in a second.

"I hope so." For being stuck in the kitchen, waiting for Alyssa to tell me what to do, I'm not as worried as I thought I'd be. I'm still pumped up from the music and dancing.

Alyssa laughs. "Me too."

I grin and she taps her fingers on the door. Her eyes glass over, and she loses focus for a second before pulling herself together. She groans and plops down on the floor, tucking her feet under her.

"What are you doing?"

She sighs. "It's going to be a while."

HUNTER

Jacqueline stares at her hands, delicately folded in her lap, before shifting her head up to look into the eyes of a bearded man. He looks two hundred years old with deep wrinkles that cut through his suntanned face. His thick, scraggly eyebrows shade his beady brown eyes and his big, round nose is as wide as his narrow mouth covered by a graying mustache.

"I've heard the council can provide shelter and safety. I'm just so tired of being on the run. It wasn't so bad when my brother was alive, but the agents—" Jacqueline pauses and waves her hand in front of her face. She takes a deep breath. "The HPA agents killed him. A reaper just ripped his soul from his body right in front of my eyes." Her voice cracks, and I sigh loudly.

"Really, Jackie? You just described what you did to me, you soul snatcher," I say.

Jacqueline groans in her mind at me. "Shut up, Hunter. It's the truth. How do you think I ended up at the facility in the first place? Your agents killed my brother to get to me. I may have stolen your soul, but at least I didn't kill you. I'm a redeemer—a sin-eater. I save people from themselves."

"I don't feel redeemed. I feel like crap," I say. I don't believe Jacqueline. I've done nothing remotely wrong. I didn't need to be saved.

"I couldn't redeem you. Whenever I take a soul, I can see the soul's worst offenses—some people call them sins—and you've never done anything wrong. Like I said before, your soul is pure. Now you're my punishment for taking a pure soul. I'm stuck with you until you either decide to free yourself and die at your own freewill or if I return to the HPA and put you back in your body." Jacqueline's voice echoes around me.

My imprisonment is some sick and twisted punishment for Jacqueline's mistake. She was hoping for an impure soul that she could have control over and redeem whenever she wanted, but got me instead. The board was right about her. She's a monster. She was planning to eventually kill me. I'm not giving her the satisfaction now. I refuse to die. *"Why don't you go back to the HPA then and ask for someone else?"*

"Stop being ridiculous. You know I can't return empty handed. Now please, Hunter. Let me talk to Mr. Soto."

"...you'll have to earn your keep. There are lots of responsibilities to choose from. Everyone always finds something they love," Mr. Soto says. I missed the beginning of his speech, and I'm sure Jacqueline did, too.

Jacqueline clears her throat. "I'm not looking for a hand out. Just somewhere safe where I can settle down. The world is so weary these days. I can't handle it anymore." Jacqueline rubs her cheek.

"That, I understand, Ms. Matthews."

"Call me Jacqueline."

Mr. Soto reaches out his wrinkled fingers and touches Jacqueline's smooth hand. The gesture is fatherly, and it's obvious Jacqueline won the old guy over. No one stands a chance against her fragile demeanor. Everyone wants to protect her. It should be their own backs they should be looking out for.

"Well, Jacqueline, if you're ready, I think I can get you an appointment in the morning with the rest of the council. We have guest apartments you're welcome to stay in until you're issued permanent residency."

"Yes!" she yells in her mind.

"Calm down, Jackie," I say. *"It's not like we won the lottery. There was never a moment Mr. Soto wasn't going to let us in."*

"You're right, Hunter, but it feels great that it was so easy. And don't be such a downer, if I can win more over, maybe, just maybe, I'll earn my freedom with the board and I'll be nice enough to return you to your body if they still have it," she thinks.

Unlike Mr. Soto, I'm not easily persuaded. Jacqueline is a survivor. I doubt she is brave enough to return me to my body once she gives up the council's secrets. While her original plan to kill me backfired, she can now use me as leverage against my mom. I'm her backup plan. I should accept this small glimmer of hope, but the reality is that I'm stuck here. This is my life now.

Mr. Soto slides from the booth and offers Jacqueline his hand to help her up. The world shifts as she stands, and she glances once more around the room. I take the opportunity to search for the pretty girl I saw enter the kitchen, but she's not here. I don't know why I bother feeling anymore. I'll always be left disappointed.

Jacqueline picks up her small suitcase from underneath the table, and Mr. Soto takes it from her. He walks ahead of us to the door, where a short bouncer stands guard, and we exit the club.

"The compound is about thirty minutes north of here. Is there anywhere you'd like to stop before we head out? We only take people out twice a month for shopping and the next time isn't for another week," Mr. Soto says, opening the door to the stairwell.

"I have everything I need," Jacqueline says. "Let's go home."

"Ha, ha, ha. Home," I mutter to her. *"More like a place to gather information to gain amnesty from the board so you can make a home wherever you want."*

"Don't ruin this," she thinks to me. "If I fail, this really will be our new home."

Great. I'm going to be stuck with Jacqueline until I die.

4

NOT A DREAM

HUNTER

THE LOCATION OF the Creature Council's headquarters feels like it's worlds away from the city. The road to the compound didn't have road markers, and if I still had my body, I would've had a heart attack when Mr. Soto sped into a tangle of trees going at least thirty miles per hour. It was magical and frightening how the trees swallowed the car and threw us onto a paved road in the middle of a forest.

It would take a lot of heavy machinery to cut through the trees and greenery to find this road, and even then, I doubt the trees would let anyone in. I've never seen anything like it. No wonder the HPA facilities are all made of cement, metal, and bulletproof glass. Supers can easily turn nature against us.

A woman in a short blue dress leans against the chain-link fence surrounding the headquarters. Her silver hair is pulled into two buns and adorned with white lilies. She's barefoot and unarmed, which is an unexpected sight for me since the HPA agents all wear standard issued black pants, shirts, and boots along with a weaponry belt. This woman is the most non-threatening security guard I've ever laid eyes on. It must mean she's deadly.

The woman waves, and Mr. Soto nods to her before driving closer to the opening gate. Up ahead looms a four-story industrial building with reflective windows and a huge patio in front with small umbrella tables. Smaller one and two story buildings surround it like miniature replicas. I count five that I can see and I bet a few more buildings hide behind it.

Sprawling green lawns fill the space around the buildings. To the right of the buildings are three giant vegetable gardens and a greenhouse. Fruit trees grow along the perimeter, while different kinds of flowers scatter throughout the property in colorful bursts. Beyond the fence lies nothing but a dense forest. This is more than some top secret headquarters; it's a safe paradise for supers. No wonder Jacqueline agreed to come here.

"It's better than I imagined," she thinks.

"I definitely didn't expect this. Why did you even consider a deal with my mom? You could live here forever," I say.

"First of all, if I didn't make some sort of deal, your mother would've killed me. Second, while this place looks amazing, I don't want to stay hidden in some small creature-made village. I need my freedom. I couldn't refuse amnesty from the board. They're who I fear the most."

"Won't the supers turn against you?"

"They'll be more worried about themselves than me by that point."

Jacqueline is either really, really, evil and inconsiderate or amazing and ingenious. I haven't decided yet. She's an honorary spy and agent for the board and no one here would be wiser since I've never in my life heard of a super working for the HPA. Most don't stay alive long enough to have that kind of conversation.

Mr. Soto pulls into a small parking lot with about fifteen other different vehicles. Their transportation is nothing special. I wonder if it's to fit in with the human population. The board is fond of their identical white vans, and I don't see a single van here. I bet it's on purpose.

Jacqueline gets out and joins Mr. Soto. The sun set a few minutes ago, and we're losing light quickly. Without any outdoor lighting, it's hard to see. I find it impossible to think all supers have night vision.

"Hey, Jackie, what's with the lack of outside lighting here?" I ask.

She chortles in her mind. "Why? You afraid of the dark?"

"I wasn't until you started throwing me into the void." I hate admitting it, but there's no point in denying it. It's not like I'm confessing my deepest, darkest secret. Jacqueline can't even tell anyone, so I won't be embarrassed.

"I promise I won't do it so often. Just when I'm indecent.

I've grown used to your company."

I stay quiet for a moment. *"Don't get too used to it."*

Mr. Soto grabs Jacqueline's small suitcase, averting her attention to him. For looking so old, he is fast-paced and doesn't even lose his breath on our speed walk to a building with a daisy painted on it. Instead of marked with address numbers, each building has an image related to nature.

"This is the guest unit. Each room has a private bathroom, but you'll have to go to the communal dining hall to eat. We have a library in the main building, and if you take this path to the right, you'll find the fields. That's where the daily activities are held. If you like swimming, we have a pool on the north side of the property." Mr. Soto points at a building with a full moon painted on it, but I'm guessing he's envisioning something past it.

Jacqueline spins, giving me a better view of the property. Only a few supers meander the premises, so I'm guessing they're all in their rooms or something is going on we haven't yet been invited to. This place is too big for only a handful of them.

Jacqueline reaches out and touches Mr. Soto's arm. "Thank you for bringing me here."

"Everyone deserves a safe place to call home," he says. He holds the opaque glass door open. The lobby's tan walls complement the brown couch, and an entertainment center with a TV takes up an entire wall. "You can pick any room you like. I'll send someone to show you around the property and to the dining hall. Need anything else before I go?"

She shakes her head. "No, this is great. See you tomorrow,

Mr. Soto."

Jacqueline picks up her suitcase and strolls to the hallway. Without checking all the rooms out, she steps into the first room she sees and closes the door behind her. She brings her eyes from the floor to stare around the room. It's boring and plain with a twin bed, vanity table, dresser, and an open door to an ivory tiled bathroom.

She plops on the bed. "It's so strange not being scared," Jacqueline thinks.

"What's strange is that such a powerful super is scared of humans," I say.

Jacqueline doesn't respond. It's going to be a long night. Hopefully our welcoming committee comes soon. After a few minutes, Jacqueline closes her eyes, and I stare at the backs of her eyelids until she falls asleep. It's the only time I feel somewhat normal.

When Jacqueline dreams, I can immerse myself in her dream and almost feel whole again. It's the only time I get some sort of peace from her while being entertained by her weird and troubled imagination.

I sometimes shut down when Jacqueline sleeps, but I'm too amped up from the trip. Now is the time I can have a moment to myself and at least be back in my body, even if it's just for a few hours and only a figment of Jacqueline's dream.

I'll take what I can get.

NADIA

We waited in the kitchen of the club for over thirty minutes before we could safely leave, and then Alyssa had to speed the entire way back to the compound.

She skids to a stop in the clearing and jumps out of the car before I have a chance to unbuckle my seatbelt. She starts positioning the car cover over her car and when she's done, she grabs my hand and we run as fast as we can down the dirt path, stopping just before the clearing that leads to the back gate.

Alyssa runs her fingers over a tree branch and pulls off the small talisman that allows us to enter the compound, then hands it to me. My fingers fumble as I try to tie it around my neck and I drop it. Alyssa swipes it off the dirt and puts it on for me, and I open the gate and walk through before throwing the talisman to her. She runs through and hangs it back in its hiding spot.

My heart pounds so hard I can hear it in my ears. Alyssa grins, jogging next to me while I glide onto the green stretch of grass leading to our dormitory. I slow down and inhale through my nose to catch my breath.

Alyssa squeezes my arm. "We're in the clear."

I smile and wag my eyebrows. "How close were we?"

"Ms. Petrov," a rich voice calls.

I turn toward the voice and see Mr. Soto running in our direction.

"Ms. Petrov, I need a favor from you," he says.

I roll my eyes. For being nearly a hundred and twenty, the shaman has more energy than I do. Mr. Soto stops a few feet away from us. He shifts his weight between legs and avoids eye contact with me. I've always made him nervous.

"What is it? Does the council need something?" I ask. I

know the council has noticed my lack of participation in the last two weeks. It's coming back to bite me now.

"A young woman named Jacqueline Matthews will be moving here. She's in the guest house now and needs a tour guide and someone to sit with at dinner. Will you do it?"

I glance at Alyssa. "Can you do it?"

Mr. Soto puts his hands on his hips. "Ms. Petrov, if you'd stop being antisocial, maybe you'd fit in better."

"You're right. I'll try harder and will be happy to show the new girl around." I only say it because I know Mr. Soto will complain to my father about me not helping out more around the compound.

He rubs his beard. "All right then. But please, Nadia, don't scare her. You already make people nervous as it is."

Thanks a lot. "I'll try my best not to."

Mr. Soto glances at his watch. "Yes, right, thank you. I'll also need you to escort her to the meeting hall in the morning. Nine o'clock, sharp." He turns and strolls away without another word and doesn't give me a chance to complain. He's always been short with me, and it sucks because I haven't done anything to him.

I turn to Alyssa. "I guess I'll meet you at the dining hall."

I watch her walk away and then I head toward the guest apartments to meet the new girl. For once, I hope I make a good impression and actually add to my short list of friends. It's better to meet someone here in person than let them find out what I am from one of the compound's gossips.

It's silent when I enter the guest apartment building. The

TV is off and the place looks empty like always. All of the doors are open except for the first one, and I stop in front of it.

I knock. "Hello? I'm here to show you around when you're ready. I'll be out—"

The hairs on my arms rise, hunger now burning in my stomach. Jacqueline is asleep in her room, and I can't stop myself from quietly opening her door and gliding in.

A girl with a mass of dark curls and flawless bronze skin lies on top of the sky blue comforter with her hands clasped loosely on her chest. I pause in the doorway. She looks so familiar, but I can't put my finger on it. I don't let it stop me though.

I shut the door and glide across the room. Jacqueline is deep in a dream, and I can almost taste her fears even before I transport myself into her dream. I fall into her mind, my stomach flipping as the air shifts.

I'm in the middle of the city, but it's nothing like what I saw today. This dream city is abandoned and haunted with remnants of what used to be human civilization. The windows on a nearby building are boarded up and police tape on the glass doors warns people to keep out. I run my fingers along the brick wall, setting it ablaze, and creep my way deeper into Jacqueline's dream world.

HUNTER

I stare over the ledge of a roof of an abandoned building. I don't really know what Jacqueline dreams about, but it's easy enough to immerse myself in whatever world she imagines without actually having to talk or see her.

The building shakes, the world trembling around me.

Something's different. Something has changed. I feel someone else's presence.

I pull myself from Jacqueline's dream. *"Hello?"* I whisper. *"Jacqueline, are you messing with me?"*

A strange energy sucks me back into Jacqueline's dream. I try to disconnect, but I'm stuck. I search around the imaginary buildings for misplaced things. Nothing has changed.

I jump from the roof and land on my feet in the middle of an empty street. Jacqueline's dreams are usually eerily quiet, and I wonder if it has to do with the fact that I'm not the one dreaming, so maybe I'm missing big chunks of what goes on. I don't ask her, though. It would make it awkward.

Loud footsteps echo through the world, and I jog to the end of the block and press my stomach to the wall of a building. I wait a few seconds, listening as the footsteps move closer, and then I peek around the corner.

I can't believe what I'm seeing. It's the girl from the club.

Her shimmering, white hair blows behind her. She slides her slender fingers over the red bricks of a rundown building. A burning trail glows in their wake, and it's like the girl sets Jacqueline's world ablaze.

An ivory strapless dress hugs her hips, contrasting her black lace-up combat boots. She smiles as she looks around, but it's not happiness. It's an eerie satisfaction. I count to three before stepping around the corner to face her. She stops and stares at me with a wild glint in her eyes.

My hands shake, and I want to turn and run. Years of being taught that supers are horrible, vile creatures crowd my mind, making it hard to remain calm. This girl won't hurt me. She can't...at least I don't think she can. I refuse to let my fear of the unknown overpower me. This is the first opportunity I've had to talk to someone besides Jacqueline. Apart from the board, this girl may be the only person to ever find out I'm here and that I'm trapped.

I clear my throat. It takes a lot in me to speak. "Are you real?" I ask.

She tilts her head to the side, her smile faltering. "You shouldn't be able to see me." Panic sweeps across her face, and she crosses her arms. She's afraid of me, too. I don't know why, but it makes me feel better. It makes me want to comfort her. "That's impossible. Who are you?"

"My name is Hunter Sullivan. I'm a soul trapped inside Jacqueline's mind." I reach out to offer my hand, but she doesn't move.

Her fear melts into surprise, and she puckers her bottom lip. "This is the strangest dream."

I step closer. "I'm not a dream."

Her gray eyes flash as she smiles the most beautiful smile—one that lights her face, squinting her eyes, yet still, it doesn't encompass happiness. It's something fierce. A force I can't deny. "I love when dream people are in denial."

She reaches out, a haunted look in her eyes, and grabs my shoulders.

NADIA

I reach out and grab Hunter's shoulders, anticipation coursing through me. His dream essence will be as satisfying as everything else in Jacqueline's dream world I've come to devour. My fingers dig into the soft cotton of his shirt, and he lowers his eyebrows, frowning.

Nothing happens.

I give him a hard shake before letting go and stepping back. Hunter feels so utterly real. His firm, muscular shoulders tense in my grip, and he locks me in his gaze, his hazel eyes the prettiest color I've ever seen. He's as cute as Alyssa's dream boy, if not cuter, but something about him ignites warning bells in my very essence.

"You're not—not a dream," I stammer.

He shakes his head. A soft, dark brown curl falls into his eyes. "Nope."

I wipe my arm across my forehead. "I'm so confused. I need to leave."

He reaches out and tries to grab my hand, but I'm much faster. "Please, hear me out. Don't go. It's been a long time since I've been able to talk to someone besides Jacqueline." He looks so sincere that I can't turn my back on him. He presses his full lips together, his jaw twitching, and he doesn't break eye contact. His soulful eyes plead and beg for me to remain in my spot.

I can't resist. Everything in this dream is so strange, yet exciting. I've never experienced anything like it. What is Jacqueline? Who is this soul? Why does she keep him?

I lean closer, a tremble rushing through me. "Can she hear us?" I ask, whispering the words.

"She doesn't know I spy on her dreams," he says.

I release a breath and stare at the bulging veins in his arms. Everything tells me to abandon Jacqueline's dream and forget about Hunter, but my curiosity overwhelms me. His soul sees my darkest side—the side people fear the most—and he's not running away in terror. He hasn't even looked away once.

I step even closer, trailing my stare from his handsome face to his casual jeans and T-shirt. "What is she? Why are you here?"

He tries to run his hand along my arm, like he can't believe I'm real, either, but I stiffen and he drops his hand to his side. "She claims to be a sin-eater. I don't know much more except that she stole my soul and now I'm trapped."

I think about his words for a moment. I've heard of sin-eaters before, but they are even rarer than nightmare inflictors. They can rip away the soul of a sinful person and consume their sins before letting the soul die in peace. But, I didn't think they could harbor souls.

"So, you're here for a reason," I say. It's not unheard of for a creature to harm a human; most only do it out of necessity. The council does its best to stop creatures from going on murderous rampages, but hurting the occasional human happens. Some creatures have to do so to survive. I'm one of those creatures.

"Yeah, but it's not what you think. I'm a good person." He shifts his weight between his feet.

"You don't know what I'm thinking."

We stare at each other, neither of us making a move. He's assessing me as much as I'm assessing him and his body language gives his nervousness away even though his face remains expressionless.

After a moment, he draws his eyes toward the clouded sky. "I didn't mean to assume," he says. "It's just you look so—" He brushes his hair from his forehead. "Frightened."

I twist my lips to the side. "I'm not afraid of you." And I'm not. I was more surprised if anything. *Keep telling yourself that...*

His Adam's apple bobs in his throat. "You shouldn't be, promise. I—I'm just lost. A prisoner here. I never thought I'd ever get the chance to talk to someone again. You're like an—"

A scream echoes through the abandoned city street, cutting Hunter off. My stomach aches as Jacqueline's dream calls for me to finish it. I shift my gaze away from Hunter and see Jacqueline standing at the end of the street with her hand over her mouth. A white van zooms by and barrels in her direction. I lick my lips, enjoying her fear wafting through every particle in the air.

It's enough to remind me that I need to focus. I shouldn't even be in Jacqueline's dream. "I'm sorry, Hunter, but I can't stay. I'll ask Jacqueline about you when she wakes up. I'm sure it's a misunderstanding."

Admitting I dream dropped on her puts me at risk, but I'm sure the council would flip out if they knew Jacqueline was holding a human soul hostage. It could be my leverage to keep her quiet while I sort this weird situation out.

Hunter rushes at me and grabs my arm. "Don't!" he yells. "She can't know you know. Please, I'm begging you. She'll never return me to my body then."

I gasp, feeling the weight of his touch, the intense urgency of his words. I nearly rip myself free of him, but he yanks his hands back to link them together, realizing his mistake.

"Okay, okay. I won't. But I have to go. I'll try to come back and then I want you to explain everything," I say.

A strange look flashes through his eyes, and he nods without a word and blinks out of existence.

Turning away from the spot he stood, I peer around the dream world. If my hunger wasn't so intense, I could refrain from destroying the dream a while longer, but I can't stop now. Not with Jacqueline right in front of me.

I glide to her and watch as people dressed in black emerge from the van and rush her. She screams as they tackle her to the ground, and I falter seeing the glint of a familiar knife. It's the exact one the HPA agents carry. I'd recognize it anywhere.

And then it hits me. I know what Jacqueline's worst nightmare is, because it's mine, too.

Jacqueline screams a high pitched, horrifying scream as she sees me saunter closer. Her worst nightmare is the board of the HPA, and here I am, acting like one of them. I suck in deep breaths of her crumbling world. Dust rains through the air, clouding my vision, and then the dream collapses into darkness. Snapping my eyes open, I stare down at Jacqueline flailing in her sleep. I can't get the image of the trapped boy out of my head, and now I need to know all her secrets. I want to know what she's hiding.

I'll find out.

Nothing is safe in a person's dreams.

5

SO MANY SECRETS

NADIA

FLYING INTO THE hallway seconds before Jacqueline wakes up, I turn and hold my fist up to knock on the door like I wasn't in her room. I hope no one finds out what I've done. I'll get in serious trouble for creating a nightmare without the sleeper's permission.

I wait an excruciatingly long moment for the door to swing open. Jacqueline appears, standing there with her mouth wide open in a yawn. She looks so familiar, but I still can't put my finger on it. It wasn't because I saw her in her dream either.

Jacqueline laughs before grinning. Her smile falters for a split second, and she composes herself. Her gorgeous lavender eyes, lined with thick black lashes long enough to create shadows on her cheeks, complement her deep purple shift dress she styles with black-patterned tights and ankle boots. A strand of amethyst colored beads drapes around her neck, sparkling like the silver rings on her fingers.

"I'm Nadia," I say, shoving my hands into my jeans instead of offering one in greeting. "Mr. Soto asked me to take you to the dining hall."

Jacqueline's eyes shift back and forth like she's lost deep in thought. She subtly shakes her head and focuses on me. It's a strange gesture, a quirk even, but I can't help wonder about Hunter and if he's really a soul in her head. "Oh, cool, yeah. Mr. Soto said he'd send someone. I'm starving from my trip."

I purposely step back, touching my feet to the ground, to let Jacqueline out of her room. "Where did you come from?"

Jacqueline's eyes dart behind me. She pauses for a second before saying, "I was picked up in the city and before that, well, I moved a lot. Nowhere I'd really call home."

"The city is amazing," I say. "It's been a long time since I've been there." I'm not a good liar, but I think Jacqueline believes me.

"I wouldn't know. I was only there for a few hours." Jacqueline's eye color shifts to hazel for a split second. It happened so fast, I'm not sure if I imagined it as I stare at her lavender eyes again. I don't want to ask either way. I wouldn't want her asking about my physical changes. "I met Mr. Soto at The Haven. Quaint little place. A little too busy for my liking."

My palms sweat, nerves getting the best of me. That's

where I recognize her from. I hope she doesn't recognize me, or if she does, I hope she doesn't say anything.

"I've heard of that place." I keep a straight face. It's hard to mask my emotions. I clear my throat, uncomfortable about where the conversation is heading. "We should probably get going. It's getting late, and I'm kind of hungry too." I lie about my hunger for food out of habit. If Jacqueline doesn't know what I am already, I'm not going to tell her.

She'd grow suspicious fast after a few nightmares, and I plan on invading her dreams again as soon as I catch her sleeping. I can't get Hunter's image from my head. I wonder if he can see me through Jacqueline's eyes. I wonder what it's like to be trapped. Worse than spending my life behind the chain-link protecting me from the outside world.

"Sounds good to me," Jacqueline says. "We can talk more there."

HUNTER

I can't believe it.

It's her.

I didn't expect the beautiful girl from the dream to be standing outside of Jacqueline's room minutes after she left me in a crumbling nightmare. This is fate, or a very cruel joke, that she's now walking in front of me and I can't even talk to her.

I hope Nadia keeps her promise to visit me again. I need to find out if she'd be willing to help me despite my being human. I never thought I'd ask a super for help, but I'd do anything, say anything, to get out of here.

Nadia's different than I expected her to be. She's not the

terrifying monster I had assumed hid under incomparable beauty. She's hot, cautious, and almost human-like. Her presence in
the dream didn't scream danger. It gave me nothing but relief.
Hope.

I thought most supers stood together against humanity and
would help each other out, meaning she'd have told Jacqueline
that she met me, but she's pretending I don't exist. It's almost
like she's not influenced by our two different worlds. Maybe
she's been sheltered all her life at this compound. Maybe she
doesn't know about what happens in the real world to people
like her.

Nadia's pale blond hair, a few shades darker than her
dream persona's hair, sways back and forth with the same
rhythm as her hips. I imagine how soft it would be to touch, to
run my fingers through. Her light gray, long sleeved shirt
matches the color of her eyes in the dream and her light denim
jeans hug her body perfectly. A sliver of alabaster skin peeks
from between her shirt and jeans, and I bet it feels as smooth as
it looks. Everything about her makes it easy for me to fall into a
fantasy, the only thing I can do without my body.

"What is she?" I ask to test if Jacqueline knows about the
dream invading girl.

"I honestly don't know. Maybe a demon or something."

There's no way Nadia's evil. I've seen evil. Jacqueline's evil.
"Are you afraid of her?"

"No."

"Are you lying?"

"No!" Jacqueline's voice echoes in the quiet night, and I

prepare myself to be thrown into the void. She's never slipped up before in front of someone, but I think Nadia has her on edge. Jacqueline closes her eyes and thinks, "Ugh! I can't believe you made me do that!" Her voice booms around me, digging into my essence with the heat of annoyance.

Nadia looks over her shoulder. "What's wrong?"

Jacqueline swallows. "I'm sorry. Bug."

Jacqueline stares at the grass for a moment and picks up her pace so she's walking next to Nadia. It's harder to be distracted by me if she's distracted by someone else. I don't apologize or say anything else either. It's better if I keep to myself for a while so she'll forget about her outburst. And then maybe she'll find out more about Nadia for me. I can learn a lot about someone from their interactions with Jacqueline.

It's nice looking forward to something other than death.

NADIA

I wish Mr. Soto hadn't forced me to take Jacqueline to the dining hall. It's extremely uncomfortable sitting at a table with a plate full of food in front of me that I push around with a fork instead of eating. I'm too distracted by thoughts of Hunter to even try to act normal.

Jacqueline's eyes shift from lavender to hazel, and I blink a few times and hope she doesn't notice how intently I'm staring at her.

With the way her eyes let Hunter shine through, I wonder if he's trying to communicate with me. I'm intrigued by who he is and whether or not he's portraying himself accurately. In dream worlds, I can manifest however I want because I'm not what the dreamer sees. The dreamer sees what scares them most. Whether it's a person or animal, even a certain situation—I create it to torment them. I don't like to, but it's necessary. The hungrier I am, the quicker the dream goes, but the more intense it is. If I visit too often, the sleeper will eventually go insane.

"Well, this is fun," Alyssa says. She twists the ends of her red hair around her index finger. "You both look out of it."

Jacqueline shakes her head. "What?" She blinks and picks up a fry and then drops it. "I'm sorry."

My eyes shift to Alyssa and back to Jacqueline. "Is something bothering you, Jacqueline? You've been quiet."

"I was just thinking about how different this place is from the outside world. I don't feel scared. I haven't even looked behind me once since I got here. It's nice not having to worry about humans."

I stare at my hands. I shouldn't hold it against her, but I can't stop my heart from hurting as her words sink in. She doesn't know that my mother was human—and a good person. She accepted my father regardless of what he was, and even went as far as dying to keep his—our secret—safe from the HPA, the council's one true enemy.

Alyssa clears her throat. "You have to know all humans aren't out to get us."

"I've been able to survive because I don't trust them," Jacqueline retorts.

Alyssa eyes me, and I shrug. I fidget in my seat. I don't know if it's worth the effort to continue this discussion. It'd only be fair to warn Jacqueline that the compound isn't antihuman and one of our very own council members is human, but instead I slide my chair back and stand up. "We should probably get back to the dorm, Lys." I turn to Jacqueline. "Can you find your way back to the guest apartments?"

She nods, absently nibbling on a fry.

I turn my back on Jacqueline and walk toward the door with Alyssa on my heels. I can't shake the bad feeling in my stomach created by Jacqueline. Without even saying a word, I know she's keeping so many secrets. Not only Hunter, but about what her plan is and why she's really here.

But I'm determined to find out.

HUNTER

Disappointment washes through me as I watch Nadia and her friend, Alyssa, walk away. I knew Jacqueline would ruin it for me. She hasn't even been here a few hours and Nadia already doesn't like her as far as I can tell. How can I keep reminding Nadia I'm stuck inside Jacqueline's head if she doesn't want to be around Jacqueline?

I want to mock Jacqueline and tell her to work on her people skills, but I'm still concerned she'll lash out at me in the crowded dining hall full of supers.

It's weird, how normal everything looks. I expected the world's worst supers to be holed up here, waiting and planning an attack on the HPA, but these are people just making a home. They're not even scary like the pictures my mom keeps in a photo album on the coffee table to remind my brother Mason and I about how awful the world supposedly is.

The realization that my mom fed me lies about the supernatural world all my life sinks in., I never once questioned it because she was so convincing. Maybe they are her truths. I'll never know if I don't get back to my body. Even if it wasn't Jacqueline's plan, my imprisonment opened my eyes to a new reality.

Jacqueline gives up on eating her dinner and stands without making eye contact with the few supers staring at us. She walks straight to the door and heads out into the cool night in the direction of the guest unit.

It's going to be a really long night together. I can feel it in my soul.

Why couldn't I be trapped in someone else's head? Why did it have to be Jacqueline? I hate her more than ever, something I never thought possible.

NADIA

Dinner was so, so awkward. I couldn't wait to get back to my room. Jacqueline is more closed off than I am, and she danced around every question thrown at her. Her disconcerting hatred toward humans doesn't do much for her, and her abhorrence toward them cuts deep into me, making me want to see Hunter even more. He could be a victim of her prejudice. He *is* a victim of something. People don't take souls like this. It isn't right. She's giving everyone a bad reputation.

Someone knocks on my door, but before I can get up, it swings open. Alyssa struts in, slamming the door behind her. She adjusts the dark blue towel wrapped around her hair and plops on the bed next to me and tucks her bare feet under her.

"I'm exhausted." She leans her back against the wall, fiddling with the strings of her green star-pattern pajama bottoms. "Up until dinner was a lot of fun. I've missed hanging out with you, Nadia."

I rest my chin on my knees. Guilt about shutting myself in for the last two weeks swirls through me. I pushed Alyssa away until I needed her. It was selfish of me, and I want to apologize, but I don't. She knows I'm sorry. Instead, I smile. "I wish it wasn't cut short. I liked being away from here. This place is suffocating me."

She leans back on my pillow. "You're one of the reasons why I stay, you know. Besides you being my best friend, I don't see a future without you. I owe your dad for saving me."

I frown. "You don't owe anyone anything. If you feel like you need to leave, then you should go."

"No, that's not what I meant. What I was trying to say was that I'd leave if you weren't here. I believe in good karma and your friendship means the world to me. You're like my sister."

I smile. Alyssa's right about being like family. We owe it to each other to look out for one another. I wonder what it would be like to live outside the compound without the laws of the council hanging over our heads. I wonder if we'd get to experience real relationships, make more friends, and actually live life.

An image of Hunter crosses my mind.

I was only with the mysterious dream boy for a short time, but he left such an impression on me. My desire to see him again scares me. I know nothing about him, but I want to. That's my problem. My curiosity is overwhelming. It's making me careless.

The hairs on my arms rise, and I glance at Alyssa on my bed with her eyelids half closed. She'll fall asleep any second, and then I won't be able to resist her dream. I promised myself I wouldn't do it to her again, not after how off she seemed this morning. I just can't.

I jump up and leave her on my bed.

As a nightmare inflictor, it's nearly impossible for me to wake up someone who is sleeping—not because I can't, but because I don't want to.

I race from my room and down the hall to the lobby and out the front door. I touch my boots to the ground in an attempt to look normal. Night air hits my face, wind blurring my eyes, and I miss a step. I tumble and land with a thump on the wet grass. I roll to my back, staring up at the bright stars and catch my breath. I can't deal with temptation tonight. I can't even deal with being me.

6

TWO DIFFERENT WORLDS

HUNTER

I CAN'T GET Nadia off my mind.

The way she pauses before she speaks, choosing her words carefully. The way her soft voice sounds. The way the white moonlight glimmers on her pale hair. The way her nose crinkles when she laughs. How vulnerable and guarded she is and how I want to break down her walls. She's the girl of my dreams, well, I guess Jacqueline's dreams.

I hate my uncontrollable feelings. Nadia is off limits—she's a super. She could never survive in my world.

Despite my upbringing to fear supers like Nadia, I want to get to know her more. I know it's a horrible idea. I don't even know what she is except that she can invade dreams, and the HPA would kill her because they'd find the ability detrimental to the human population. But she can see me. I'm desperate enough to put my life in her hands. I might even trust her.

It takes a bit, but I finally get up the nerve to talk to Jacqueline. I kept quiet all through dinner because I knew she would've thrown my presence into the void. I hope she's still not mad. *"We should go explore,"* I say.

Jacqueline stares in the mirror and sets her comb down. "We'll get a tour tomorrow," she says out loud, taking me by surprise.

"Then how about a night walk? I'm bored. I can't stand watching you brush your hair anymore. It looks fine."

She ties her hair back. "Okay, but don't expect me to make a habit out of complying with your demands."

"I'm not demanding anything."

"Whatever," she thinks before she stands up and slides her boots on. "Please, try not to distract me if we run into someone."

"I won't. I am sorry about earlier, so you know. It's just, Nadia—"

"Forget about Nadia, Hunter. You're from two different worlds, and it would never work out. Trust me."

I don't need the reminder. *"So, you're psychic, too? It's not like anything can come out of this. I'm in your body, remember?"*

"I could never forget."

Jacqueline pulls her door open and steps into the hall. Hovering in the lobby, she peers around for a second before exiting the building. With the lack of outside lighting, the stars shine brighter than I've ever seen them. The brilliant, round moon casts enough light for Jacqueline to easily stroll down a path without trouble seeing.

Surprisingly, the grounds lack life. Silence overtakes the world so the only thing I hear is Jacqueline's breathing. I expected a few creatures of darkness to be skulking around, but maybe I made them up in my head. I always assumed things that go bump in the night were supers. Granted, there aren't humans running around the compound to stalk anyway.

Jacqueline rounds a building and slows down. A soft thud and a moan sound out from nearby. Jacqueline stops in her tracks to listen. Whoever made the noise is just out of sight, so we can't get a good view of what happened.

"Afraid of something?" I ask.

Jacqueline sighs in her mind. "No."

She steps forward and strolls toward the sound when I catch sight of flowing, blond hair glowing in the moonlight.

It's Nadia.

She lies on her back in the wet grass, staring up at the cloudless night sky. Even in a white T-shirt, black athletic pants, and sneakers, she looks incredible. Moonlight bathes her bare arms in silver, reminding me of the hauntingly beautiful dream girl she is.

"Stupid steps," Nadia grumbles to herself. She doesn't move but just stares at the sky.

"Jacqueline, you should go help her," I say.

"Why?"

"Don't you want to make friends? Won't it help you to find out the information the board wants?" I only say it because I want Jacqueline to trust Nadia. Nadia can visit me any time if Jacqueline does.

"I guess you're right."

Jacqueline meanders over, but Nadia is so deep in her thoughts, she doesn't even glance at her. Bending down, Jacqueline grabs Nadia's hand. "Here, let me help you," she says in her most sickly sweet voice.

Nadia jerks her hand away, eyes wide, and before Jacqueline can even take a step back, Nadia screams.

NADIA

The grass rustles next to me and before I can turn my head to see what's causing the noise, a warm hand latches onto me. A rush of energy pulses through me, and the taste of tangy orange floods my mouth, a memory of a dream overwhelming me, as I stare into Jacqueline's vibrant eyes.

I scream and jerk away, crab walking back as far as I can. My breath heaves, my heart racing. I resist the urge to lash out at her, call her crazy, and run away.

I wasn't expecting Jacqueline to be outside, and she startled me. But now that she's here, I search her eyes for glimpses of hazel. I can't get her dream off my mind. The mysterious boy who could see me for who I am. He is all I thought about through dinner. I shouldn't have gone into her dreams, but I couldn't resist the call of her dreams inviting me in. It doesn't help I'm still recuperating from my hunger strike, and Alyssa is off limits. I can't put that strain on our friendship. But Jacqueline? She's holding a soul hostage...I think.

"You scared me!" My shrill voice rips through the air.

Jacqueline winces, crossing her arms. "I'm so sorry. I heard you fall. I was only trying to help."

It takes everything in me not to scowl. "It's—it's okay. I didn't think anyone was out here. People don't usually venture out this late." I wish I didn't say that. The last thing I want her to ask is why I'm out here. She can't know what I am or what I can do just yet.

Stepping closer, she holds her hand out to me again. I try not to flinch as I take her proffered hand and let her pull me to my feet. I already sense she's still tired and will probably fall asleep within the hour. I can almost taste her dreams. I *will* taste her dreams.

"I needed to clear my head," she says. Her eyes shift from lavender to hazel and back again.

"Me too." My heartbeat stabilizes, and I force my mouth to smile. Craning my neck, I look at the front door to the dorm. "You don't get a lot of privacy around here."

Jacqueline plays with a fallen curl from her bun and tucks it behind her ear. She shifts her weight from foot to foot and stares past me. Her eyes change again, and she subtly shakes her head. If I wasn't staring at her so intently, I wouldn't have noticed it.

She blinks rapidly and shrugs. "I'm okay with that. I'm tired of being alone."

"I don't think I could ever get tired of that. When I'm eighteen, I'm getting out of here." I don't know why I tell her, but I do, and it's too late to take it back. I've never told anyone my plan, not even Alyssa.

The corner of Jacqueline's lips curl, and she looks away. After a long pause, she says, "You're better off staying here where you're safe."

I raise my eyebrows. "I'm not better off staying somewhere I hate."

Her eyes shift colors again, and I think of Hunter. It's all it takes to keep me from running back into the dorms. Guilt floods through my mind. I should resist my craving to give Jacqueline nightmares. If I back away now, I have a fighting chance at controlling myself.

"Let me walk you back to your room," I add, instead. *You're doing this to investigate. You just want to figure everything out. It's not a big deal.*

But it is a big deal.

I'm letting my nightmare inflictor side control me. It won't be long until it takes my humanity, too.

HUNTER

Jacqueline snores so loudly in her state of deep sleep that I almost miss the sound of the door to her room clicking shut. The air shifts, and I recognize Nadia's presence immediately. Relief and hope flood around me, pulling me from my dark thoughts. I wasn't expecting her to return so soon, but I'm glad she has. I've been anxious to see her again in the dream world.

"I don't have long." Nadia's voice wraps around me and tugs me into Jacqueline's dream.

She leans against the railing of a pier, facing a busy boardwalk. Her shimmering, white hair blows in an imaginary sea breeze, and she wears a simple white cotton dress without shoes. I shift my eyes from her narrowed stare and to her lips, trailing my gaze to her smooth shoulders and then the rest of her.

She pats the spot next to her, reciprocating my once over like she still can't believe I'm real. But something in her gray eyes, a light shining from within her, pokes my very essence in a good way. I wish she didn't turn her gaze to our surroundings. Being trapped in her stare is way better than being trapped in Jacqueline's head. I'd rather be lost in her eyes than lost in this dream.

The dull roar of the ocean hums through the dark night and colorful lights illuminate Nadia's porcelain skin in rainbow colors. A large Ferris wheel hums as it spins and game stands blare repetitive tunes. It's a place I'd hang out at if I had my body. I guess Jacqueline's dreams aren't always so morbid.

I rest my back on the railing next to Nadia, so close that our arms brush against each other. "You came back."

She tucks her hair behind her ear and leans her shoulder against mine, like she needs to feel how solid my soul is in this world. "I have a lot of questions, Hunter."

I gaze at her in my peripheral vision. "Ask me anything you want."

Nadia watches a man kiss a woman under the lights of the concession stand sign. The corner of her lips pull up slightly in a tease of a smile I wish she'd give me. She tenses as they whisper into each other's lips. Nadia is more intense in the dream world than she is in real life. I want to tell her it's okay, but instead I turn to stand in front of her so she has to look into my eyes.

"This is really strange for me," she says. "I try not to stay in someone's dream. Observing without turning dreams into a nightmare isn't exactly easy." The fact that she muses her thoughts instead of immediately interrogating me speaks volumes about her. I like it.

"I don't mean to make you uncomfortable," I say. "It's just been too long. You have no idea how happy I am that you're here." And I mean it. I'm sure I'd be happy for anyone to see me other than Jacqueline, but having Nadia see me? I think my bad luck might be changing.

She raises her eyebrows. "I bet. I can't imagine what it's like."

"Horrible."

Reaching out, she touches my shoulder and runs her finger down my arm. I hold utterly still, letting her explore my soul manifested in this dream. I don't know what she feels, but her brows pucker, creasing her forehead almost curiously.

She drops her hand back to her side, though the coolness of her touch lingers. "You feel so real."

The wind blows around us and strands of her hair fall on her cheek. She doesn't move to fix them, and I wonder what she'd do if I tucked them back behind her ear. If I wasn't so nervous, I'd do it. I'm too afraid of scaring her away. I'd do anything for her to stay.

I cross my arms over my chest, putting a sliver more of space between us. "It's because I *am* real."

She steps closer again and touches my cheek next, like she can't stop herself. I lean into her hand, never realizing how much I missed feeling the physical sensation from another person. She feels as real as she claims I do, yet it's different than I remember a touch feeling like before I was imprisoned by Jacqueline.

Nadia pulls herself away, tilting her head to the side, her inspection of me over. "I think it's because you're an entity separate from Jacqueline. It's like you're doing the same thing I am by manifesting into her dream. I have no impact on you, because you're not the dreamer. My father never told me that it was possible. Maybe he doesn't know."

I'm taken by surprise. I don't know exactly what I expected from Nadia—maybe something closer to an interrogation—but she hasn't even asked me a single question. She's working through her thoughts out loud, and I let her. Anything to get her to trust me.

"It's not every day you stumble upon a soul trapped in a monster's head, huh?"

She winces, and I regret my words immediately. Her eyes dart from mine, turning her attention to the crowd behind us. After a few seconds, she meets my gaze again with a new darker expression. She glares at me, pursing her lips. A blip of fear seizes my chest—not because she unleashes unsuspecting fury on me but because I unintentionally caused such a fierce reaction. And even though she's angry, she's still so beautiful.

I close my eyes, expecting her to react. To disappear. To slap me, even. But she doesn't do any of those things.

"Do you think I'm a monster?" Her low voice, nearly a whisper, sinks into me.

I open my eyes again. I should say no, but I lose my words. Fidgeting under her glower, I cross and uncross my arms, her eyes piercing into me. I suck in a breath and blow it out, trying to control the tone of my voice, and then finally say, "I don't know."

Raising her hand to my cheek again, she brushes her fingers along my jawline, making me shiver. "Most people lie and say no because they really do think I'm a monster."

I push my hair off my forehead. "I'm not a liar. I really don't know the answer to that. What I do know is that you act differently here than you do in the real world. I don't know what to think."

She twists her lips and drops her hand back to her side. "It's because I am different."

A scream rips through the night, and Nadia jerks her head to look past me. I glance over my shoulder and see the crowd start to move and run in panic. The wooden beams quake under my feet, and I reflexively clutch Nadia's arm. She smiles, but it's not at me. It's at what's going on behind me.

"Looks like Jacqueline's mind is reacting to my presence. I have to go, Hunter," she says, sliding past me.

I spin with her as she glides a few feet toward the crowd, still facing me. "Please, stay. You have to stay. You never asked me the questions on your mind." I'm not too good to beg, and I consider doing it.

Her bottom lip pouts. "The nightmare is starting." She

points behind me, and I peer over my shoulder as a massive wave grows and swells taller than a four-story building. I'm actually a little afraid even though I know this isn't real. Turning my back on the swelling ocean, I watch Nadia move closer to the crowd and away from me. "I'm sorry, Hunter. I'll visit again as soon as I can. I need to think more."

"Nadia, please." My words drift away on the wind.

A deafening cracking sound rips through the air and part of the boardwalk disintegrates. The glowing Ferris wheel topples over and crashes into the dark ocean. A fire ignites at the concession stand, and Nadia disappears into the crowd. Each person she touches explodes in a dark cloud of smoke.

I pull away from the dream as the giant tidal wave begins to crest. Jacqueline moans and the world shifts and then it suddenly feels empty. Nadia's presence disappears, and I'm alone with my own thoughts again. And now? I'm even more miserable knowing what I'm missing when she's gone.

7

NOT GIVING UP HOPE

HUNTER

JACQUELINE TAPS HER fingers on the white painted nightstand. She hasn't slept since waking up from her nightmare a few hours ago and her random thoughts annoy me. Not to mention how sporadic they come, because she can control what I can and can't hear in this shared space of ours, which I'm glad for. I don't know if I could handle hearing her more than I already do.

"Maybe you should give up your freedom and settle down here. Everyone seems pretty nice. The board can't do anything if they can't find you." Jacqueline's private thoughts rush around me. She's talking to herself.

I can't help myself from responding. *"Hold on a second, Jackie. The deal was to stay here until you got the information you needed. Don't go convincing yourself otherwise. If we stay, you can't put me back into my body."*

She smacks her forehead, releasing a groan. "But if I stayed here, you could see Nadia all you want. The council can offer me protection for life. I'd never be scared again."

While she makes a good point about Nadia, it would be torturous to know I won't have the slightest chance of ever getting to be with her outside of the dream world. *"That'll get creepy after a while. Hell, it's a little creepy now. What's the point if I can't even talk to her?"* I say it the way I do so Jacqueline doesn't realize I've met Nadia. I can't risk Jacqueline doing something stupid to spite me.

"What if I found you a new one?"

Huh? *"A new body?"*

"It's a very simple process. You can pick anyone you like."

"I like my body."

The way she says it, it sounds like someone else would have to lose their body and then what? I'm not cool with that. Someone shouldn't have to die when I have a perfectly good body back home. Jacqueline has caused enough harm as it is.

"Well, Hunter, I'll think about it but don't hold your breath. I like the idea of staying here forever, and you can't do anything about it. I won't dare go back to the HPA to put you back in your body. They'll kill me for not holding up my end of the bargain."

"You can't do this! You made a deal." Fury sweeps over me,

my emotions getting out of control. I'm so livid that I could combust and take Jacqueline down with me. I had hoped that this wouldn't turn into a long-term situation, but if she really decides to stay here, all hope for me is lost.

"I'm sorry. I really am. I can teach you to free yourself if you want."

"*No!*" I'm not going to learn to free myself. I'll die if I do. I don't want to die. If Jacqueline has made up her mind to stay here, then I'll wait it out a while longer as her prisoner. I'm not giving up hope yet. I'm only seventeen and have a life ahead of me. This isn't how I'm supposed to end, sad and alone, trapped in a monster. I'm supposed to die in a blaze of glory or something. Die with meaning.

I really, and I mean *really*, wanted to live to see my eighteenth birthday. It's only a few months away.

Someone knocks on the door, drawing her attention away from me. I hate how she can go about her day like my life isn't hanging on the line. If I ever get out of her head, I'm going to bring her back to my mom myself and make her plead for her own life.

Jacqueline opens the door. My anger fizzles out at the sight of Nadia hovering in the doorway. In the harsh hallway lighting, her hair appears darker, golden-blond, and her light gray eyes now shine a mesmerizing indigo color. She looks the same, yet different. More alive and vibrant. More real.

Nadia wears a sky blue, long sleeved T-shirt and light colored jeans with dark gray lace-up boots that stop before her knees. She twines her pale fingers together, a ghost of a smile playing on her lips. "I thought I'd bring you some breakfast, and we could eat outside." She holds up a small paper bag in one hand and a bright pink blanket drapes over her other arm. She peers over Jacqueline's shoulder and into the room.

Jacqueline steps out and closes the door. "That was thoughtful, thanks. I'd love to."

Nadia reaches over and loops her arm with Jacqueline's, surprising the hell out of me. Last night she freaked when Jacqueline barely touched her hand. I'm not sure what's changed, but I don't like it. It's going to give Jacqueline more reason to stay here if she has friends.

"Aren't you a little old to be friends with Nadia?" I ask.

"Stop acting like nineteen is ninety," Jacqueline thinks.

I resist arguing with her so she doesn't thrust me into the void. I doubt it'll make a difference, anyway. I just have to wait and see where fate takes me whether I like it or not.

NADIA

Jacqueline's puffy eyes tell me she hasn't slept at all since I saw Hunter. The nightmares I inflict on people make it hard to want to sleep. As long as I continue to visit Hunter, she'll never get any peaceful rest. But I don't want to stop. I'm even going as far as faking my friendship to find out more about the boy trapped in Jacqueline's mind.

Her dark hair strays in all different directions, and she absently uses her fingers to comb the unruly mass of curls. We stroll to my favorite spot to the right of the gardens in a grassy area people avoid for no other reason than nothing is there.

Jacqueline helps spread the blanket, and I set the bag of

blueberry muffins down. I sit cross-legged and Jacqueline kneels, adjusting her legs to the side, before smiling at me.

She pushes her hair from her face. "I never thought I'd actually like living here."

"It's fine if you're into boring. There aren't many young people around. I have a tutor because there aren't even enough kids to hold a class."

"Try sitting through a lecture on human history. It's not even right. They leave out all the good parts relating to our world."

"Well, I doubt anyone would believe the most influential people are manipulated by enchantresses or how Napoleon Bonaparte was a troll."

We both laugh. Despite my hesitation toward Jacqueline, it's nice hanging out with someone who doesn't know what I am. Jacqueline is guarded, but I don't think it's to protect herself from me—she seems to be in a constant battle with herself, her personal demons taking precedence over everything else. Maybe it's Hunter.

"Nadia?" Alyssa's voice drifts through the air to me.

Peering over my shoulder, I meet Alyssa's gaze. Her eyebrows rise while my forehead wrinkles. She presses her glossed lips together and says, "I've been looking everywhere for you." Touching her fingers to her hair, she plays with her side braid, shimmering a coppery color in the pale morning light.

I grin at her dramatics. The compound isn't that big, and she probably knew I was going to pick up Jacqueline the moment I made the decision to do so. The corners of Alyssa's eyes crinkle when I roll my eyes, a gesture Jacqueline can't see because she's behind me. "I have to take Jacqueline to the meeting hall, remember?"

Alyssa plays with the hem of her short, Chevron-patterned dress. "I figured we could do something after. The council is going to be pretty busy today." She doesn't even have to say what she's thinking. I know she wants to leave the premises again now that she knows I won't say no anymore.

I glance at Jacqueline and meet Alyssa's gaze again. "We should all hang out after."

"I'd love to," Jacqueline says.

I lean back and look at her upside down before looking back at Alyssa, waiting for my best friend to say something.

Alyssa presses her lips together, tightening her jaw. "I don't think Jacqueline will like what I was planning."

"Why?" Jacqueline asks.

I shift to look at her. "Because you went through all the trouble to get here, and we want to go out."

Jacqueline's eyes widen. "I—" She pauses.

I touch her knee. "It's okay. We can hang out tonight."

She shakes her head. "No, it's cool. I think I can handle it."

"You're right. You *can* handle it," Alyssa says. She plops on the blanket next to us.

I grin. "Perfect, we'll go after Jacqueline's meeting."

Jacqueline shifts, stiffening. "Only if I survive it."

Alyssa reaches out and touches Jacqueline's shoulder. "Everything will go smoothly. Promise. You'll just be painfully bored."

"Thanks for the reassurance. I'm really nervous. What should I expect? What do you think they'll ask me?" she asks Alyssa.

"The meeting is open to everyone, so it's possible you'll have an audience. They'll ask what are you, where'd you come from, how'd you find us? The standard stuff."

"Oh." Jacqueline's voice is so soft that I swivel on the blanket to look at her. Her eyes shift color, and she looks off into the distance.

I reach out and touch her arm. "What's wrong?"

Jacqueline hesitates for a split second before she says, "I'm a necromancer. People tend to be afraid of me. I thought that information would be for only the council and whoever I chose to tell."

My mouth forms an O, but I don't say anything. I'm caught off guard, because she's lying. Necromancers can communicate with the dead, use the spirit world to heal people, and reanimate corpses, not hold souls hostage. It takes a lot in me to keep my cool. If she wants to pretend to be a necromancer, that's her prerogative, and I'll give her the benefit of the doubt that she lied because she is scared to admit what she is. It's not like I've been very forthcoming either. I get it.

"That is so cool." I hope I sound genuine.

She shrugs. "Not really. Someone always bothers me."

Alyssa clears her throat. "It's better than constantly seeing future predictions. I'd switch abilities with you any day."

I'm surprised by the tone of Alyssa's voice. I've never heard her snap like that before, and I wonder what's going on in her head. I raise my hand up before Alyssa can say anything else. I need to tell her what's really going on. "I need to get Jacqueline to the meeting hall."

Jacqueline releases a breath and gets to her feet. As I get up, I raise an eyebrow at Alyssa in the silent question of what the heck she's doing, and she shrugs. She helps me with the blanket, and I give her the extra muffin from the bag to keep her quiet on the short walk.

We stop in front of the main building, and I turn to Jacqueline. "Take the elevator to the basement, and Roxanne will be waiting for you there. She's the council's assistant."

"You're not coming in with me?" Jacqueline asks.

I shake my head. "I'm not really on anyone's good side there. You'll be fine. I'll meet you right here after, okay?"

She frowns but doesn't ask any more questions. "I guess so."

My chest tightens, watching her pull open the door to enter the building. I can't believe she agreed to leave the premises with us, and I hope she buys my fake friendliness. I can't ever trust a girl who weaves lies and keeps secrets. I'm only nice so I can invade her dreams.

HUNTER

"Why didn't you beg her to come with us?" I ask.

"Because I don't need anyone to hold my hand." Jacqueline's voice whispers in her mind quieter than usual. She's nervous.

"Why didn't you tell them what you really are? Afraid of something?"

"It's easier this way, Hunter. People know what necromancers are and they aren't as threatening as me. They only play with the dead when I focus on the living."

"What if they ask you to raise the dead?"

"They won't."

The elevator doors ding open, and Jacqueline steps on and hits the button for the basement. I'm actually kind of surprised the council has such a tall building. Most the facilities back home are a few levels underground. You have less to worry about that way. It's easier to lockdown the facility and keep people out...or in.

The red light on the elevator camera blinks. Jacqueline peers at it for a second before staring at her reflection on the mirrored wall. Exhaustion mars her face. Dark under-eye circles glare like bruises, and her curly hair takes on a life of its own. The council is sure to sympathize with her. Anyone with a heart would.

When the elevator doors slide open, Mr. Soto greets Jacqueline with a huge smile. He talks to a woman dressed in a purple gown way too formal for a meeting. Her strawberry blond hair, tied in a thick braid, reaches the floor. I'm guessing she's the receptionist Nadia told us about.

"Jacqueline, welcome!" Mr. Soto's voice booms through the small waiting room. A suede couch rests against the wall across from a small desk with a computer and telephone. The rest of the room lacks any sort of décor. No artwork or anything. "I hope you found your way around all right."

"Yes, Mr. Soto, thank you. Nadia has been very kind to

me. She even brought me breakfast," Jacqueline says.

Mr. Soto clears his throat. "Yes, right. Hopefully she didn't do anything to scare you off. She isn't very social."

"Oh, Javier." Roxanne grabs his arm. "Nadia is a sweet girl. What would Dmitri say if he found out how unkind you're being?"

Mr. Soto huffs, adjusting his bow tie. "He won't hear about this now, will he?"

An awkward silence falls over the room, and Jacqueline stares at her trembling hands. "What do I say?" she thinks, rubbing her hands together.

"You're asking me?" I ask. Well, this is a first.

"Yes. Hurry."

"Make it out as a joke," I say. The best way to ease a tense situation is to joke about it. It's always worked for me.

Jacqueline shifts on her feet. "I'm sure Mr. Soto was only joking," she says, her voice as smooth as velvet. "If Nadia isn't very social, then I'm a pariah."

Mr. Soto barks a laugh and rests his hand on Jacqueline's shoulder. "Come on, Jacqueline. The council is waiting. They're sure going to love you."

LIFE WITH A DREAM BOY

NADIA

ALYSSA GRABS MY hand. "She lied to us."

She yanks me away from the building, and I follow her down a small stone walkway until we're away from anyone that could overhear. I turn to face her without saying anything. A million thoughts run through my mind. I knew I was right about Jacqueline. Relief rushes through me that Alyssa sees it, too.

Tilting her head close to mine, Alyssa whispers, "She's not a necromancer."

It takes me a minute to collect my thoughts. I have so much to tell her, but I want to know her thoughts first. "Did you see something?”

She puffs air through her lips, shaking her head. “I’ve met a necromancer before and their eyes don’t shift color like hers do. Have you noticed them?”

I look away. I want to keep Hunter to myself a little longer. “I have.”

“Why would she lie?”

I glance around. “She’s afraid of something.”

“You think so?” Alyssa’s eyes glass over, and she stares off into space for a moment before bringing her attention back to me. She blinks a few times before adding, “You don’t *think*, you *know*. What aren’t you telling me, Nadia?”

I never thought I’d dread this conversation with my best friend as much as I do. How can I tell Alyssa what I know? She’ll realize I’ve been invading Jacqueline’s dreams without her permission. I already know it’s wrong. I’m afraid Alyssa will judge me, or worse, tell me to stop. But I’m not the only one in the wrong.

I swallow, licking my lips. “It’s all so complicated, Lys. I accidentally caught Jacqueline sleeping last night, but when I invaded her dreams, there was a boy there. He was real. A soul trapped in her head. You’re right about her not being a necromancer. She’s a sin-eater.”

She tugs on her braid. “We have to tell the council she’s lying.”

I press my lips together and turn away. Alyssa doesn’t even think twice about the wrong I’ve done to Jacqueline. “No. We can’t. You don’t understand. Hunter needs me.”

Her forehead crinkles. "Is that the soul? They can help him."

I sigh. "Please, let me figure this out on my own. You don't know that the council will help him. They don't always intervene in this kind of thing."

"You like him," Alyssa says, smirking at me. "Of course you do. You felt his soul. God, I couldn't imagine how intimate that is."

I blush. I never thought about that. I close myself off from dreamers when I'm in their heads, but Hunter? I've let him in. "I don't know. I'm trying not to. I've only visited him twice."

Her eyes widen. "Twice already? You know you can't have a life with a dream boy."

I lift up my hand to stop her. "Just forget about it."

She taps my arm. "What if Jacqueline is dangerous? She's lying to everyone for a reason. I want you to be careful."

I purse my lips. "Let's just get through the day. Maybe she'll tell us the truth, and then I'll decide what I'm going to do about Hunter."

Staring at me with wide eyes, she thinks about my words for a moment before turning to face the perimeter wall. "I don't like this, Nadia. I don't trust her. Maybe it's not such a good idea to take her with us today."

I sigh. "You said it'll be fine."

"For now it is."

HUNTER

A small auditorium makes up the council's meeting room. Three people sit behind a table for four draped in a navy blue table cloth. A chair is placed to their right with a small table positioned next to it, and a pitcher of water and an empty glass rests on top the table.

The size of the Creature Council is underwhelming considering it's three times smaller than the board. Mr. Soto guides Jacqueline on stage, and I chuckle at her inward groans. This is less of a meeting and more of a performance. Jacqueline's awkwardness is hilarious.

She glances at the few random supers in the audience before taking the single seat, facing the council. I bet she's freaking out and wished she had begged Nadia to tag along with her now.

"Please, state your name," Mr. Soto says, drawing Jacqueline's attention to the council.

"Jacqueline Matthews." Her voice is a notch louder than a whisper. She stares at a woman in a black pantsuit with straight, blond hair and rimless glasses. "I don't believe it," she thinks to me. "That woman is human."

I'm just as surprised that there is a human on the council. I thought they were here to protect and act as a governing body for supers. Next to the woman, a young man with a shaved head and clean face yawns from boredom. He's more casual than the others in basketball shorts and a tank top, and he looks ready to leave. Beside him, a young girl with jet black hair and electric blue eyes smiles at us, adjusting the beaded necklace cascading down the front of her flower-patterned dress.

"Please, state the desired length of residency," Mr. Soto says.

Jacqueline rests her hands in her lap. "Permanently."

Mr. Soto thumbs through a stack of papers. "Please, confirm your species."

"Necromancer." Jacqueline still holds onto the dead people whisperer façade. I wonder what would happen if someone found out she was lying or if they happen to have another necromancer here that asks too many questions.

Smiling, Mr. Soto turns his head toward the audience. "The floor is open for questions."

Jacqueline glances at the almost empty audience again before staring back at her hands. I'm seriously dying to talk to her, but I'm scared she'll toss me into the void. She plays with the hem of her dress and shifts, crossing her legs at her knees instead of her ankles.

Jacqueline clears her throat when no one raises their hand. "Can I ask questions?"

Mr. Soto nods. "Why yes, anything." She really does have him wrapped around her finger.

"I've only been submerged in the supernatural world for a few years, and I've only heard rumors about the Creature Council after I lost my brother to an HPA agent. Can you explain the structure more?"

I'm glad she asked. I was wondering the same thing.

"Is that what you really want to know?" the human woman asks. "You've been staring at me like I have two heads."

I chuckle.

Jacqueline links her fingers together, meeting the woman's gaze. "I'm sorry. I didn't mean to stare. I just didn't expect there to be a human on the council—I don't know if you read my file, but I've had some bad luck with them." If I had eyebrows, I'd raise them.

The woman presses her lips together. "It's that kind of attitude that hinders the supernatural race from melding with human society."

I almost feel bad for Jacqueline.

"Forget I asked," Jacqueline says. "I have no other questions."

"Oh, Veronica, you know she didn't mean anything," the girl with jet black hair says. She looks at Jacqueline. "How much do you know about the HPA and its board?"

Jacqueline swallows. "Only that they want to eradicate all supernatural creatures by any means necessary."

The girl smiles. "That's only partially true." She nods at Veronica. "Veronica was a lead scientist for the HPA and worked on an experiment using DNA from supernatural creatures to create a virus to make humans less susceptible to illness and cancer. Things went wrong when the HPA took extreme measures to capture different creatures, and of course people were going to fight back. After an attack on their facility, killing nearly all their scientists, the founder of the HPA put together the board with generous financial sponsors and now spends all their efforts on wiping out all non-human people."

Veronica folds her hands on the table. "As Ana mentioned, the HPA was headed in a direction I couldn't live with. I lost my husband and son to them."

Jacqueline covers her mouth. "How awful."

"We live and learn," Veronica says. "I was only able to leave because one of my patients helped me. I was able to find protection here and eventually a spot on the council."

"We've been around much longer than the board," Mr. Soto says. "We have no qualms against humanity, and you shouldn't either."

A silence falls over the room, and I draw into myself. I've never heard about half the things they said. They make the HPA sound corrupt and violent, but really, most of the agents and scientists are conditioned to fear supers and follow orders. Being stuck in Jacqueline's head has given me a different perspective. Maybe I'll be like Veronica when I get my body back.

"Yes, Mr. Soto," Jacqueline says quietly.

He claps his hands and pushes from the table. "Well then, let's go ahead and introduce you to everyone you'll need to know to fit in around here."

NADIA

We've been waiting for over an hour for Jacqueline. Just when I'm about to give up on her, she pushes through the door, her brows knitted together and a frown on her lips. She jogs down the steps, her messy hair bouncing with her sudden movement, and then she fakes a smile. It's more like she bares her teeth at me.

"You don't look very happy," I say.

Jacqueline crosses her arms and looks between Alyssa and me. "I'm so embarrassed. I didn't know a human was on the council. I wanted to crawl in a hole and die when she practically yelled at me for being surprised."

I grimace. "I should've warned you."

Alyssa grabs both our arms, half dragging us toward the back gate. "Enough talk. We only have a few minutes to get out of here if we want a few hours to do whatever we want."

"Are you sure we won't get caught?" I ask.

"Shhh." Alyssa holds her index finger over her lips.

Jacqueline steps closer to me, her arm shaking as she brushes it against mine. A small group of people loiter near the apartments, and we sneak past them, heading in the direction of the back gate. Alyssa swipes the talisman from the tree, and we take turns going through the gate. Running through the trees, we race down the beaten path to where Alyssa keeps her car hidden. I get in after her while Jacqueline slides onto the backseat.

"Where are we going?" Jacqueline asks.

Alyssa starts the engine. "You'll see," she says, eyeing me in her peripheral vision.

I grip Alyssa's knee. "Are you sure we have to ever go back to the compound?"

I don't know why I ask. The compound is the safest place for us to live, but it always seems so complicated. I'd love to live somewhere I don't have to worry about my nightmare inflictor side.

Jacqueline laughs nervously. "Maybe I should stay here."

I turn in my seat and grin. "It was just a thought." I laugh and shift back to look at Alyssa.

She raises her eyebrows and smiles. "It's funny how you can still surprise me, Nadia. We can do whatever you want."

I'm tempted to really go through with it. I'd love to see what the world has to offer, and I wonder how long I could survive before having to call the council for help—if they'd even help me. And then I think about Hunter and the urge to runaway subsides. Jacqueline would never agree to go with us. "It's tempting, but let's see how another trip to the city goes first."

HUNTER

"I can't believe you're leaving," I say.

Jacqueline wrings her hands together in her lap. "Alyssa is a seer. She can keep us safe," she thinks.

"What if she can't?" It'd be perfect for Jacqueline to get caught again by the HPA. It'd serve her right for tormenting me with her desire to settle down at the compound.

"She can."

Nadia laughs at something Alyssa says, but I can't hear them over the radio. She's happy and carefree, and I wish she were laughing with me. Watching Nadia makes me regret my desire for Jacqueline to get caught. It'd put Nadia in jeopardy, and I don't want her getting hurt. I still haven't had the chance to get to know her.

"But if she can't? What'll you do if you're caught by an HPA agent?"

Jacqueline taps her fingers on the door panel, her annoyance tangible. "They won't hurt us. I'm working for them, remember? Your mom has given me two months to find out information."

"Whatever you say, Jackie. Just don't let them get hurt."

"Hey, I'm not the one putting them at risk."

I groan.

"Come on, Hunter. You know I always come first."

9

I AM A MONSTER

NADIA

I STAND NEAR the edge of a gleaming reflection pool in front of a monstrous mausoleum. The block-like building is a dark gray granite masterpiece with a small set of stairs leading up to double doors. Giant rectangular stained-glass windows glitter in the sunlight, evenly spaced apart on the wall, and I bet they're more beautiful from the inside.

Alyssa came up with the cemetery idea shortly after we left the compound since Jacqueline was clearly nervous about the city. She figured taking me to one with such history and beauty would be a lot cooler than the small one we passed the last time we were out. And she was right. This cemetery is so peaceful with its meticulously cared for gardens, sprawling green lawns, and fascinating human memorials.

I smile and step toward the entrance of the mausoleum. Jacqueline waits next to Alyssa and we all step inside through the double doors. Cold, deathly silence surrounds us. I gape in awe at the gleaming Italian marble floors and the warm wooden walls. The massive windows let in pale light into the main entry adorned in cream colored furniture and a tan rug. If I took a picture, no one would know I was at a place where the dead go to rest.

A short glass wall surrounds a set of stairs that descend deeper into the mausoleum. Textured granite walls complement the Italian marble floor, and the temperature noticeably lowers as we enter a long hallway.

"I brought you here because I wanted to show you something," Alyssa whispers.

Jacqueline walks silently behind us without a word.

I don't stop to look into the quiet rooms we pass, slightly afraid of what I'll see, until we reach the last open entryway. It leads to a small room with marble floors and a giant stained glass window that allows in soft, colorful light. What I thought were marble walls are actually memorials with people's names and birth and death dates. A cement bench sits in the middle of the room, and Alyssa guides me over and we sit down together.

Jacqueline strolls along the perimeter of the room and touches the walls. "Whose crypt is this?"

"The council's," Alyssa says.

I frown. "The council cremates remains."

"They do that for creatures, not humans."

"What?" My voice echoes, and I cover my mouth, like I'll disturb the dead.

If Alyssa is implying what I think she is, that would mean my mother could've possibly been put to rest here. I push to my feet and read each of the etched names. My mouth dries when I see the name I was terrified, yet hoped, to find. I trace my fingers over the letters, my heart hammering, and look up at Alyssa with tear filled eyes.

"Emily Petrov was my mother," I say out loud. "My father never spoke of her having a resting place. I don't even know if there was a funeral. I was young when she died."

"Is that how you ended up at the compound?" Jacqueline asks, her voice barely above a whisper. She stands next to me and touches my shoulder. "I'm sorry about the human remark from yesterday. I didn't know you were half."

Tears blur my vision. "They're not all bad."

"I know that now."

Alyssa comes up on my other side. "We can go, Nadia. We don't have to stay here. I didn't realize this was where your mom was put to rest."

HUNTER

A tear rolls down Nadia's cheek, and if I had control over Jacqueline's hand, I'd reach out and wipe it away. She sits hunched over on the block-like bench and leans her elbows on her knees while hiding her face with her hands. Her shoulders shake. In this moment, I wish we were in a dream so I could comfort her. She's so vulnerable and fragile, I know with certainty that Nadia isn't a monster.

"I'm okay. I want to stay," Nadia says. She pulls her hands away and peers at Jacqueline. Nadia's tears burn pink trails on her cheeks and her indigo blue eyes shine in the rainbow light coming in through the stained-glass window.

Jacqueline's eyes shift from Nadia to the engraved stone on the wall with the name Emily Petrov on it. "How did she die?"

"I don't think that's an appropriate question to ask right now, Jackie."

Nadia rubs her eyes and stares at the floor. "She was murdered."

NADIA

My mouth quivers, and I lick my lips a few times to moisten my mouth. I've never shared this story with anyone, but I can't stop the words from coming. People should know the truth about my mother. "My mother had lost her sense of reality after being in our world for so long. An HPA agent found us at home when my father was out one night, and she didn't know the agent was real. She thought she was hallucinating. She didn't even try to run and just stood there while he cut her throat. The agent killed her to prove to my father that we'd never be safe." I leave out that it was my father's fault that my mother went crazy. I can't bear to share that detail with Jacqueline. I shake the image from my head. I can picture it so clearly. I don't even know why I'm telling them this, but I don't stop. "I was still hiding under the table when my father came home. We left within minutes, and I never saw our house again."

"Oh, Nadia," Alyssa says. "I didn't know that's how she

died. I'm so sorry."

"You couldn't have known." I cover my face and squeeze my eyes closed. "Can I have a minute," I whisper.

I need to be alone with just my memories.

HUNTER

As Jacqueline follows Alyssa into the corridor, intense, confusing emotions rush through me. I'm losing hope. Nadia was my hope, and I think I'm going to lose her. She'll never side with me once she discovers that my mom is an HPA board member. She'll think I'm the monster.

I *am* a monster, though, at least by association.

It's sickening what the HPA is capable of. I've never heard of agents killing humans before. What's the point in trying to preserve humanity if they're going to kill innocent humans because of their association with supers?

"You have to tell Nadia that not everyone involved with the HPA is bad."

Jacqueline sighs in her mind. "Don't you get it, Hunter? They *are* bad, though."

"You know I'm not bad. You said it yourself. I'm a pure soul."

"You would've turned out just like the rest of them if I hadn't taken you."

"You don't know that."

"I do."

I hate to admit that Jacqueline is right. If I hadn't been imprisoned by her, I'd have continued on the path the HPA set for me. I would've enrolled in their training program the day I turned eighteen. I'd have turned out to be just like the agent who killed Nadia's mom. It would've been all I knew.

"Jacqueline?" Alyssa taps Jacqueline's shoulder.

She blinks a few times and meets Alyssa's green eyes. "I'm sorry. I was lost in my own thoughts."

"Is it the dead? I didn't even think about... Did you want to go outside and look at the gardens?"

Jacqueline nods. "I'm fine. Used to it. But I'd love to see the gardens. This place is really depressing."

NADIA

I couldn't enjoy the rest of the mausoleum. It's different when you're not connected to someone buried there. It went from fun to miserable in a matter of minutes, and I feel bad that I've ruined what was supposed to be an adventure. No wonder I don't have many friends. I don't want to be around me either.

I blankly stare out the window. I don't have much to say anymore and just want to head back to the compound.

Alyssa switches lanes. "It's okay to be sad," she says quietly.

"I don't mean to be a downer. It's just that I wasn't prepared for that. And, I'm not really sad. It's been a long time since her death, but I'm pretty angry with my father for not telling me."

"Would it have made a difference?" she asks.

I glower. "You're defending my father?"

"Dmitri doesn't need me to defend him. All I'm asking is if it would've changed anything."

Her words soften my anger. "I think if I'd had known, I would've wanted to visit her. You know my father doesn't want me to even step outside my room, much less the compound these days. He's overprotective."

"He loves you."

"Alyssa?" Jacqueline asks from the backseat, interrupting our conversation. "You should look out the back window."

Alyssa gazes in the rearview mirror. "Oh, no." Her eyes glass over and then she blinks a few times. "We're okay. Everything is okay."

HUNTER

Nadia and Alyssa cut their quiet conversation short and a thick silence surrounds us. Jacqueline shifts in her seat and peers out the back window. She rubs her hands together, her fear intense enough to slice through me.

"Is that what I think it is?" Jacqueline thinks to me. "Please, tell me I'm hallucinating."

She stares at a white van weaving in and out of traffic. I recognize the vehicle immediately. It's one of the HPA's vans. It's still too far back to see who's driving, but I know for a fact that only field agents drive them. If the girls are spotted, they'll be in serious trouble.

"Hate to tell you this, but that is definitely an agent," I say.

"No, no, no, no. This isn't happening." Jacqueline chants the words in her head over and over.

"You said that an agent wouldn't harm you."

Jacqueline nervously cracks her knuckles. "I don't really know that, Hunter. I'm hoping."

"Well, for your friends' sake, I hope that's true."

NADIA

A horn blares, drawing my attention out the back window.

Jacqueline clutches the seat and stares out the window as well. My heart sinks into my stomach. A white van drives behind us, a little too close to the car. The driver honks his horn again and waves his arm for us to move over.

I rest my hands on the dashboard and turn to look at Alyssa. She stares into space seeing something I can't. What I wouldn't give to have her ability, to see the future. She claims it's a horrible gift, seeing things she can't always control all the time, but it can't be worse than surviving on scaring people in their sleep.

"Stay calm," she says. "It's important."

"What's wrong?" My dry mouth makes my words hoarse.

"What did you see?" Jacqueline leans between the seats. "Are we going to die?"

Alyssa grips the steering wheel. "Really, you both need to stay calm," she says again.

Panic seizes my chest. "Just tell us what you saw."

"There's road construction ahead, and they're redirecting traffic. Among the workers is an HPA agent marking the cars of any person he suspects could possibly be a supernatural being. It's the perfect way to track and kill without people being suspicious."

"What? They'll know what we are!" My voice rises.

Alyssa cringes, grabbing my knee. "I don't think so. We're not the normal creatures they look out for. The agent won't suspect a thing as long as we stay calm."

Shadows edge my vision. "But did you see it for sure?"

"No decisions were made yet."

I hit the dashboard. "Alyssa!"

Jacqueline groans from the backseat. "Why can't we turn around?"

My chest is so tight, it hurts to breathe. The world weighs heavy around me, suffocating me with fear and anxiety. I rest my fingers on the door, clutching the handle. It takes all my will power not to fly out of the car and run.

"It'll cause suspicion. Trust me," Alyssa says. "All we need to do is act normal."

I blink back my tears and grip the arm rest. This is a big mistake. I know it. They'll recognize what I am and murder me like they did my mother. I'm going to die in the front seat of this car. I can feel it.

Staring straight ahead, I search for the person I should be most afraid of. A solid wall of cars blocks the street in front of us, and we can't turn around even if we wanted to. Traffic eases forward, and I fidget with my seatbelt.

"You're making me nervous, Nadia," Alyssa says. "Please, relax. We're almost through."

I take a deep breath. "I can't. I can't stay here and hope for the best. You said it yourself. No one has made a decision. When they do, it'll be too late. You need to pull over."

Alyssa grips the wheel. "Don't do this, Nadia. We're too close."

My mind is already set. I'd rather risk the streets alone than face a potential threat, trapped in a car, with nowhere to run. I couldn't defend myself if I wanted to. I don't even know how to fight.

We're less than five car lengths from the construction zone where it looks like a water pipe burst. I unlatch my seatbelt, fling my door open, and jump out.

HUNTER

"Stop her, Jackie!" I yell.

Nadia thrusts her door open and catapults out of the car. Her wide, frightened indigo eyes peer around, and she spins on her boots. She's crazed with fear, acting on her instincts to flee, and I know in this moment she really has lived a sheltered life. I wish I had my body so I could jump out after her and reassure her that she's safe. Fight for her against any and all agents if I have to.

My uselessness pains me, a deep ache cutting through my soul. If Nadia is caught by an agent, I'll never see her again, and then what will I do? I need her to help me. But I need her to be okay, too. Her presence, her soul—how can I feel like this already? It goes against everything in me. She's softened my hardened façade, even just only being able to watch her from within Jacqueline.

Unbuckling her seatbelt, Alyssa shifts to look at us. "Stay here."

Jacqueline nods. "I wasn't planning on going anywhere."

Alyssa rushes from the driver's side and leaves the car idling in the middle of traffic. Jacqueline watches the two girls argue through the window.

"You should help Alyssa," I say.

"Be quiet, Hunter. She told me to stay here."

NADIA

I cover my ears, protecting them from the hammering sound of breaking concrete and spin around, not touching my feet firmly to the ground.

A car door slams, drawing my attention to the traffic in front of me. Alyssa races around the hood of the car, leaving Jacqueline in the backseat. Cars honk and a few people yell, but she doesn't acknowledge them. She reaches out to grab me, and I glide back, finding myself at the mouth of an alley between buildings.

Her eyes glass over, her eyebrows pinching together in worry. "Get back in the car."

I glance behind me. "I can't do it, Lys. Just leave me alone."

"I'm not leaving you. You're having a panic attack, Nadia."

I heave a breath. "Please, I'll be the reason you're caught."

She tugs my arm. "Don't make us abandon the car."

I push her a little too hard, and she stumbles back, slamming into the wall. But I'm not going to let her pull me back to the car. My heart races, threatening to explode from my chest. I need to get out of here, but I don't have a plan. All I know is I'm not getting back into the car. I can't.

I run my fingers through my hair, pushing the pale blond strands away. "I'm not making you do anything, Lys. I'm trying to help you. Don't try to make me get back in. They will know. Look at me. I'm barely passable as it is."

Alyssa frowns and glances toward the street. "Fine, just let me get Jacqueline. We can all go to The Haven by foot and see about getting a ride back home."

A cold chill slithers down my back. I stare down the empty alleyway. It dead ends into a chain-link fence with another street on the other side of it.

I shake my head. "You're going to hate me if you lose your car."

"It doesn't matter." Alyssa's eyes glass over. "Oh, no. Nadia, run."

Someone clears their throat, freezing me in place. I turn my head toward the direction of the traffic. A tall, well-built man with his dark brown hair pulled back into a small bun stands on the sidewalk facing me.

"Run," Alyssa whispers.

I take a step, pulling Alyssa with me. A pop resonates through the air, startling me, and a metal dart clatter into the wall, missing my arm by an inch.

"Let the girl go," the man says, glaring, crinkling his dull brown eyes. "And don't run. If ya do, I'll kill ya."

I shake my head, dropping me hand from Alyssa's arm. "This is a misunderstanding." I glide a foot back and immediately regret the action. Fear made me careless, stopping me from being more aware of my footing. From the way the man's eyebrows arch, I know he noticed my fluid, unnatural motion.

"Slowly raise ya hands and walk to me. If ya can follow those directions, I won't hurt ya." His accent is subtle, but noticeable, and creepier with the way he reaches into his long jacket.

I see the glint of a knife before he even shows it. My world closes around me, making it hard to focus on anything but the sparkle of the blade. This man isn't some Good Samaritan thinking I'm fighting with Alyssa like I was praying for. He's an HPA agent. I'd recognize his knife anywhere. It's like the one that killed my mother. It's going to be the one that kills me, too.

10

CAN'T STAY FOREVER

HUNTER

"OH, MY GOD." Jacqueline's words ring out through the car as she unbuckles her seatbelt.

Nadia pushes Alyssa against the wall, and a man in an all black uniform slides from in between cars and struts past us without a second glance. He stands in the mouth of the alley, blocking Nadia and Alyssa in, and he reaches for the knife attached to the weaponry belt hidden under his long jacket.

"Don't just sit here. Do something!"

"Like what? He has a knife. He'll kill us all," Jacqueline thinks.

"No, he'll kill your friends if you don't do something."

Jacqueline opens her door but doesn't get out. "And he'll kill me if I do."

NADIA

I brace myself as the agent marches closer. He grins, wagging his eyebrows, as he pulls his concealed knife from under his jacket. Twirling it between his hands, he makes a show of the power he thinks he holds over me. He's trying to intimidate me, get in my head, scare me more than I am.

I clench my jaw. I'm not going to give him the satisfaction of seeing me cry.

"Don't hurt her!" Alyssa rushes the agent with a broken brick. She chucks it and hits his chest.

He growls a groan, jerking his arm out to grab Alyssa. "Do you even know who you're dealing with? I'm trying to help you."

I scream, the sound ripping from my throat, echoing off the walls. Flying forward, I crash into the man's back. The second he touched Alyssa, I lost it. I couldn't stand by and do nothing. He stumbles, losing his balance, and we both fall to the ground. The man jerks his elbow behind him and hits me in the ribs. I heave a breath, unable to cry as pain washes through me.

Rolling to my side, I press my back against the brick wall of the building. Loose gravel embeds in my cheek, and all I can do is watch the man jump to his feet to chase Alyssa, because she keeps throwing whatever she finds at him.

Even though she's not a skilled fighter, Alyssa can see his moves before he makes them. She dodges the knife with such grace and agility that she could easily run to safety if she wanted to. Sliding past him, she runs deeper into the alley. If she'd just turn and run, she could escape, but instead, her eyes shift to mine.

"Go," I mouth. I'm useless until I can catch my breath and get back to my feet.

The man launches at Alyssa and grazes the knife along her arm. She jumps backwards and hits the opposite wall. I watch in horror as the man jabs his knife at her again, almost stabbing her shoulder. She drops to her knees and rams into the man's legs, knocking him down.

It takes everything in me to find my footing and get up. The man should have less of an advantage facing two people, but he does have a weapon. I search the alley as Alyssa dances out of the reach of the agent, and I spot an empty bottle a few feet away.

I pick it up and smash the bottle over the man's head. He huffs and swivels, grabbing my arm. Screaming, I stab the broken bottleneck into his shoulder, but he only tightens his grip, yanking me onto him.

"I don't really want to hurt ya, girl," he says to Alyssa.

Alyssa clutches her arm. "Yet you won't stop waving your knife around."

The man's fingers dig into my arm. "If you'd just walk away, no one gets hurt."

Alyssa stares past the man to me, and she holds my eyes while she says, "Okay."

I blink to keep my tears from spilling. It's what I want her to do, but it doesn't hurt any less. I'd rather die knowing my best friend is alive and safe than die knowing that she died with me.

The man relaxes and pulls me up with him, aiming the knife at Alyssa before training it against my neck. The cold blade presses to my bare skin, and he walks backwards with me against him toward the opening of the alley.

"I'm sorry, Lys," I say, closing my eyes. I can't bear the thought of her watching me die.

"Let her go!"

HUNTER

The agent spins while holding Nadia and keeps his knife trained on her neck. With a single jerk of his arm, he could kill her. He should kill her for fighting back. It's what he was trained to do. But he doesn't. He takes sick pleasure in taunting her.

The agent grins. "Now, why would I do that?"

Jacqueline meanders forward with her arms raised in a non-threatening manner. "Because she's not the one you should be afraid of."

Alyssa jumps on the agent's back and throws him off balance. He releases Nadia, and she falls to her knees. Alyssa runs to her friend. Jacqueline rushes the agent and grips his arm and digs her nails into his skin. The agent freezes and stares into Jacqueline's eyes. She glares and tugs him closer to her until they're only a foot apart.

"I have a deal with Dr. Sullivan," Jacqueline whispers. "The board will be furious if you mess up their plan."

The man scowls. "Ya lying monster."

"I don't think he knows, Jacqueline," I say.

Jacqueline ignores me. "Are you willing to find out?"

The man pushes Jacqueline, and she stumbles back and hits the wall. Jerking his arm up, he aims it at Jacqueline's chest. He steps forward, causing Nadia to scream again. The world shifts as Jacqueline rolls to try to get away. Nadia throws herself at the agent. She's inhumanely fast, her feet not touching the ground, but the agent manages to grab her hair. He thrusts her head back, presses his knife to her alabaster skin, and then Jacqueline closes her eyes.

NADIA

My neck stings as the agent's blade nicks my skin. I should've run. Alyssa and I could've made it back to the car, but I couldn't leave Jacqueline. It wouldn't have been right. If Jacqueline dies, Hunter would die, too.

I close my eyes.

"Nadi, no!" I swear it's my father's voice.

The man's chest hits my back, the force pushing me forward. We collide with the ground, him on top of me, crushing me. Just as quickly, someone yanks his heavy weight off me. I gasp for air, feeling around the ground for anything I can use to protect myself. The man moans, and I blink a dozen times to regain my vision. The world spins as someone pulls me to my feet.

Alyssa's wide green eyes stare past me and into the alley. My mouth falls open, my heart nearly thrashing from my ribcage at the sight of my father wrestling the man to the ground. My father's punches fly so fast, his arms almost blur as he fights the man into submission.

Without looking up, he yells, "Run! Get out of here."

"I don't want to leave you!" I cry.

He glances at me, his eyebrows pointed in anger. "Alyssa, get her out of here. This isn't the only agent."

Jacqueline runs ahead of us, and Alyssa drags me from the alley and back to the car. She pushes me onto the backseat next to Jacqueline and rushes to the driver's side and hops in. Starting the engine back up, she merges into traffic. Even though I can't see what's happening in the alley, I stare at the entrance, hoping to see my father come out. By the time we pass through the construction zone, no one has come out of the alley. Alyssa turns left, leaving my father behind with an agent trained to kill him.

HUNTER

"I think your mother lied about our deal," Jacqueline thinks. She twists her fingers together. "She was never going to give me my freedom."

"You don't know that. The board isn't always so open with their plans."

"At least I don't have to worry about them now."

I want to yell. *"Must be nice to not have to worry about what happens next."*

Jacqueline ignores me, shifting in her seat to look at Nadia. "You saved my life," she says to her.

Alyssa looks at us in the rearview mirror. "I think we kind of all saved each other."

Nadia doesn't say a word. She leans her head back, staring

at the roof of the car. Her hands shake on her lap, and she doesn't move. Jacqueline reaches over and touches Nadia's knee. Nadia glances over at us in her peripheral vision and then looks back at the roof.

Not only did an HPA agent murder her mother, the fight with the agent today rattled Nadia so much that I'm sure she'll never agree to help me if she finds out that my mom is a board member. She'll take Jacqueline's side, and I'll be living out the rest of my life as a body-less soul with the worst luck.

I hate the HPA.

I hate my mom.

I hate my life.

NADIA

We make it back to the compound in time to find Mr. Soto heading toward the guest apartment. Jacqueline stays with him, and I stroll next to Alyssa as we walk around the perimeter of the compound.

I can't stop thinking about how I almost died today. I would've died if my father hadn't had showed up to save us. I'm confused about Jacqueline, too. She put her own life in danger so I'd have a fighting chance. She didn't have to do that. Now, my head and my heart are at constant battle over whether or not I should visit Hunter again. *You promised him...*

I push Hunter's image from my mind. "Is my father going to be okay? I'll never forgive myself if something happens to him because of me."

Alyssa bumps my shoulder. "He'll be back by morning. We were really lucky he was in the city."

I blink tears from my eyes. It's been a few weeks since I've seen my father and having him rescue me in a back alley was not ideal. He's going to be furious. My hands tremble. "I was so stupid for getting out of the car."

She touches the cut on her arm. "You were scared."

I purse my lips. "Still an idiot, though."

She tilts her face to the darkening sky. "Just a little."

We both laugh, and it calms my nerves. It feels so normal, making today feel like it never happened and was just something I saw in someone else's head during a nightmare.

When we reach the dormitory steps, Alyssa turns to me. "I'm going to go to the dining hall. I'm starving. Join me?"

I cross my arms. "Maybe next time. I've had enough excitement for one day."

Alyssa laughs and touches my shoulder one more time before breaking away and heading toward the dining hall.

Silence greets me in the lobby of the dorm, the TV off, and everyone probably already at dinner. Gliding down the hallway, I head toward my room. The fight with the agent completely drained me. I haven't been this scared since I was a little girl. Memories of my mother flood my mind, and I envision the way her daisy yellow hair smelled like coconut and how she had small crow's feet at the corners of her eyes from how much smiling she did. She never stopped smiling, even at the very end. It'll haunt me forever.

Hunger burns in my stomach, and I touch my feet to the floor and bend over, clutching my knees. The feeling hits me hard and fast. Sweat breaks out on my forehead as I sense someone sleeping in the room next to Alyssa's. It's always been empty, and I'm thrown off guard by its new inhabitant.

I know it's Jacqueline without having to open the door. Mr. Soto must've assigned her this room when we left her with him, and she moved in while Alyssa and I were walking around. I knock and wait a second to see if it disturbs her. She's too tired to wake completely. Her dream beckons me forward. Before I can stop myself, I open the door.

Her dark, curly hair sticks out from under her green comforter. She's in such a deep sleep that I doubt anything could wake her. Today wore her out just as much as it did me. Her exhaustion makes going into her dream easy. It was only a matter of time before I caught her sleeping again. My mouth waters in anticipation.

I shut the door behind me, glide across the room, and hover over her. Rolling her onto her back, I press my cool fingers to her temples. I close my eyes and my stomach flips as the world shifts. When I open my eyes, I'm in her dream.

HUNTER

I sit on the tailgate of an old truck parked in the empty lot of a gas station. In front of me, an endless desert stretches to the horizon about to be hit by a thunderstorm. Dark clouds churn over the infinite dry ground, and a bright streak of lightning sparks in the distance. I feel Nadia before she shimmers into view.

A pale gray dress, cinched at her waist, hugs the curves of her hips. Her long, white hair hangs loosely down her back, sweeping back and forth with her movement. Her bare feet don't touch the pavement as she glides closer like a hauntingly beautiful spirit.

I pat the spot next to me, but she doesn't sit down. She stares at me for a moment and then looks up at the storm brewing in the sky. Thunder claps and lighting strikes a power line, creating a shower of sparkles.

And then it starts raining.

Nadia pouts, staring at the water pooling in her palms to rush over like small waterfalls. The rain streaming down her cheeks could be tears. Melancholy hides the smile I wish I could see, gripping her tightly enough that I can feel the sorrow in my own soul. She looks so lost and helpless, a victim of grief.

I reach out for her hand, testing to see if she'll let me hold it. She does, sending my heart racing. Having her in this torrential downpour, watching the rivers of rain soak her dress, making it cling to her skin, does something to me. I want to pull her into my arms, hug her, hand her my shirt from my own back. Something to make the sunshine return to light her beautiful eyes.

"I was so frustrated I couldn't help you today," I say after a minute of holding her hand. I know she won't speak unless I do. "I don't know what I'd have done if something happened to you."

She tilts her head back and lets rain pelt her face. "I almost got Jacqueline killed."

"Why did you save her?"

Her eyes meet mine, and she presses her lips together. "I don't know. All I could think about was you."

She pushes her wet hair from her face, raindrops clinging to her pale lashes, causing her to blink. Heaving a breath, she steps forward and sits down on the tailgate next to me, pressing her leg into mine.

I continue to hold her hand, thinking she needs it more than I do. "I'm glad you did. She might be the bane of my existence, but if she dies..."

"So do you," she finishes for me. She sniffles, wiping the rain—maybe tears—from her cheeks. "I'm really sorry you're in this situation. I want to help you—"

"But you don't know me or anything about my situation," I say.

She might not know me or anything about me, but the fact that she saved Jacqueline because of me, gives me hope. I don't know what to say to her. I'm afraid anything I tell her will mess this all up. Nadia's unlike anyone I've ever met. Jacqueline and I are strangers to her and she faced one of her own personal fears head on so that we could live. I'm grateful but guilty. What would she say if she found out the truth about me? She'll hate me. I can't stand the thought. Not because it'd mean I'll be stuck with Jacqueline until I die but because I feel a connection to Nadia, feel it in my soul, one I don't want to lose. It seems to be all I have left.

She must feel my intensity, because she remains silent without prying for anymore, just waiting for me to continue. I cup my free hand and let it fill with rainwater. "Are you doing this?" I ask. I need to change the subject. I'm not ready to go there.

She shrugs. "Does it bother you?"

I shake my head, afraid I'll say something wrong. I'll let her lead the conversation now and be here and let her get to know me on her terms. It may be the only way she'll forgive me for my association to the HPA. At least I hope she will.

After a moment, I finally say, "I miss the rain."

Her gaze drops to the wet ground. Even when she's sad, she still looks beautiful. I sit quietly and watch as the rain pelts her face and drips off her chin. It's strange how real the dream feels and looks. How she feels, twining her fingers with mine. I can almost forget that it's all within Jacqueline's imagination. But maybe this is my new reality. Because right now, with my dark thoughts threatening to shut me down and lock Nadia out, I'm not sure I'll be free again.

I push the morbid feelings away.

Right now, Jacqueline doesn't matter. The only thing that matters is that Nadia's here and she hasn't forgotten about me.

NADIA

Hunter brings our hands up to my face and runs the back of his hand across my cheek to swipe the rain off my skin. I offer a small smile, looking at him and the earnestness in his hazel eyes. His dark hair slicks against his forehead and water runs down his face and over the shadow of day-old stubble peppering his cheeks and neck. His green T-shirt sticks to his stomach, show-ing off the ridges of his abs, the kind of muscles I don't usually see on creatures in the compound. He hasn't changed much since the last time I saw him, and it helps me believe he is who he says he is and he's not manipulating his true self.

The memories of seeing my mother's memorial stone replay in my mind the longer I have time to think. I can't help but wonder if Hunter has one, too. The body can only live so long without a life force. I'm afraid to tell him what I suspect. I don't think I can handle watching him grieve when I'm reliving the grief of my mother all over again.

I cup his chin, nudging him to look at me. "I can make it stop if it's too painful thinking about what you're missing."

He tips his head toward the sky. "I like pretending I'm whole again."

"Can you be?" It's easier to tiptoe around what I really want to ask.

He shrugs. "If Jacqueline would take me home."

"So, you have a body?"

He nods. "Looks just like this." He waves his hand from his chest to his feet. "I'm sure someone is taking care of it for me."

I puff a breath of air through my lips. "Who?"

Sirens ring out in the distance, and I turn to face the two-lane road separating the gas station from the barren desert.

Jacqueline's nightmare kicks into motion regardless of whether or not I do anything. My presence alone is enough to mess with her head. The rainstorm probably didn't help either.

"You're leaving me, aren't you?" Hunter asks.

I meet his gaze and nod. "I don't have a choice. I can't stay here forever. Jacqueline's sleep cycle is almost up."

Jacqueline's presence draws near without me even having to see her. Like Hunter, I can feel her presence. Now that I know Hunter's here, I can feel him stronger than ever. More so than Jacqueline. I wish I had more time.

An old Camaro barrels into the empty parking lot, the nightmare landing right in front of me. I can't stop the smile forming on my lips, seeing the fear in Jacqueline's eyes. Hunter's gaze bores into the side of my face, and I suppress the urge to defend myself and why I look at Jacqueline the way I do. But Jacqueline catches sight of me, her worst nightmare unfolding. I wonder who she's imagining me to be.

"Hunter, please leave. I don't want you to see me like this," I say.

He touches my shoulder. "You don't scare me," he whispers.

"Please," I beg.

I reach out to touch Hunter's shoulder, to plead with him to leave, but he's already gone.

Turning back, I face my dreamer. A white van pulls up behind the Camaro and blocks Jacqueline in. She can't do anything, not even run.

Slamming my hand on the hood of the car, it explodes into flames, the smoke coating my tongue, tasting as sweet as milk chocolate.

The sky above begins to crack, and I can't help the satisfaction rushing through me as I destroy the rest of Jacqueline's dream.

"Bye, Hunter," I whisper into the collapsing dream around me.

His presence doesn't appear before me, but I can feel his

soul lingering nearby. "Please, don't forget about me, Nadia."

I don't think I could if I wanted to.

11

UNLOCKING SECRETS

HUNTER

THE MOMENT NADIA left, emptiness settled into my soul. I think I might've wasted too much time letting her control everything, but I couldn't help it. She felt so sad until the moment the dream shifted, and then it was like she was someone else, like the girl I met in the first dream. But she doesn't scare me like she did Jacqueline. The only thing I'm afraid of is if she doesn't come back. I might go crazy thinking about the possibility.

I push my worries away. She saved Jacqueline because of me. I'm just as real to her as she is to me. I can feel it. I could hear it in her voice when she asked me to leave. She's afraid I'll see her as a monster, but I'm more afraid that's how she'll see me.

As much as I hate to admit it, I know that if I want to get my body back, Nadia needs to know where I come from. I'll be more of a monster to her if I don't tell her the truth, convince her I'm not like my mom or the HPA. If I keep this secret any longer and she finds out, thinks I'm purposely hiding it from her, I don't think I'll even have a fighting chance.

I see how Nadia feels about secrets. I'm going to have to take a huge leap of faith and hope for the best. I have nothing more to lose anyway. I wish I could bring her back right now. I want to meet the real Nadia, not her dream version. But I can't.

I doubt I ever will.

NADIA

I sit on the wet grass as the moon sets, the midnight sky gradually lightening to lilac. I hug my knees to my chest. Confusion and anger sweep through me, and I'm unsure about everything.

Thoughts of Hunter cross my mind. I'm not even sure if I want to get involved, risking myself for a strange soul I know nothing about. But I feel bad for him. His essence lingers with me from the dream, and I wish I had more than a sleep cycle to talk to him.

Apart from Hunter and Jacqueline and this nearly unbelievable situation, what really has me down is that my father hasn't returned from the city. So many things could've gone wrong. Alyssa's vision, though accurate most of the time, can change in a split second. Most of the time, she doesn't tell me what she sees at all because of how quickly things change.

"Care for some company?"

Turning my head, I meet Jacqueline's lavender eyes. It's been a few hours since I invaded her dream to be with Hunter, but it doesn't make seeing her again any less awkward. Her secrets have turned into my secrets, and what that means for me? I'm not sure.

I study her eyes, waiting to glimpse the hazel color of Hunter's to peek through. His soul flashes for a split second like I expected, and I pat the grass next to me. I do it for his sake, though I fear she'll realize what I'm doing to her. At least she hasn't now. If she figured out that I was messing with her dreams, I doubt she'd be asking to sit with me.

"Sure, but I have to warn you, it's highly possible that my father will be arriving any minute, and he's scary as hell when he's mad."

Her lips twist to the side. "It takes a lot to scare me." Her eyes shift to hazel and back to lavender, Hunter shining through again.

I rest my chin on my knees. "I wanted to apologize for everything that happened today. Facing an HPA agent isn't my idea of fun. You were so brave."

"It wasn't my first run in with one," she says, looking at me.

I hold her gaze to watch her eyes. "Is that why you're here?"

She blinks. "What do you mean?" Her face remains expressionless. It's a strange reaction to a simple question.

I tilt my head to the side. "I was just wondering if you

came here because you're afraid of the HPA."

Her eyes flash from lavender to hazel, blinking between colors. "Oh, yeah." She shakes her head. "Sorry, I must still be tired. I came here because they took everything from me."

I fiddle with the laces on my boots. "How were you so calm facing the agent? I was terrified."

Tears rim her eyes, and her fingers tremble when she reaches out to touch my arm. "I was too, but it was nothing compared to being caught. If you think agents are scary, you should see the board."

"How did you escape? My father said it was a death sentence for creatures caught." I study Jacqueline's face, and she sucks in her bottom lip. I wish I could hear what she is thinking, see what she's imagining. I wonder if she's lying. If there was a way to escape the HPA, the Creature Council would know. My father would tell everyone to better prepare.

She straightens her back. "I got lucky, I guess." Her eyes shift to hazel and stay there until she blinks a few times. I wonder if Hunter's talking to her as I do. If I were her, I don't think I could even function with someone inside my mind. She's obviously a pro at hosting stolen souls.

"Luck? You must've raised an army of the dead or something," I quip.

She wipes the back of her hand on her forehead, smearing imaginary sweat, and stares up at the sky to avoid my unwavering gaze. "As long as you don't try to fight back, they don't kill you immediately," she says, not really answering my question, making it incredibly hard for me to feel as much for her as I do for the boy in her mind. Maybe he's the reason she was taken by the HPA in the first place.

I shake my head, matching her serious express to not give away my true feelings. "Oh, I'm pretty sure that isn't always true. That man would've killed us no matter what today." I touch the gauze on my neck where the knife nicked me. "I guess you really did get lucky."

HUNTER

I'm screwed.

Nadia and Jacqueline are bonding over their fear of the HPA. I should've told Nadia about me sooner. She's going to take Jacqueline's side, and I'll be stuck here forever. My hope slips away from me, and I can't stop it. I need Nadia to understand the circumstances. She has to know I'm not like my mom. I'll convince her I want nothing to do with the HPA anymore. I'll beg her to believe me.

"But, really, how did you escape?" Nadia asks, extending her long legs and leaning back on the palms of her hands.

I push away my racing thoughts at the sound of her curiosity—no, at her doubt. Maybe I'm not lost after all. Nadia might share the same negative history as Jacqueline with the HPA, but I doubt Nadia would ever give someone up to save her own life. I know it, because I saw it. I felt it in her.

"Right place, right time," Jacqueline says, missing the doubt that sparks a whole new flame of hope to light up the stupid void she always throws me into.

I laugh out of nervousness. Jacqueline still dances around the truth with Nadia. *"Why don't you tell her the truth? She's go-*

ing to get suspicious."

"Shut up, Hunter. You're distracting me," Jacqueline thinks.

I'm testing Jacqueline. I can use her lies against her when I tell Nadia the truth about who I am. Nadia won't trust Jacqueline, and it'll work out better for me. It'll give me time to convince Nadia I'm not the one she should be afraid of and prove Jacqueline isn't some weak, frightened person. She's strong, intelligent, and cunning. Manipulative.

When Nadia discovers the real truth, Jacqueline's perfect, safe existence will shatter. Her vulnerability and weakness will come to light, and I can use it against her. I *will* use it against her. It's the only way to get her to take me back to the HPA. She won't just return me to my body out of the goodness of her heart. She needs to be left without another choice.

Nadia tilts her head back and stares at the sky. "I didn't mean to pry," she says. "I can tell you're uncomfortable sharing things from your past. I get it. I'm the same way."

Jacqueline laughs in her mind. "She won't be suspicious of anything, because she trusts me, Hunter."

"Jacqueline?" Nadia asks.

"Sorry, I sometimes get lost in my thoughts," Jacqueline says.

Nadia presses her lips together, her nose crinkling. She saw me again. It takes everything in me not to boast to Jacqueline that she's wrong about Nadia. Because Nadia is suspicious, and the questions running through her head are starting to pile up. By nightfall, she'll be dying to see me again. It'll be my chance to gain her trust, to beg her to do something.

"It's okay, but you should probably head back inside. My father is coming."

NADIA

The last time I was this relieved to see my father was the night my mother died. His pale skin looks ashen against his inky black hair. His obsidian eyes crinkle at the corners when he sees me, and he opens his long, sinewy arms. It wasn't the greeting I was expecting, but I'll take it.

I get to my feet, letting him wrap me in his arms. He kisses the top of my head once and pulls away. Looking down at me, he searches my face before inspecting me from head to toe. His thin lips disappear in a frown, and he reaches out and touches the bandage on my neck.

"Oh, Nadi, you were hurt," he says.

"I'm okay, Dad," I say. "It's nothing."

He stares at me for a long while. "Alyssa? What about the other girl? Are they hurt?"

I stare past him at the purple sky. "They're fine."

He hugs me again. "You have a lot of explaining to do. What were you three doing in the city? You could've been killed."

I sigh. "I'm so sorry, Dad. We wanted to have some fun. It's so boring around here."

"I don't understand. You didn't even want to leave your room the last time I was home."

I tuck my hair behind my ear and step back. "I know, but things happened. Alyssa helped me see, and I don't want to be some sheltered little girl anymore. I'm wasting away here."

He releases a small laugh at my dramatics. "But you could've gone with the escorts."

I grimace. "That's the last thing I want to do."

He crosses his arms and stares at me. "I only want two things in life for you, Nadi. For you to be safe and happy. I can see that I'm failing you on both accounts."

I grab his hand. "You're not. I promise."

"I wish you'd have talked to me."

"You weren't exactly here."

He frowns.

"Which is fine. I swear. I'm not a little girl anymore."

"Obviously. I didn't think I was gone so long, but you're too—"

"Too sheltered. You know, I didn't even know how to protect myself in the city. How terrible is that? The daughter of the council's police force can't even tell an agent from a normal human until it's too late. I just—I don't want to stay hidden here forever."

He hugs me. "Things are going to change."

I smile. "They already are."

"You're right. I see you've fed enough to hold your color. Someone from the city?"

I blush. I know what my father is thinking with the worry swimming in his onyx colored eyes. He's afraid I'm terrorizing strangers in the city, since I'm sure he's aware I haven't seen a volunteer within the compound in a while. I was always surprised by the thrill seekers who like being tormented in their dreams.

"No," I say.

"Care to elaborate?"

I shrug. "Why does it matter? I don't ask you about what you do when you're on the road."

He puffs air out his nostrils. "You're right. It's not my business. But I'm worried, Nadi, people in the city are dangerous. If you really must go there, please, let me take you."

"Sure," I say. "But I don't need you to chaperone me."

He rubs his chin. "No, but you need to know where the safe places are if you ever get into trouble again. I can introduce you to people who can protect you and help you outside the council. You have to know a lot of people like I do. It's how you survive in the real world."

The real world—a place I've only ever really encountered in dreams.

"So, you're really going to take me to these places and let me meet people outside the compound?" This is going a lot better than I imagined. My father hasn't even raised his voice. And from what he's saying, it sounds like I'm not grounded for eternity. He's actually going to let me go back.

He clears his throat. "Yes, because I now see that I can't scare you into staying here forever, and I guess even an HPA agent can't keep you away."

I cringe. "Is he dead?"

My father pulls me into a hug again. "I wanted to kill him. I've never wanted anything more in my life, but no. We only kill if we're out of options. We aren't like the board."

"So, he can come back?"

My father eases away and shakes his head. "You don't have to worry about him, I promise. And when I show you what you need to know. You won't have to worry about other agents, either. I would prefer you never go to the city alone, though."

He'd really keep me in a bubble if he could. "When will you even have time to show me? Next week? In another month?"

"Today."

"Seriously? The council will let you?"

He laughs. "No one is a prisoner here. As long as you follow the rules, help out, and don't do anything that could jeopardize the compound, like sneaking out, we can do as we please." I glance away when he mentions sneaking out. I hope he doesn't report Alyssa or Jacqueline to the council.

"About the whole sneaking out," I say.

"I think the agent was punishment enough for you girls."

I blow a breath out in relief. This is by far the best conversation I've ever had with my father. I wonder what changed. I open and close my mouth, trying to think of the right words to say. "Is that why you're being so cool about everything?"

He looks down at me with a tight smile. "Is it really that weird for me to be understanding?"

"Yes, actually."

He laughs and kisses my forehead. "Well, I'm going to try to change. I don't want you to feel like you have to hide things. Your mother would've scolded me for that, you know."

My heart aches hearing him mention my mother. I want to

bring up her memorial, but I don't want to ruin the moment. So instead, I hug him. "When do you want to leave?"

"Soon."

"Okay, I need to get ready. I promised Jacqueline and Alyssa I'd have breakfast with them."

"Who's Jacqueline?" he asks as I open the door.

"She's new here. You didn't get a chance to formally meet when you caught us in the city."

Before he can say anything else, I glide inside and let the door close with a thud. It's still early and most people are sleeping so I head down the hallway that leads straight to my room.

A tingling sensation washes over me, and I dig my fingernails into my palms. I can't believe Jacqueline is asleep so soon. It's been less than twenty minutes since I talked to her, and here she is again, calling to me in her sleep.

Now's your chance to talk to Hunter. I can jump into a dream regardless of my hunger. It's much easier to control the dream when I don't want to destroy it. If I can go in with a clear head, maybe I can start unlocking Jacqueline's secrets. Maybe I can focus more on Hunter without my own thoughts getting in the way.

Opening the door, I glide into her room. I hover in front of Jacqueline's sleeping body, staring at her, thinking about all the lies she has told me. But the truth lies in her dreams. Secrets can't stay hidden from me.

Just a few minutes. In and out. You don't have to ruin her dream, I think.

And then I fall into it.

HUNTER

She's back.

Nadia's back. I'm in shock and disbelief, because it's much sooner than I expected. I thought I was going to have to wait all day, but Jacqueline fell back asleep, probably because she's as bored as I am.

"Hunter?"

Nadia's voice resonates through me, and I step from the shadow of a large oak tree. Her white hair shimmers in the pale sunlight overhead, and her gray eyes meet mine. She's just a ghost of herself in this dream world but still as beautiful as when I first laid eyes on her.

"You're here," I say.

She crosses her arms. "You seem surprised."

I grin. "I am. It's like you know the moment Jacqueline is asleep and then just appear. Can I ask you a question?"

She spins an inch above the ground and looks around at the peaceful meadow. "I can't guarantee I'll answer it."

I shove my hands in my pockets and look at my bare feet hidden in the overgrown grass. "What exactly are you?"

She frowns. "You haven't guessed?"

"A succubus?"

She cracks a smile. "Definitely not. I'm a nightmare inflictor."

It's my turn to grimace. I've never heard that term before. "I always thought nightmares were caused by an overactive imagination."

"They can be," she says. "But I can create nightmares so

horrific, they affect people in their waking state, and if I visit too often, I can drive a person crazy."

I think about her words for a moment. The HPA would automatically classify Nadia as one of the most dangerous creatures, but to me? I live a nightmare life. Nadia is my relief, my day dream. "You're the reason Jacqueline's asleep?"

She shakes her head, her hair swaying back and forth. "I wish I could. It'd make things easier for me. She's probably exhausted because I keep visiting, and she's not getting enough restful sleep."

"Why do you do it?" I'm nervous that my questions will push her away, but I have to ask. I know about a lot of creatures, especially ones that are considered a threat against humanity, but I've never heard of Nadia's ability. She'd be at the top of the board's kill list if they ever found out. I can never let that happen.

"I don't have a choice. It's how I survive," she says. "I can't live a normal life otherwise. It's my sustenance. But it's not like I love what I am. I'd give anything to be completely human like my mother was."

I study her face. Her almond shaped eyes, lined in thick, pale lashes, shine in the dream sun. Her heart-shaped lips pucker, her bottom lip fuller than her top lip. I imagine what it'd be like pulling her into my arms and kissing her, but instead I say, "I understand the feeling. I'd give anything to get out of here."

Nadia looks me up and down. "What's it like?"

"Torture." I kick the grass with my bare foot. I should've imagined shoes. "I have no control over anything. I see what she sees, hear what she hears, and when she sleeps, I'm bored out of my mind. I can't sleep in this state. I can just sort of shut down, though."

"Will you tell me the truth?" she asks. The question is abrupt, and I know what's coming. I promised myself I wouldn't lie.

I swallow, knowing she's going to ask me the questions I've been dreading. "I have no reason to lie to you. I have nothing to lose since I'm stuck here. I want you to trust me, Nadia."

"Why you? What have you done to deserve this fate?"

I turn away and stare at the clear, blue sky. She's going to abandon me and never come back. She's as afraid of the board as Jacqueline, and I think knowing where I come from will cause irreparable damage. But I have to tell her. I know it. The more I tell myself that, the easier it is to open my mouth.

"You have to promise to hear me out. I'm not a bad person, I swear, but you're going to think I'm bad by association," I say.

She stiffens. "Go on."

"Jacqueline got herself into a sticky situation before she came here. To get out of it, she made a deal with a very powerful person to spy on the council and gather information of their whereabouts. The only way Jacqueline would make the deal was if they gave her someone as collateral," I say.

She scrunches her nose. "You must be important."

I sigh. "Apparently not, because that powerful person Jacqueline made the deal with was my own mom."

She tucks her hair behind her ear. "That's terrible. Why

would your mother do that? What's so important about the council that she was willing to destroy your life?"

I swallow. "That's the thing. My mom isn't just some random person. She's on the board of the HPA."

Her eyes widen, and she takes a step back. Fear and disgust mar her face as she narrows her eyes. A flood of shock, grief, and fury swirls around me, Nadia's emotions palpable the longer she remains near me.

She puts more space between us, holding herself.

And I know I've lost her. Her raw emotions cloud her judgment, consuming the goodness I usually feel radiating from her, and I don't think I can do or say anything to make things right.

I hold up my hands. "Please, Nadia. I'm only related to a board member. I'd never hurt you. Please, you have to believe me."

Thundering clouds roll over the sun, darkening the world around us.

"I—I have to go," she says.

"No!" I yell. "Nadia, don't leave me here. I need you. Please."

But it's too late. She disappears, and I'm left in a crumbling dream.

12

❦

DANGEROUS BY ASSOCIATION

❦

NADIA

"THE SITUATION WITH Jacqueline is worse than I thought. We can't trust her at all," I say, tying my hair back into a ponytail.

Alyssa stares at my reflection in the mirror. "She saved your life yesterday. She's not going to harm us. I haven't seen anything bad."

"We still can't trust her."

"Is this about the dream boy?"

I nod. "I wasn't joking about Hunter being real. I can touch him, talk to him, he sees me for who I am. And, he knows things about Jacqueline."

Alyssa's visions are never set in stone because of freewill. Every decision a person makes leads to another and so on, which can influence how something turns out. Alyssa can guide a person to make the best decision possible, but she can't actually make them do it.

"Okay, but you're going to have to give me more to work with," she says. "I can tell something is bothering you. What changed?"

"Hunter says she's working with the board of the HPA," I blurt.

Alyssa crosses her arms, her eyes widening. "Are you sure? How do you know? Maybe that's why she fought the agent yesterday. It'd make sense. She's acted way too scared to just jump in to help us without knowing she's safe."

I lick my lips. "I think you're right, but the agent didn't hold back. This is all so confusing. I believe Hunter. He's angry at Jacqueline and the board. He said the board gave him to her as part of their deal."

"Really? Then I think you're right about your dream boy. You know how sin-eaters work—they redeem bad souls so they can die in peace. If Hunter isn't a bad soul, there's no need to redeem him. I bet she didn't even know Hunter's soul was pure when she took it."

My brows scrunch. "What do you mean?"

"I know that as of right now, Jacqueline isn't going back to the board, and I don't think she would keep Hunter for fun. So, that means Hunter can't be killed by Jacqueline. It's the only explanation for his being trapped in Jacqueline's head. When I was studying different kinds of soul manipulators, there was a section about sin-eaters. The consequence for taking a pure soul is that she must live with it until she puts it back in its body or until the soul decides to move on."

A thousand thoughts swirl through my mind. If what Alyssa says is true, that means that Hunter wasn't lying. He's a good person despite being the son of a board member. But, it doesn't make me less uneasy. He's dangerous by association.

Alyssa rests her elbows on her knees and leans her chin on her hands. "I think you should talk to him again. As of right now, Jacqueline isn't leaving, but you know how that goes. We should probably tell the council, too."

My heart sinks into my stomach. "Not yet."

"If she decides to leave, it could be devastating for this place."

She's right. I just wish it were simpler. Hunter swears he's not a bad person, but sociopaths are great liars. He could easily fool me. But if he isn't, I'd feel guilty for not doing anything about it. The council wouldn't help him. He has no one on his side. If I were trapped inside someone's mind like Hunter, I'd hope someone would care about what happens to me.

"Please, Lys. You don't understand. I'm begging you not to say anything."

She looks at the carpet. "Okay, but you have to keep me involved. I can help you."

A knock on the door startles me, and I sigh. I know it's my father ready to take me to the city, but I really want to ignore him right now. Too much is going on in my head.

Alyssa slides from the bed and opens the door. She smiles at my father and moves out of the way to let him in. "It's good to see you again, Dmitri," Alyssa says. "Thanks for letting me tag along to the city."

My father glances at me in the mirror. I set my comb down. "I know nothing about this."

"I guess it'll be all right," he says. "Next time actually ask, Alyssa, instead of assuming."

She giggles. "I'm sorry. I sometimes forget not everyone can see what I see."

My father nods his head. I push to my feet, considering making up an excuse not to go, but Alyssa looks pretty excited. I also want to spend time with my father while I can. Ignoring the dread slithering down my spine, I smile. "Thanks for doing this."

My father turns to me. "Does your new friend want to come with us? What was her name again?"

"Jacqueline? Oh, I don't know. She's pretty freaked out from yesterday," I say.

"I think we can convince her." Alyssa leans close to me and whispers, "It's best to keep her near us for now."

I hope Alyssa's right.

HUNTER

"You're really brave after yesterday," I say.

Jacqueline stares at the back of Nadia's headrest as her dad speeds down the highway. I never thought I'd see the day that Jacqueline would leave the compound again, but I'm not complaining. It'll give me a chance to remind Nadia I'm here.

"Agents won't bother us. Dmitri will protect us. He's probably a hundred times more skilled and deadlier than any of your agents," she thinks.

"They're not my *agents, Jackie."*

"Whatever."

The city looms in front of us. Dmitri exits the highway and cruises on the city's outskirts to the river. Jacqueline stares at the water while tapping her finger on her knee. She's more anxious than she admits.

Dmitri clicks the radio off. "See the bridge up ahead? It's a safe route from the city. On the other side is a spelled warehouse where you can find shelter. It belongs to a good friend of mine who has set up safe camps throughout the area for people who aren't accepted into the compound."

"They reject people?" It's the first thing Jacqueline has said out loud since she sat in the car.

Dmitri glances at her in the rearview mirror. "All the time."

"I thought they were here to protect us all?"

Nadia turns in her seat and looks at us. "That's funny. The council only allows useful people to stay at the compound. Once you're not, they kick you out."

"Don't worry. Necromancers are always useful," Alyssa says.

Jacqueline fidgets, and I laugh. Her anxiety is so strong it makes me anxious, too. She plays with a curl, looking out the window. I'm enjoying this a little too much, but I don't care. She deserves it.

Dmitri pulls the car into a familiar parking structure and

waves to a security guard. He parks a level up in a spot with a reserved sign and shuts off the engine. He turns to look at Jacqueline. "They're only joking. Don't let them scare you. If the council accepted you, you have nothing to worry about."

NADIA

I'm excited.

I can't remember the last time I got to do something fun with my father. He's not as embarrassing as I expected in front of Alyssa and Jacqueline, and it was a cool surprise when he pulled into the parking structure of The Haven.

"I've been here before," Jacqueline says. "This is where Mr. Soto picked me up."

I stare out the window. A boy strolls through the parking lot, his curly, brown hair reminding me of Hunter. I'm afraid I'm going to start seeing him everywhere as the guilt of knowing he's imprisoned in Jacqueline's head weighs heavy on me. Pulling my gaze away, I glance at Jacqueline. Her eyes shift colors, and I wonder what Hunter is saying. I shouldn't think about him. It's too dangerous. But it's hard to resist.

I hate how much I'm attracted to a dream boy. How he scares me yet draws me to him. I don't even know the real him, but his soul? Maybe my darkness enjoys his light. But I can't help think how differently things would be otherwise. He'd see me as the monster I am. Yet, things aren't different. He knows me apart from what I am, and even seeing me as a nightmare inflictor, he's still not afraid. Fate brought me to him, but fate has never been kind to me.

I push the thoughts away. Nothing can ever be real between me and Hunter. He's a living soul without a body, and even if he was back in his body, his mother works for an organization that would much rather see me dead than with him. The odds are not with us. Our future together would only be made of dreams and not reality. A life of fantasy.

Despite my unbidden feelings for Hunter, it's hard to imagine my life without him now. He's invaded my very being, because of his presence inside of Jacqueline. I can't imagine creating another nightmare without him there. I hate myself less because of him. I've never been okay with what I am until now.

When I climb out of the car, I meet Jacqueline's gaze. Her eyes flash from lavender to hazel again. Hunter won't let me forget him even if I wanted to. He's not giving up on me. It'd be easier if Jacqueline wasn't here. I could forget them both. *You're lying.*

My stomach twists in knots, and I want to throw up. Jacqueline's presence has me so conflicted about everything. It bothers me more than I thought it would. She could be setting us up in the long run even if Alyssa hasn't seen it. It makes me wonder what I would've done in her situation. Would I have stolen a soul and ruined a life to survive? Maybe. I can't say for sure. I'm no different than she is. We're both monsters in the end.

Sliding his arm around my shoulders, my father pulls me from my thoughts. "Is something wrong?" He guides me toward the stairwell with Alyssa and Jacqueline trailing behind us.

"I was just thinking about yesterday." My father doesn't need to know anything about Jacqueline and Hunter. He'd forbid me from invading Jacqueline's dreams again.

He squeezes my arm. "You don't have to worry about the HPA here. This place is just as safe as the compound, maybe even more."

HUNTER

Nadia and her dad walk ahead of us, quietly whispering to each other. Every time she looks into Jacqueline's eyes, her face softens with an unintentionally irresistible pouty lip. But I know Jacqueline doesn't recognize the constant shift in Nadia's expression like I do.

Jacqueline's—or maybe my—presence pains Nadia, yet she hasn't given either of us up to the council. It gives me hope that I haven't lost her completely. Hope that she'll return to me and let me explain everything to her. Let me show her I'm not a threat.

Nadia peers over her shoulder once more, looking more human now than I've ever seen her. Her usually pale blond hair is a few shades darker and her skin has more color. It's hard to believe she's even related to her father.

Now that guy is scary. He stands a good foot taller than Jacqueline with pitch black hair. His skin is so pale, it's almost translucent, and dark blue veins trail up his arm. His black eyes suck in light, a creepy contrast to his paleness. I'd be terrified if he were the nightmare inflictor to invade Jacqueline's dreams.

Alyssa nudges Jacqueline's shoulder. "I'm glad you came. I was afraid what happened yesterday scared you off."

Jacqueline stares at the ground. "I almost didn't, but I can't let my fear control me...and the compound is a little boring. I feel like all I've been doing is sleeping and eating."

Alyssa laughs. "I'm sure the council will give you something to do soon enough."

"God, I hope so."

I want to say something sarcastic, but I don't want Jacqueline to throw me into the void, not when we're somewhere besides her room. It's interesting to super-watch and see how different creatures act outside of the HPA's Guide to Surviving the Supernatural World. I'll have to remember to burn the handbook when I'm free. Whoever wrote it had no idea what they were talking about.

"This is what life would be like if I stayed..." Jacqueline's thoughts interrupt mine. They weren't intended for me, but I'm still annoyed by them. She's also the calmest I've ever felt her.

"Until they discover the truth. You can't hide it forever."

"I can try."

I don't respond, because I can't help the despair rushing through me as she continues to steal my hope away.

NADIA

We enter the small lobby and cross it to the hallway where Cian sits perched on a barstool. He shoves his magazine under his arm when he sees us and smiles widely. "Dmitri Petrov, my friend, what brings you here?"

My father shakes the troll's hand and nods his head at me. "My daughter does."

The troll grins at me, his eyebrows jutting up his forehead. "Nadia, doll, you didn't tell me your father was Dmitri. He's well respected around these parts. Just yesterday he removed two agents from our city."

I cringe. "I know."

My father looks down at me. "You've been here before?"

"My fault," Alyssa says, interrupting. "Don't be mad at Nadia."

My father runs his hand through his inky black hair. "I'm not, just surprised."

I step past Cian and put my hand on the door. I wouldn't mind if my father wanted to stay here with Cian. "If you two want to catch up, we can go inside without you. I don't mind at all. Take your time, Dad."

"No, no," Cian says. "Enjoy yourselves. Everything's on me today."

Sighing, I walk into the room packed with people. I scan the crowd, and Alyssa nudges me and points in the direction of a few cute boys on the dance floor. My father slings his arm around my shoulders, and I grimace. The Haven was a lot more fun without him chaperoning.

My father lifts his hand and waves at a few people before guiding me across the crowded dance floor and to a booth in the corner. He nudges me to sit down, and Jacqueline slides in across from me.

My father presses his hands on the table. "Wait here while I get a few of my friends for you to meet. They can help you girls if you need someone separate from the council. It's good to always have a backup plan." He glides away.

Alyssa hovers next to the table but doesn't sit down. Leaning over, she says, "I'll bring us some drinks." She smiles and saunters away, leaving Jacqueline with me, and we glance at each other awkwardly.

"This is better than fighting agents, right?" Jacqueline asks with a forced laugh.

I nod but don't say anything. It's hard to make small talk with a girl I don't trust, whose changing eye color constantly reminds me of the boy I should be afraid of but instead feel connected to. The day is already dragging and we just got here. I hope it's over soon.

13

EVERYONE HIDES SOMETHING

NADIA

MY FATHER'S CELL phone rings, and he pulls it from his pocket and answers it. "I'm in the city now. No problem. See you soon." He hangs up and looks at me. "Will you be okay here for an hour?"

Finally. I'm miserable. My father introduced us to a handful of people, but it felt more like he was showing me off. It was so embarrassing. "I'll be totally fine. Go."

He chuckles. "You're making me feel unwelcome, Nadi."

"You are welcome here, just not when the world needs you," I say, grinning.

"Fair enough." My father kisses my head and glides to the

exit. He waves from the door, and I release a breath when he disappears.

"Are you sure we're going to be safe without your dad here?" Jacqueline asks. Her hands tremble as she absently twirls the straw in her cup.

Alyssa laughs from across the table. "I'd tell you if we weren't. As of now, nothing is going to happen except someone is going to ask you to dance."

Jacqueline frowns. "What?"

"She's right," I say, bumping her arm. "I am."

HUNTER

Nadia's friendliness toward Jacqueline kills me. Sometimes it feels forced, and I see the distrust in Nadia's gaze. Other times, she relaxes and laughs, smiles, and seems to forget about me. It's like she's punishing me for being who I am, even if she doesn't intend it this way. It's possible that I'm a little jealous, even though I'd never admit it, but it should be me dancing with Nadia, not Jacqueline.

"You've been acting strange since yesterday. Are you okay?" Jacqueline stares past Nadia at a guy who has been checking her out all afternoon.

Nadia frowns and stops dancing. "No, not really."

"Ask her why," I say.

"She doesn't look like she wants to tell me, Hunter," Jacqueline thinks.

"You won't know if you don't ask."

"Why do you care?"

I don't respond. I can't. It's pointless arguing about a situation that is out of my control, especially under these circumstances because Jacqueline doesn't know that Nadia has been visiting me.

"You need to give up, Hunter, and stop being so obsessed with a girl you'll never meet. You're stuck with me."

"I hate you," I say.

"I'm sorry. I really am."

NADIA

Shaking off the bad feelings Jacqueline rips from me with her simple question, I remember to move my body and sway, dancing to the music. But I don't take my eyes off Jacqueline, though her gaze constantly darts away from me, like she's avoiding making eye contact. Her eyes shift from lavender to hazel and back to lavender as she has a conversation with Hunter. I wish I could listen to her thoughts and see what has her now so serious.

She bats her lashes a few times. "Anything I can do to make you feel better?"

I shake my head. "Don't worry about me. Just enjoy yourself. I'm sure I'll get over it."

A boy with short, dark brown hair, wearing a T-shirt and jeans, comes up next to Jacqueline and leans toward her. His full-sleeved tattoos ripple under his muscles as he touches Jacqueline's sides. He whispers something in her ear, and she blushes and turns to look at me. I smile and wink, letting her know it's okay to leave me. She lets the boy tug her away toward a booth in the far corner.

I glance around to look for Alyssa. She's nowhere to be

found, so I make my way off the dance floor, ignoring looks from a few boys hanging out at a table nearby.

"Your friend should be careful." A boy with shaggy, blond hair stands up from the table and grabs my hand. "Ryder is an incubus. He's been known to cause a few problems for people around here."

I tug my hand away and don't meet the boy's eyes. "My friend is a necromancer. He should be the one to worry."

The boy leans closer. "You're new around here."

His face hovers inches from mine, and I pull away from his sudden closeness. I know he's trying to be friendly, but I'm not exactly in a friendly mood. I press my lips together. "You're really brave talking to me."

His brows knit together. "Why?"

"My dad is Dmitri Petrov."

He steps back and glances at the two boys sitting at his table. Before he has a chance to do or say anything, I shrug past him and walk to the kitchen. I don't want to be here anymore.

I need to clear my head.

HUNTER

"Nadia's leaving, Jackie," I say.

"I'm sure she's not going to abandon me. She'll be back."

"You should probably stick together."

"Shut up, Hunter. I'm trying to have a conversation."

Jacqueline stares at some guy named Ryder with a lip and eyebrow piercing, tattooed sleeves, and a crooked nose like he's the greatest thing on earth. He's definitely textbook bad boy, and I bet a lot of girls fall for him. Maybe I'll get a tattoo when

I get my body back. I need some street cred after everything that has happened to me.

Ryder taps his fingers on the table. "You work for the council? I saw you with Dmitri. You know people around here call him the Night Terrorizer? He's pretty badass as long as you're not on his bad side."

"I only live at the compound," Jacqueline says. "Moved in a few days ago. What do you mean the Night Terrorizer?"

"You know, because he's a nightmare inflictor. I had a friend volunteer to be his victim once, said it was the craziest, freakiest thing he'd ever experienced."

Jacqueline blinks a few times and then thinks, "I've been having a lot of nightmares lately. I wonder if Nadia..."

Oh crap. This isn't good. *"I'd know if someone was intruding your thoughts, Jackie. I'd definitely know if it was Nadia,"* I say.

Her suspicion melts away. "You're right, Hunter. I'm being paranoid."

I really hope she believes me, and I hope Nadia comes back to see me soon, so I can tell her that Jacqueline suspects something. Nothing good can happen for anyone if Jacqueline finds out.

Jacqueline leans back and stares at the crowd of dancers. "I've never heard of that ability," she says to Ryder.

Ryder lowers his eyebrows. "Funny how the council makes you register and inform them of what you are but aren't exactly open about their employees."

Jacqueline shifts nervously. "How do you know if someone

invades your dreams?"

"I told you I'd know."

She ignores me.

"Why do you ask? You been having nightmares? I know someone who can give you something to find out if you want."

Jacqueline peers at the dance floor. "I don't know. My friend never mentioned her ability, but I don't think she's hiding it from me. I've just never asked."

Ryder grins. One side of his mouth rises higher than the other. "Everyone hides something though, like you for example. It'd be a shame if anyone found out your little secret. Lucky for you, the council doesn't allow incubuses there."

What? Who is this guy?

He licks his lips and leans forward to grab Jacqueline's hand. "But don't worry. Your secret is safe with me."

Jacqueline laughs nervously. "I don't know what you mean."

"That body isn't yours. You stole it from a human, huh? Their aura keeps peeking through."

A rush of alarm courses around me. "Oh, no. I'm losing it. I'm being careless. No one should be able to see Hunter, not even an incubus." Jacqueline's thoughts ring clear as day even though she didn't intend for me to hear them. Something is going on with her. I hope it doesn't affect me.

Then it hits me. Ryder is an incubus. His kind is well-known with the HPA because they're lethal. They siphon energy from people, and that's why he can see me.

I can't believe it.

"Oh, God. This is so embarrassing." Jacqueline squeezes Ryder's hands. "How awful it would've been if someone other than you found out. How can I thank you?"

Jacqueline lays it on pretty thick, wrapping Ryder around her finger already. She doesn't correct his assumption about stealing a body and probably never will. I bet he thinks he has a chance with her. He better not have one though. This situation sucks enough as it is. I'll be permanently placed in the void if that were the case. It's what I would do.

He grins at Jacqueline. "Dance with me?"

NADIA

I sit in the dimly lit stairwell outside the exit from the kitchen. I'm pretty sure my father told Cian to stop me from leaving, but it's not like I'm brave enough to go anywhere alone. So, here I am, avoiding contact with everyone except a brief greeting to the cook.

Something is seriously wrong with me, because I can't even relax and have fun for a few hours. Maybe I'm the one who's actually going crazy from visiting Jacqueline's dreams over and over again. I only know of the consequences for the dreamer, not for myself. *You can't live with him in a dream forever.*

But I want to.

Part of me is terrified of visiting Hunter again. I'm terrified because of the board and what they could do to me, yet I'm scared of the council, too. They'd never allow it. It would be breaking a serious rule—putting the compound in jeopardy. It's impossible to even consider a future with Hunter, but I still want to imagine it.

I wish my mother were here. She'd know what to say or what I should do. She picked a hard life for herself falling in love with my father. Her life was one consequence after another. *Look where it got her.* I wonder if she thought it was worth it. I wonder if my father would agree.

"Nadia?"

I tilt my head up and stare at a silhouette in the bright light of the kitchen. Alyssa steps in and closes the door behind her. Her stilettos echo off the concrete stairs as she takes a few steps to join me.

I pat the spot next to me. "A lot is going on in there."

"Sorry I left you," she says.

I look at her and smile. "As long as you had fun, it's okay."

She leans her head on mine. "But you didn't."

Huffing, I tap my foot on the stair. "It's not that, it's just—this is going to sound crazy." I take a deep breath and blow another puff of air through my lips. "I can't stop thinking about Hunter. I know I should forget about him."

I press my lips together and stare at my hands. Alyssa doesn't say anything, and I know she agrees that my thoughts are crazy. To her, liking Hunter is like being infatuated with an imaginary person, a dream boy. He's only real to me. No one but me can see or hear him inside Jacqueline's mind. Alyssa couldn't possibly understand.

After a minute, Alyssa says, "I don't think you sound crazy. I think you *are* crazy." She giggles and then touches my knee. "You do realize that life will be hard and the only way you'll have some semblance of normalcy is if you figure out how to free Hunter, right?"

I sigh. "I can just live in the dream world." I'm mostly joking, but the thought is way better than having to confront Jacqueline and then force her to let him go. If she's working with the board, that'll most likely start a war I can't win. It's also possible that Hunter's not interested in me in any way except wanting me to help him return to his body. I might just be a way out. I'll never know for certain unless I do it.

"Can you at least pick a place I can visit?"

We both laugh, lightening the depressing mood I'm in. Maybe after I make a decision, Alyssa can tell me whether or not it's a good one. If only her visions were concrete. Life would be a lot easier.

Grabbing the rail, Alyssa pulls herself to her feet. "My advice is to not make any decisions yet. First think about the future you'd have with Hunter and if it would be worth risking everything you have for it."

She's right, like always. "You can't tell me that?"

"That's only something you can decide." She takes my hand and pulls me up. "Now, come on, your dad is about to notice we're not inside."

14

LOST IN DREAMS

NADIA

JACQUELINE WAS QUIET the entire ride back to the compound. The moment my father parked, she was greeted by Mr. Soto and whisked away. She was acting bizarre after I pulled her away from the incubus on the dance floor, and I'm pretty sure I was mentioned in conversation. She wouldn't even meet my eyes.

My father strolls next to me in the bright moonlight. "I have to escort one of the council members to a sanctuary in Arizona."

I sigh. I thought I'd get to spend more time with my father than a measly day. "They can't get someone else? You just got home."

"It's a short trip. A few days tops."

I run my fingers along the chain-link fence of the perimeter. "That's what you said last time."

He slings his arm around my shoulders and hugs me. "It won't always be like this, Nadi, promise."

He sounds so sure that I almost believe him. But, as long as the HPA is around, it'll always be like this. He'll be sent out for weeks at a time to places I'm not allowed to know, doing who knows what. I'm afraid it's going to eventually wear him down.

I stop in my tracks and look past him. "I hope you're right."

HUNTER

"What's wrong with me?" Jacqueline says out loud. She stares at herself in the mirror, combing her curly hair with her fingers. "I can't focus. I feel so tired, but I know I slept. I'm losing control."

"Hey, Jackie, just thought I'd mention that you're talking out loud."

"Shut up, Hunter! I can't think!"

She rubs her eyes and blinks a few times. Leaning close to the mirror, she nearly presses her nose to the glass. Her purple eyes look different, wider, scarier.

"Too much fun hanging out with Tats?"

"His name is Ryder." Her voice echoes around me again.

"Well, there you go. You're thinking again."

"Go away, Hunter. You're distracting me."

Jacqueline tosses me into the void, the light of the world

disappearing. I should've kept my mouth shut, but she was freaking me out a little. It was like she was trying to pluck me out of her head and failing miserably.

Fear and loneliness swirl around me in the darkness, and I try to imagine being with Nadia. She's the one who understands what I'm going through. Just the thought that she might come back to visit me gives me enough hope to not lose myself in this black abyss.

The air around me shifts, and I hear a pop before I see the familiar darkness of the inside of Jacqueline's eyes. She finally fell asleep and let her guard down, allowing me my freedom to enter her dreams.

NADIA

I hug my father outside of the guest apartment building. He doesn't have a permanent residence on the compound because he's not here enough. The council thought it'd be a waste of space for us to use one of the family cottages for that reason. I don't mind much, though. I like having my own personal space.

Gliding across the grass, I head toward the dorms. It's well past midnight, and I consider not going to my room because sometimes the temptation of sleeping people is too hard for me to manage.

I wring my hands together outside the door and take a deep breath before going inside. Silence awaits me in the empty lobby. I force myself to keep moving toward the hallway to my dorm room. My stomach burns with the sudden awareness of a dreamer, and I grab the wall to support myself. Excitement and anxiety pulse through me, sensing Jacqueline's familiar dreams calling to me. I've been dying to see Hunter again. Now is the perfect time to visit him with morning a few hours away. I could probably stay a few sleep cycles with him if I try.

Jacqueline hunches over in a chair, resting her head on her vanity table. She's sleeping deeply, and I close the door. Gliding across her room, I touch my fingers to her head and fall into her dream.

HUNTER

I can't help being pissed at Jacqueline for throwing me into the void. Now that she's decided to stay here, I bet she'll do it more and more, and I can't do anything about it. From how crazy she was acting, I bet she'll keep me locked away during her wakeful hours.

"Hunter?"

I was so wrapped up in my thoughts I didn't even feel Nadia arrive.

"I'm here," I say, slipping into Jacqueline's dream world.

Nadia stands on the edge of a cliff overlooking a greenish-gray ocean. The sky behind her swirls with dark clouds, and in the distance a rundown power plant gives the dream an apocalyptic setting.

Wringing her pale fingers together, Nadia's unease drifts over me. Her light gray eyes shift away from me, and she presses her pink, heart-shaped lips together. I'm afraid to say anything, afraid she'll abandon me here forever.

But I can't stop from stepping closer to close the space between us. She spins, touching the tips of her boots to the ledge of the cliff, balancing the edge like she'll jump any second. She gazes at the murky ocean, refusing to acknowledge my presence at all. I half expect her to dive off the cliff, abandoning me again.

Gently, I touch my finger to her shoulder. She doesn't move away from my touch but reaches up and rests her hand on mine, surprising me. Her cool fingers brush mine in the same exploratory touch as before. It reminds me how real she is, and I hope it reminds her the same of me.

She looks at me in her peripheral vision, though I wish she'd meet me straight on. "Tell me why I should trust you."

I clench my teeth together, a million reasons rushing through my mind. I want to tell her to trust me because I'm not a bad guy and that I would never hurt her. I want to tell her everything there is to know about me, about the HPA, and how I've changed. None of those words feel right. I don't think I could say anything to earn her trust. She must build it on her own.

"I don't know," I finally say.

Stepping away from the ledge, she swivels to face me, still holding my hand. She tilts her head up to look into my eyes. "Do you trust me?"

I don't even have to think about it. "Yes."

"I'm dangerous."

"Everyone can be dangerous." I bring her hand to my cheek, feeling her cool fingers on my skin. "It doesn't make you bad, though."

Her guarded expression cracks, and she smiles. A new light casts from her gray eyes, glimmering like a full moon in a midnight sky. I could stand in the light from her eyes and smile forever if given the chance. But it's not in this dream world I want to experience it. I want to meet Nadia in reality. Feel all of her instead of only her beautiful soul.

I smile back at her without saying anything more.

She turns her gaze toward the ground, a slight blush warming her colorless cheeks for the first time since I've met her in a dream. "This is crazy. I can't seem to keep away from you as hard as I try. Deep down I know this is a dream and this connection I feel for you can't be real. We can't be real, Hunter."

I tuck a strand of her shimmering, white hair behind her ear. Her words sting, but I keep my expression neutral. I don't want her to see the pain in my eyes. "You're real to me."

She cups my face in her hands. "I wish things were different. You know I don't want you to be here, and I'm scared about what will happen if I don't do something, but—I'm just a nightmare inflictor. I can manipulate souls for dreams, but I can't pull you free. The council won't help you, either. You're the son of a board member."

I frown. "Don't remind me."

She leans forward, resting her head on my shoulder. "I wish we could've met someplace else, living a normal life. It'd be my luck that the universe gave me a dream boy."

I chuckle. I can't help it. Nadia's been thinking about what life would be like if I weren't trapped in Jacqueline's head. It's what I constantly think about—how life could be. How life should be if I wasn't lost in this dream.

"I wouldn't call your luck bad for me," I say.

She groans. "Hunter, am I making up our connection in my head? Is it wrong that I want to stay in this world?"

I frown. "I wish you'd never leave."

"It's unfair to stay."

"Then help me."

She turns away from me and faces the ocean again. "I don't know if I can, Hunter. I just don't know."

NADIA

My heart races, thinking about all the things that could go wrong if I decide to help Hunter escape from Jacqueline's mind. First, I have no idea how to help him. Only Jacqueline can free him. And second, I can't forget about where he comes from. He'll always be the son of a board member.

Hunter's hazel eyes reflect the dark clouds looming over the ocean. He brushes his dark hair out of his face before shoving his hands into the pockets of his black corduroy jacket. The warmth from his touch dissipates from my cool skin.

"As much as I want to get on my knees and grovel, I know how afraid of the HPA you are. I wouldn't blame you or hold it against you if you don't want to help me." He frowns and presses his lips together. "I'm grateful you're even hearing me out. That you haven't abandoned me."

"You know an agent ruined my life." I don't know why, but I need to remind him why I'm terrified of the board. It's not an irrational fear. It's not something that was pushed into me by my father or the Creature Council. My fears are warranted.

He rubs his stubbly chin, his lips tilting down. "I don't

know what to say, Nadia. I know how evil the HPA is. Look where I am because of them. I wish there was something I could make things right for you."

I lift and drop my shoulders. "What's done is done. All I can do is move forward."

HUNTER

I want to pull her to me, wrap my arms around her, and kiss her. I despise the HPA more than ever since being trapped by Jacqueline. I'm ashamed my mom is on the board and is okay with all this. Just thinking about the agency ignites fury in my soul. How they caused so much pain and did something so horrible to Nadia and her family—to many others. It isn't right.

I swallow the burning hatred before Nadia feels it pouring from me. "I promise you that if I get out of here, I will do everything I can to change things. It shouldn't be like this."

Standing on her tiptoes, she leans forward and kisses my cheek. I reach up and press my fingers to the cool spot her lips left behind on my skin. A whisper of a smile plays on her pink lips. We watch each other for a moment and both close the space between us. Nadia finally lets her guard down for me now that our thoughts fill the air. I slide my arms around her shoulders, wanting to feel her presence close to mine. She leans into me and rests her forehead to my chest. I wonder if she can hear the phantom sound of my beating heart.

Time slows with the beautiful nightmare inflictor in my arms. We don't even have to speak to each other to grow our connection. Being in this state is a level no one in the world can ever experience or understand. It's all for us.

I just hold her and breathe in the flowery scent of her hair for what seems like forever, but eternity still isn't long enough.

Thunder booms over the ocean, and the wind picks up, gusting around us. The dream shifts and grows darker. I know Nadia will have to leave soon. I can feel it. Her presence already pulls away. It's a cruel fate that we can't stay like this when I'm imprisoned in Jacqueline's mind. I want to do everything I can to protect Nadia from the dangers of the world, dangers I'm asking her to face on my behalf, but I can't even get myself out of this mess.

She tugs at a few strands of her hair. "You've done something to me, Hunter. I should be afraid of you, but I'm not."

I smile. "I'm glad. I was nervous you'd never come back and wouldn't ever find out that I'm different. Meeting you changed me."

She shifts in my arms and peers over the ledge of the cliff. "I'll always come back. I just wish I didn't have to go."

I hug her tighter. "Then stay."

Stretching up, she kisses my cheek again. "I can't. It'll be too much on Jacqueline. I can feel the nightmares starting to affect her."

I want to tell her they are, but I don't. Jacqueline deserves this for imprisoning me here. I can't feel bad for her.

A scream rips through the quiet air, drawing my attention from Nadia. I glance over the ledge at the soft, tan sand below. Jacqueline runs on the beach, wearing a flowing, purple dress, and two people in biohazard suits chase after her.

She trips and wails again, scrambling to get back to her

feet. "Leave me alone! I haven't done anything."

"We don't want to hurt you!" A deep voice echoes over the waves.

Nadia stiffens next to me.

I reach for her hand. "This is a strange dream."

She plays with her hair with her free hand. "My presence alone is enough to disturb dreamers without doing anything. The longer I stay, the more intense it'll be for Jacqueline. It's why I try to get in and out quickly, but you make it so easy to stay."

I watch Jacqueline's nightmare unfold. She slows down as the sand gets softer under her feet until she's knee deep in it. Her loud cries dig under my skin. It's hard to watch her struggle to escape the two people, but I can't save her from herself. This is a nightmare and not real life, despite how much I'd like it to be.

"Please, get away from me. I don't want your help."

The two people swoop in, unfazed by the sand, and one of them grabs Jacqueline by her dark brown, curly hair. She screams, jerking back, and a clump of her hair rips from her scalp, leaving behind a bloody wound.

My stomach churns.

"I have to go, Hunter," Nadia says, her voice barely above a whisper. "Jacqueline has been through enough tonight."

"Ouch! My fingers!" Jacqueline yells.

The biohazard man reaches to grab Jacqueline again and falls back when her skin peels away in his grasp. She cries out, waving her bloody hand, trying her best to keep the people away from her.

"Stop fighting. You've been contaminated. We need to take you back to the lab," the man says.

"Goodbye, Hunter. I'll try to see you again soon." Nadia's cool lips press my cheek, but I don't turn away from Jacqueline.

The air shifts and the dark sky cracks, sending pieces of clouds into the roaring ocean. Within seconds, the world collapses. Nadia's presence disappears, and I'm alone with Jacqueline again.

I miss Nadia already.

15

DESTINED FOR DREAMS

NADIA

I'M OUT OF control. Visiting Hunter every opportunity I have makes me a bigger monster than Jacqueline. I promised myself I would only give nightmares out of necessity, like when I'm starving, but now I barely even think about it—I just do it.

Hunter changed me. The world doesn't feel so dull, but colorful and vibrant, full of life and happiness. Guilt wages a war with my good senses. I shouldn't enjoy visiting him, seeing him, touching him so much. But no one has ever known me in a dream world. He sees my nightmare inflictor side and isn't scared. He likes me, and not only because I can help him. He genuinely cares about me. I can feel it. It's so tangible, because it is part of his soul. That kind of connection with someone is rare.

I watch the stars fade in the early morning sky. People should be waking up soon, and it should be safe enough for me to go back inside. I want today to be normal, like any other day. I want to get ready and get back to the routine I've slacked off on. I need to do something to get my mind off Hunter. It's better if I at least try to help out around here again before people start whispering behind my back more than usual.

Squeezing my eyes shut, I force the image of Hunter away. I need to focus on me right now and whether or not I can make the decision to help him. I need to think about what would happen after. Can I live my life in more fear than I do now? Can I forget about him and move on like all this was just a dream? Can I live with myself if I decide not to help him? These are some heavy decisions, and I wish someone else could make them for me. I need someone besides myself to blame if things go wrong or aren't the way I want them to be.

All these questions on my mind make my stomach flip. It's wishful thinking and unreasonable to even consider things might turn out well. I'm toxic. I survive by giving people nightmares. I don't even know if I'm capable of being with Hunter in real life. Look what happened with my mother.

I hear the door to the dorms creak open, and I crawl closer to the building and into the shadows. I'm not up for company and don't want to deal with facing anyone.

"I said I was sorry. I've had a lot on my mind. Give me a break." A familiar voice echoes in the quiet morning. "Are you sure? I haven't been getting good sleep at all."

I press my back to the wall. Jacqueline stands in the middle of the walkway, clutching her head. She's talking out loud, and with the way the conversation sounds, it's not only to herself.

"Yeah, okay. You're right." She takes a few steps. "Of course I feel guilty. I'm not some heartless person." She spins on her feet, facing me, and moves her hands to her eyes and rubs them.

"Okay, yeah. Dang it, Hunter. Shut up." She pauses. "Shut up!"

Jacqueline's getting careless by talking out loud. After such a long nightmare, it'll take her fragile sanity a few extra minutes to recuperate. She should bounce back, though. It took years for my mother to descend into madness. Jacqueline's obviously much stronger, too.

Crossing and uncrossing her arms, Jacqueline paces in a circle. Her dark brown curls hang in a mess over her shoulders. Wearing black yoga pants and a burgundy T-shirt, she's the most casual I've seen her. She runs her barefoot over the edge of the cement and into the grass.

It takes everything in me to open my mouth, and finally after awkwardly watching her for another minute, I ask, "Who's Hunter?"

Jacqueline spins on the balls of her feet and stares at me with a scary wildness to her expression. Her lavender eyes shift to hazel and back again, and she brushes her untamed hair back with her hands. "What?" she asks, peering into the shadow to see me. "Oh, Nadia, don't mind me. I was just talking to myself."

I stand and walk closer. "You told Hunter to shut up. Who is he?"

She looks ready to run. "I don't know."

"How'd he die?" I ask. If I thought confronting her about Hunter would help him, I'd press harder since it was her slip up, but she looks like she's willing to murder someone to keep her secrets safe, so I play along with her lie about being a necromancer.

She pauses for a minute, relaxing. "Oh, uh, I haven't asked." Her eyes shift to hazel again, and she blinks until they revert back to normal. "And I honestly don't want to know. It's morbid enough as it is."

Jacqueline's sneakier than I thought. If I didn't know who Hunter really was, I'd have believed she was a necromancer speaking to the dead.

"Is that why you're not sleeping well? Too many ghosts?" I purse my lips. "I honestly didn't think they'd be able to come through the magic protecting this place."

She frowns. "I—I guess. I don't know." She thrashes her head back and forth. "Actually, it's not ghosts. I thought maybe you could tell me why I can't sleep."

I raise my eyebrows, a rush of fear sinking from my heart and into my feet. "You don't think that I'd actually..." My voice trails off, and I look at the ground. "Of course you would. Who wouldn't? Always blame the nightmare inflictor when you can't sleep." As the words come, fear slithers into anger in my mind even though it shouldn't. It's not like I'm innocent. I'm lying.

But thinking about Hunter trapped in her head irritates me. "You do know people are capable of creating their own nightmares? A lot of things can cause them. You talk to the dead, that's enough to give even the most fearless person bad dreams." I don't meet her gaze, because now is my chance to erase all doubt she's had about me. I need her to keep trusting me. I can't risk her mentioning her sleep issues to the council. Who knows what they would do.

"I'm sorry," she sputters. "I shouldn't have said anything. I just—my past is haunting me, and I feel like I'm going crazy sometimes. If it makes you feel any better, I don't even care what you are." She sounds so sincere. I believe her until I see Hunter's hazel eyes flash through. Her eye color shifts when she's having an inner debate with him. I bet he's calling out her lies. It's what I'd do if I were in his place.

"You'd be one of the few," I say, tucking my hair behind my ear. I shift on my feet when silence falls between us.

Finally, after a long moment, Jacqueline nods. "I completely understand. Most people are terrified of me as well."

And they should be, I think. *I should be.*

HUNTER

"Can you blame them?" I ask. *"You're the scariest super I know."*

Jacqueline growls in her mind. "You haven't seen scary, Hunter."

"I'm pretty sure I have."

"They're probably scared of the dead people," Nadia says. She looks so human with her blond hair pulled up into a high ponytail. Her indigo eyes complement her deep blue shift dress, opaque black tights, and knee high black boots. I wish I could cup her face again...kiss her if she'd let me.

Jacqueline straightens her shoulders, bringing her attention back to Nadia. "You think so? People should know the dead are harmless. It's the living that people should be afraid of." Jacqueline touches Nadia's arm, reminding me I'm stuck inside Jacqueline's head and that I'll never get to be with Nadia in real life at this rate. We are destined for dreams.

Nadia twists her lips to the side. "That's not what I hear. My father is great friends with a necromancer, and she says no one can keep a secret around her because the dead see everything. Sometimes secrets are all a person has."

Panic rushes through Jacqueline's mind, and she shifts her gaze to the ground. "Oh, no. What if the necromancer comes here? I didn't realize there was another one around." She isn't keeping her personal thoughts from me. It's annoying because I want to respond, but it'll get me sent to the void again.

Jacqueline blinks a few times before asking Nadia, "You know another necromancer? Where is she?" Her voice cracks.

Nadia stares up at the sky. "She's not too far from here, but she doesn't have connections to the council and probably never will. I can get her information if you want."

It takes a lot of effort not to laugh. Jacqueline is so uncomfortable, her anxiety hits me in palpable waves. I might not feel anything else, but her unease feels like getting slapped. I'm enjoying how Nadia purposely pushes her buttons. I like to think she's doing it for me. Jacqueline didn't think her plan through and sooner or later, she's going to get caught in a lie by someone other than Nadia. And when she is, I hope I'm already back in my body.

"That would be great." Jacqueline's enthusiasm is obviously fake. "Maybe I can meet her sometime."

"Oh, I bet I can have it arranged. I'm guessing it's not often you get to meet someone like yourself. I'd kill to meet another nightmare inflictor. The only one I know is my father, and he doesn't count." Nadia beams a bright smile. She's so beautiful in the morning light.

Jacqueline's personal thoughts ring through to me again. "What am I getting myself into? I could never meet a real necromancer. They'd know I was lying immediately. Ugh!"

"I can hear you." I laugh. I can't stop myself this time. *"I hope you get caught, Jackie."*

"Shut up. I swear I'll kill you if I'm caught."

"You know you can't," I say.

"Then I'll make you want to die."

I don't argue with her. It's not worth it. She could probably push me enough to where I'd want to die, but Nadia gives me the hope of that never happening.

"Nadia?" A melodic voice calls out. "You should come back inside."

Alyssa flips her fire red braid over her shoulder before placing her hands on her hips. When she meets Jacqueline's gaze, she frowns. Her bright green eyes narrow for a split second and then her lips curl into a quick smile. Without saying anything else, she spins on her bare feet and struts back inside.

Jacqueline gazes at Nadia but doesn't say anything, either.

Nadia plays with her ponytail and shrugs. "When Alyssa tells you to do something, you do it."

It hurts to watch her walk away. I want her to keep me company forever even if she can't hear me inside Jacqueline's head. It's the thought of her knowing I'm here that counts, and she's willing to fake an effort with Jacqueline that gives me hope that I'll get through it—that Nadia will be the one to free me.

NADIA

"The tension between you two was obvious. Are you okay?" Alyssa hugs me with one arm as we walk toward our rooms.

"I am now. I had to convince Jacqueline I wasn't giving her nightmares. I think someone at the club told her," I say. "Then, she lied to my face again about the whole necromancer thing. She's really something. I feel bad for her, but then I don't."

"She should've been born a demon. She has the mindset of one." Alyssa opens her door, and I follow her into her room. I try not to stare at the hundreds of drawings taped to the walls. She sits on a pile of clothes on her bed and folds her hands into her lap. "Not to mention her influence on people. The council loves her."

Rolling my eyes, I suck in a breath through my gritted teeth. "That's why I'm so conflicted. She's so nice, and I can see myself being good friends with her, but then there's Hunter and her deal with the board. She's going to mess up soon. I can feel it. I caught her talking out loud to Hunter."

"Did you call her out on it?"

"I wouldn't do that to Hunter. He's different. He's so—" I press my lips together. "I can't describe it. Think I can save him?"

She fiddles with her hair. "I can't tell you that. You're too ambivalent. You need to be absolutely certain you want to and then you need to be absolutely certain you're going to try."

I sigh. It's not what I wanted to hear. I want to know it's possible to save someone's soul without being put in danger. I don't even know where I'd begin to help him. I can't manipulate souls. "I wish you could meet him, then you could tell me if it would be worth putting myself on the line."

She smiles. "Even if I did meet him, I couldn't tell you that. You're the one that has to live with this. Can you? If you think you can live out the rest of your life without any regret toward not helping Hunter, then I say don't help him."

I tug on my ponytail. "That's terrible advice."

"Why? Because I know you're a good person?"

I moan. "I'll decide later. I think I need to see him one more time."

Alyssa eyes me through her thick eyelashes.

Blushing, I say, "If you met him you'd get it."

"I like my dream boys, too," Alyssa says with a smirk.

I narrow my eyes. "He's not a dream. He's so real, I can touch him, Lys." I can feel his soul against mine, see him for who he is. This is something I don't think anyone could grasp. Maybe Jacqueline. But she's the real nightmare. Even though she obviously knows Hunter is innocent, she doesn't care. She's selfish. Dangerous.

"I know. You've told me a dozen times already. It's..." Her voice trails off.

"Amazing," I finish for her. It's the only way to describe it.

"And what happens if he gets his body back?"

I glance at the carpet. "I want it to work," I say softly.

Alyssa stands up and pads over to me, hugging me. "You couldn't meet a normal boy, could you?"

I laugh and blink away my oncoming tears. "Because they're all afraid of me. I'm scared Hunter will be, too. It's why I'm hesitant to think of the possibility." I wipe my eyes. If Hunter gets his body back, he'll be normal. And then what? He'll risk the same fate as my mother. "I could turn him insane, and he could die. It isn't fair for me to put someone in that position, no matter how much I care about them."

Alyssa pulls away. "You don't know that, Nadia. Only I can predict that kind of thing." Straightening her back, she smiles. "And I predict it'll all work out how it should."

"Until it doesn't," I say.

"And then we figure it out from there."

I love when Alyssa is right, because it makes the future seem less ominous and foreboding. I wish things weren't so subjective. I think I would fare better in a world where everything is set in stone. *You would hate that*, I think. *You need a life with options. You live for those options.*

And I do.

Right now, I'm choosing to help Hunter. I just hope it's the right choice.

16

BREAKING POINT

NADIA

I STEP INTO the hallway to make my way back to my room when the pull of Jacqueline's dream hits me hard. She's sleeping more and more and will never feel fully rested, but I can't stop myself. I'm addicted to invading her dreams. It's too easy.

I glide into Jacqueline's room. Pale sunlight shines on her face. She sleeps with half her body off the bed like she was too tired to get all the way in it. Reaching down, I touch my pale fingers to her temples.

The world shifts.

Hunter leans against a gray boulder, staring at an empty playground. A baseball field stretches to his right, but it doesn't look like it has been used in ages. The grass is dead, the dugouts contain broken benches, and the bleachers have seen better days.

Hunter stands straighter. "Jacqueline's having a hard time staying awake."

Twisting my lips to the side, I nod. "It's because of me."

He steps closer and stares down at me. Reaching up, he tucks my hair behind my ear. "Don't feel bad, Nadia."

I pucker my lips. It's easier said than done. Jacqueline hasn't done anything wrong to me and even if Hunter thinks she deserves the fate we're forcing on her, I don't. "This is why I'm a monster."

His brows furrow. "You're not, though. You're only coming here because of me. If I weren't here, you'd never invade Jacqueline's dreams."

Tears blur my vision. "I hate this."

He looks into my eyes for a few moments before leaning closer. "I don't want you to feel this way. It was never my intention for you to feel guilty or hateful. I want you to be happy, just like you were when we first met."

I close the space between our faces even more. "I don't think I can."

Hunter tilts his lips toward mine and whispers, "I wish I could fix it. You're—God, Nadia. I'll stay here forever. You don't have to visit me anymore. Just forget about me. I can't ask you to help me if this is what it's doing to you."

I blink my tears away. "I'm beyond considering helping you, Hunter. I—"

Brushing his lips to mine, Hunter cuts off my words with a kiss. His life force grazes against mine, and I can feel everything good swirling in his soul—his innocence, his desires, his hope— all these emotions light up our world through our kiss. His hands glide to my waist, pulling me closer, deepening our kiss until the world around us fades away, and I'm left hovering in a strange blend of shadows with Hunter outside Jacqueline's dream.

As quickly as we leave the dream, we fall back into it. Hunter slowly pulls away, smiling while peering into my eyes, staring right at my soul in a moment I never want to end.

He kisses me again, feather soft, light, just teasing me with his lips. "I—"

The ground shakes, the sky cracking to cloud the world around us. It's too soon. I just arrived. Something must be happening in the real world that's causing Jacqueline's dream to collapse. While she won't wake up with me in her mind, I need to get out of here. And quickly.

Hunter grabs my hands. "What's happening?"

Fear squeezes my chest. "I have to go. I'm sorry. It's not safe for me."

I pull out of Jacqueline's mind without saying goodbye to Hunter. I didn't have a choice. Shaking my head, I look around Jacqueline's room. Someone taps on the door, causing my heart to fall into my stomach. I can't leave without being seen.

Rushing to the window, I open it and climb out. Jacqueline moans from her bed, but I don't stick around to see her wake up. I make my way back inside and catch Jacqueline in the hallway, picking up a package left in front of her door.

I wait for her to go back into her room before heading to mine.

I feel so sick to my stomach, thinking about how close I was to getting caught. In a split second, my life could've been over, and I'd never get to see Hunter again.

I can't let that happen.

HUNTER

A minute after Nadia left, Jacqueline's eyes fluttered open. She wouldn't have woken up if it weren't for the banging on the door. I'm pissed that the unexpected visitor was just someone delivering a package. I don't know when I'll get to see Nadia again. I wasn't ready for her to go. Not after her kiss.

"What is it?" I ask as Jacqueline scratches the tape off a package wrapped in brown paper.

"You'll know when I do," Jacqueline thinks. "It's from Ryder."

That incubus is really getting on my nerves. I didn't think Jacqueline would ever hear from him again. What kind of guy sends gifts to a girl after only dancing for one song? I doubt it's because he's kind and generous. He's sneaky and conniving— probably the perfect match for Jacqueline.

"I bet it's a body part or something to go with this stolen body he thinks you possess."

"Only you'd think something like that was romantic, Hunter."

Jacqueline rips the paper from a white gift box. She tugs the lid off and runs her fingers over the black tissue paper. She's taking her sweet time and needs to hurry up. I want to know what gift was so important that it forced Nadia to run away.

Lifting up the tissue paper, she uncovers the weird object from Ryder.

"That's an odd gift," I say. *"I guess nothing says I love you like something handmade, probably from someone else's heart."*

Jacqueline holds up a large ring wrapped in thread. Turquoise string knots from one end to the other, over and over again like a carelessly made spider web. A single leather string hangs from it with a few glass beads knotted on it.

"To catch unwanted nightmares," Jacqueline reads out loud as she rubs the card that was stuck in the web. "This must be what he was talking about when he said there were ways to find out if someone was invading my dreams."

"How...thoughtful." Sarcasm drips from my words. Is this some kind of joke? I didn't think that guy was serious. What if Jacqueline sets it up and finds out? This is inconvenient, and I have no way of telling Nadia.

"It kind of is except for the fact that Nadia is my friend."

"I'm pretty sure he wants you to leave the compound and spend the rest of your life with him. You know if Nadia finds out about this, it'll be the death of your friendship."

"Relax, Hunter. I'm not going to hang it up."

"So, you believe she's not causing you nightmares."

She puts the dream trinket back into the box and sets it on her nightstand. I'm tempted to ask her to throw it away, but then I'd look a little crazy considering Jacqueline doesn't know Nadia frequents her dreams.

"I want to, but I don't know. I've never had such a hard time sleeping."

"I think someone just has a guilty conscience. And me."

Jacqueline stares in her vanity mirror, running her hands through her dark, curly hair, before giving up and tying it into a low bun. Dark circles shadow under her eyes, making her look like she could use another fifty hours of sleep. She blinks a few times and turns toward the door.

She shrugs. "Doubt it."

I don't respond. It's too easy to argue with her.

Jacqueline gets up and walks to her door. "Can you be extra quiet today? I'm having a really hard time concentrating," she thinks.

"I'll do my best, but no promises, and don't you think about throwing me in the void or I'll never shut up again," I say.

"Fine, whatever."

"You're talking out loud again."

"Just be quiet," she thinks.

While Nadia mentioned the nightmares would affect Jacqueline, I didn't think it would last so long. Jacqueline's always been so controlled and put together unless I really, really badger her, but I'm not talking to her more than usual.

I'll have to ask Nadia about it the next time I see her. If I see her.

NADIA

"I'll see you in a few days," my father says, adjusting the black duffle bag on his shoulder. "Are you sure you can manage?"

I lower an eyebrow. "I always manage." We have this discussion every time my father has to go on an assignment. He's been whisked away for work so often over the years that it doesn't even faze me anymore.

"Can you do me a favor and stay here? I know I showed you the city, but it's different when I'm out of town," he says, staring me down.

I look at the floor. "What if I promise not to wander the city?" I don't really have plans to go back, but I want the option of not feeling guilty if I do end up wanting to go with Alyssa.

He sighs. "I don't know."

It's my turn to sigh. "I'm tired of living in this bubble. I'm tired of having to worry about fitting in. And, I'm so over people treating me like I'm some rabid monster out to eat them alive. You don't know what it's like to be here all the time."

He wipes his hand over his forehead. "That bad again?"

"It never got better. I just gave up on telling you. It doesn't make a difference, especially when the council is uneasy about me, too. I didn't even realize how bad it was until I got to be around the people from The Haven."

He switches his duffle bag to his other shoulder. "I wish you would've said something, Nadi. If you can hang on for a few more weeks, I'll make other arrangements, but I can't promise it'll be any better."

Other arrangements could mean a lot of things. I'm excited to think of the options. Maybe we could live on the beach, and I'll get to see a real sunset on the ocean. "Okay, but I want to know before you decide anything."

He smiles and leans down to kiss the top of my head.

"We'll choose together," he says, pulling me in for a hug. "And Nadi, please don't sneak out. You can go to the city when they bus people there, all right? And if you need anything the council can't offer you, give Cian a call. He can help you."

Alyssa pops out from her room a second after my father turns his back to leave. She gives him a quick hug, and we both watch him go. Sliding her arm over my shoulder, she leans her head on mine. I should be used to him leaving, but I can't help feeling sad when he actually does. Maybe because one day he may never come back. *He'll come back. He always does.*

"The council isn't going to be happy when we move," she says.

I frown and turn to look at her.

"I saw you and your dad make a decision," she adds. "I also plan on asking if I can go. I already know he'll say yes. But, I also saw the council will be less than pleasant about it."

I sigh. "When are they ever pleasant?"

Alyssa laughs. "Oh, they will be until they realize they can't convince me to stay, and I'm not letting you leave me behind."

I hug Alyssa. "You know I never could."

She beams a radiant smile. "Now if only we could skip out on our chores for the next few weeks."

"We can't skip one more day?" I ask, puckering out my bottom lip.

Alyssa raises her eyebrows. "You'll be fine. We won't split up this week."

Alyssa strolls ahead of me. We come to Jacqueline's door, and my stomach churns, nausea rushing over me. I feel so light headed that I lean on the wall for support. Alyssa turns on her heels and grabs my arm to keep me from falling. She drags me down the hall and as quick as the horrible feeling came, it disappears.

"That was strange," I say. "I almost blacked out."

"Are you hungry?" Alyssa asks.

I shake my head. "No, that's not it. I don't know. I'm fine now."

She stares at me for a minute before slinging her arm around my shoulder. "I can cover for you if you're still feeling weird."

"I think I need some fresh air."

HUNTER

"Can you go back to the dorms so I can watch a movie? You're killing my sanity, Jackie."

She hums to herself as she thinks, "What? You don't enjoy the sunshine?"

"I would if I could feel it." My sharp words snap at her with my anger. It's getting harder and harder to go with the flow of things. I'm even tempted to agree to a new body.

"If I could take you back, I would."

That's not very comforting. She can leave here if she wants and go back to the HPA. Nothing is stopping her. *"You can."*

Her frustration runs hot around me. "They'll kill me because I have nothing to offer them. I'm not going to give up the location of the council. I'm not going to risk getting all these people killed."

"Not even for your true freedom?"

Jacqueline stares at the sky. "What about—" Her thoughts cut off.

"Hi, Jacqueline." It's Nadia. Her familiar and comforting voice pushes away my anger.

Nadia stands a foot away, her blond hair shining in the bright sunlight, making it look golden. I wish I could swim in the blue depths of her eyes, gazing through Jacqueline to peek at me. In jeans, a white sweater, and sneakers, and she still manages to be hauntingly beautiful outside our dream world. Jacqueline studies her face, but I can't stop staring at her lips, the memory of our kiss still hot in my mind.

"H-hey," Jacqueline stammers. "What are you doing here?"

Nadia stares into her eyes for a moment longer before blinking. "Looking for you." Putting her hands on her hips, she squints in the sun. "I wanted to make sure you were okay. You were acting so strange last night."

Jacqueline rubs her eyes. "This place is getting to me. I'm thinking of going to the council to ask for something to help me sleep."

"You think they can help you?"

"Shut up, Hunter!" Jacqueline's voice echoes through the air.

"Take a deep breath, Jackie. You're talking out loud."

Jacqueline groans. "I said shut up, Hunter. Shut up. Shut up. Shut up! You know something is wrong with me, but you act like it's not a big deal. And you know what? I do think Nadia is inflicting nightmares on me. It's what she does!" Jacqueline slaps her hand over her mouth and grimaces.

Nadia's mouth falls open. "How can you say that? I've been so nice to you."

Jacqueline scrambles to her feet. "I—I'm sorry. Something is wrong with me. I'm losing it. The voices are too much."

Nadia steps closer and grasps Jacqueline's arms. "Get yourself together. You're talking nonsense." She stares into Jacqueline's eyes. "You can't just throw around random accusations. If anyone heard you, they'd believe you, and I'd get in serious trouble."

"Do you want your friend to get in trouble?"

"Hunter!"

Everything goes black.

NADIA

Jacqueline grips her hair, tilting her head to the sky. Her lavender eyes flicker between hazel and lavender a dozen times before sticking to lavender. She jerks her head, looking around, and then grabs my shoulders and glares at me. Her wide, wild eyes shift around my face, and she doesn't look like herself at all. She's at her breaking point, something that shouldn't have come so soon. Something's different about Jacqueline.

It's Hunter.

Tears rim my eyes. "Jacqueline, please, please calm down. You're scaring me." I'm a horrible person. I'm worse than she is. She's lost control and her sanity is on the brink of breaking. I hate myself for what I've done to her. My longing for Hunter is going to kill her. I need to back off. I need to give her time to rest.

Jacqueline pulls me to her and hugs me, moaning against

my shoulder. Her hands shake as her nails dig into me. "I think I need to sleep. Wake up and start all over again. I'm so sorry, Nadia. I didn't mean to freak out." Jacqueline's eyes remain lavender, and I wonder where Hunter is. Without his presence, she's calmer and more controlled. She's more herself. My nightmares and his presence makes this worse. I didn't know until this moment.

I touch her hand. "It's been a stressful week."

Jacqueline turns away and darts across the stretch of green grass toward the dormitory. I sink to my knees, pressing my palms flat on the ground. I gulp in breath after breath to calm my nerves. Jacqueline's not going to believe that I'm not invading her dreams for much longer.

Time is running out fast.

17

SURVIVOR

NADIA

I STAND OUTSIDE the dormitory.

I've been out here for a few hours, trying to give Jacqueline as much sleep as I possibly can. I'm not going to invade her dreams for another day. As much as it pains me, Hunter will have to wait. What's another day longer anyway? He's not going anywhere.

You're strong enough to resist. Just go in.

I'm terrified that I'm not, though. I'm weak. Not because inflicting nightmares is how I survive, but because visiting Hunter is tempting...he's a part of my life now, and I can't give him up. He's as important as the dreams I destroy.

I gaze around the property with my back to the door. A few dozen people enjoy the sunshine and blue skies. Some relax on blankets and others do physical activities—playing a game of catch, running, even flying.

I wonder what it would be like without my nightmare inflicting stigma constantly hanging over my head. It wasn't so bad when I was younger, before the dream cravings started, when I was still basically human. But even then, I was an outsider. I couldn't wield magic like elves, fly like pixies, or transform like shifters. I was a child without a mother and with a father people respected out of fear. I still feel as lost as I did then. Maybe even more now.

Turning toward the dormitory, I glide in. The empty lobby greets me with the sound of the left on TV. I rest my hand on the back of the worn leather armchair and stare at some human talk show one of the fairies obsesses over. I release the breath I've been holding to steel myself. I don't sense anyone sleeping.

I head down the hall, and a foreboding feeling twists my stomach in knots. My fingers tremble as I run my hand along the tan wall. I can hear my own heartbeat in my ears and my eyes shift from the floor to the ceiling. The air looks strange, like it's going in and out of focus.

I freeze, breathing heavily, and stare at the row of doors leading into dorm rooms. I feel sick again like this morning. I swallow, licking my lips to moisten them, my tongue feeling heavy in my mouth. It takes everything in me to step forward, yet something stops me from stepping back. I want to turn and run outside, but I can't stop my feet from moving. I'm stuck in a gravitational pull filled with dread, and it's forcing me to continue on.

Another wave of nausea rolls through me, and I cover my mouth. My skin crawls with the tension tangible in the air seemingly alive, biting and pinching at my clothes. My feet ease from the floor without warning. I swing my arms back, flailing, trying everything I can to stop. The force pulls me from my torso, and resisting bends me into a painfully odd U-shape position with my back arching. Fighting the pull will rip me to pieces.

So I stop.

I let myself go.

My stomach heaves the farther I'm dragged into the hallway. My head pounds so hard that black stars pepper my vision. I can't feel my extremities through the intense fear ripping at my very essence. Sweat beads on my forehead, dribbling into my eyes. I blink over and over until the world flashes in and out of my vision like a strobe light.

I try to scream, but the moment I open my mouth, rancid tasting air fills my throat. The air is thick enough that it's like gulping water, yet I can still breathe through my nose. The stench contaminates everything, affecting my taste buds. Whatever is happening is messing with my nightmare inflictor half.

The air drags me to Jacqueline's room. Panic seizes my chest, and I tilt my head back as far as it goes to keep myself from going into her room. I guess she didn't believe me when I told her I wasn't invading her dreams, and now she's punishing me. I can't think of another explanation for this horrible energy drawing me in.

The door creaks open to reveal black haze clouding the room. It swirls and moves, very much alive, and slithers around me, running over my shoulders and playing with my hair. Jacqueline sleeps with her face in her pillow. I couldn't sense she was asleep because of the spell she cast over me. I didn't know a sin-eater could even bewitch me. I've never been so out of control in my life.

Just when I think I'm going to be forced to hover over Jacqueline while she's sleeping, I stop. My body hovers frozen a foot off the ground, suspended in the hazy, black air. I'm nauseated and frightened and can't think of anything to do to free myself.

I open and close my mouth, swallowing rotten air, but I can't find my voice to call out to Jacqueline. Searching the room, I peer around as best I can through the fog. My gaze turns to the floor, my heart thudding so hard against my ribs that my chest hurts. Tears burn my eyes at the object below me. I'm not being held hostage by some unexplainable super power Jacqueline possesses but by a nightmare catcher.

I've never seen one in real life before now. From what my father has told me, real nightmare catchers are the bane of our existence...and deadly. Humans make hundreds of novelty ones, but if you can convince the right creature, they can charm one for you. They're supposed to be very, very, rare and are illegal to have on the premises, but here I am caught in its prison.

I hang helplessly in the air as my life drains away. I'm weaker by the minute. The nightmare catcher will siphon my energy until I'm an empty shell of myself, and without any sustenance, I'll die.

"Nadia?"

Alyssa's quiet voice trickles through the haze. I almost didn't hear her. She's like a shadow amid the fog. She reaches her hand out to grab me, but her fingers hit an invisible wall. Pounding her hands on the invisible barrier, she tries everything she can to get to me, but nothing happens. I'm stuck, and she's locked away from me.

I shift my eyes down and back to hers and then back down again. Her emerald green eyes glass over, and she stares past me for a few seconds and then crosses her arms.

"You're going to die if I can't figure out how to free you," she whispers.

I open my mouth again, but the words stick to my tongue, held hostage by the putrid air.

I can't tell her to get rid of the nightmare catcher.

I'm doomed.

"Do you know what's happening?" she asks quietly.

It takes a lot out of me, but I finally nod and drop my gaze to the floor again.

Her eyebrows knit together.

I glance at her and back to the floor again.

Dropping to her knees, she presses her hands to the invisible barrier. She can't get to the nightmare catcher. Waking Jacqueline might be my only option of surviving. I refuse to die today. Even if it means that I can never visit Hunter again. *You're a terrible person. Hunter needs you,* I think.

No, I'm a survivor.

"I see a small crack, but my hand is too big to get to it," she whispers. She paces in a circle for a minute and then stops at Jacqueline's night table. An opened gift box rests on it and Alyssa reaches over and picks up the lid, tearing the corners to flatten it.

She kneels next to me and presses the flattened box top against the barrier. It slides through the barrier under me. After what feels like the longest minute of my life, a burst of fresh air hits me, and I fall to the carpet, gasping.

"Get it out of here," I whisper, "and shut the door."

It feels like I haven't invaded a dream in months. Before Alyssa has even left the room, I glide to Jacqueline's bed, sliding my fingers under her head to press her temples. I invade her dream.

HUNTER

Whispers sound through the quiet room.

Jacqueline passed out hours ago and hasn't even stirred since. Pulling from the dream, I listen to the quiet commotion her body tunes out. Whoever speaks sounds panicked, unsettled. I wish Jacqueline would stop snoring, so I can hear better. But no, I can't do anything except try my best to figure out what's going on.

"Shut the door."

It's Nadia.

I don't know what happened after Jacqueline thrust me into the void, but I didn't think Nadia would come back for a while after Jacqueline's outburst. It was crazy to witness.

Jacqueline was fine one second and then it was like a switch flipped, and she couldn't control herself. It'll be hard to deal with Jacqueline if this is how life is. Hot and cold—the little things setting her off.

I feel Nadia enter Jacqueline's mind.

Nadia's presence swells with power, demanding my attention. It feels different than before. It's so overwhelming, it's like she's going to push me out of Jacqueline's head and kill me by accident.

"Hunter?" Nadia's voice comes barely a whisper.

I ease back into Jacqueline's dream and find Nadia hovering in the middle of a quaint living room. A plush, green couch sits against a long wall adorned with a crookedly hung painting of a waterfall. In front of it, a coffee table rests with a pile of books stacked over a foot high on one side. Pale sunlight trickles in through a curtain-less window. It streaks across Nadia's glittering, white hair.

Her white dress flows around her knees, shifting and moving when she doesn't. It's barely a shade lighter than her porcelain skin. Her haunting pale gray eyes hold an emptiness I've never seen. I step closer, gazing at the eeriness of her irises, lacking the life they should. Her blue lips press in a thin line, unmoving like her unblinking gaze. She's like a ghost here to torment me.

Uneasiness and dread wash through me.

I grab her stiff, icy hands and bring them to my lips and blow on them. Nothing happens. If we were in the real world, I could warm her up, but in this dream, I'm just a projection of what I could be.

I reach up and touch her chin when she doesn't say any-thing. "You're so cold. What happened?"

She just stares past me.

"Nadia? What did Jacqueline do?" Her unresponsiveness gets under my skin. Maybe this is my own nightmare.

Finally blinking, she draws her eyes to mine. "I'm too weak to feed. If I don't, I'll die."

Her faint voice stabs me in my soul. Pain swells through me like she just punched me in the gut. "You can't die, Nadia. Please, tell me what to do."

"Help me eat."

I look for a door leading to the kitchen, but there isn't one. It's just a room with a window and no other way out. I pick up the coffee table and throw it at the window, shattering it. The loud noise makes me cringe, but I don't hesitate. I pick up Na-dia and carry her through the window. Her shoulder hits the frame and sparks erupt. The wall begins to smolder and Nadia inhales.

And then I remember.

Nadia feeds on the destruction of dreams.

I swing her around and help her run her fingers over the red bricks. They blacken and burn and begin to crumble as she destroys the house with her touch. Warmth swells from her back and travels to her shoulders, and she curls her fingers.

She gulps in a few more breaths. "Jacqueline set up a nightmare catcher," she says through swallows. "It almost killed me." Her hand slides over my neck, and she leans her head on my shoulder.

I frown into her glittering, white hair. Jacqueline didn't set up anything. "What are you talking about?"

"There was a nightmare catcher on the floor of her room. It pulled me in and trapped me. If Alyssa hadn't come, I would've died."

She's talking about the gift from Ryder. Jacqueline knocked the box with it off her nightstand when she plopped into bed. She was too exhausted to pick it up. It never even crossed my mind that it would affect Nadia like she said it has.

I knew I should've nagged Jacqueline to get rid of it when she opened the package. I could've prevented this whole thing if I would've put two and two together. "I'm so sorry. It was an accident. Jacqueline didn't—"

She presses her finger to my lips. "Don't you dare defend her, Hunter. She doesn't deserve to have you as a white knight."

I can't resist kissing her hair. She looks so beautiful this very moment in my arms with the way she narrows her eyes and puckers her bottom lip. Her eyes search mine, and I don't say anything. She's so mad at Jacqueline that I don't think she'd listen anyway.

I shift my eyes to the red and orange flames licking the walls of the house, making it rumble on its foundation. The roof collapses, creating a cloud of smoke. I take a step back even though it can't hurt us.

And then I hear a long and loud and agonizing scream rip through the dream. I shiver from the shrillness of it and press my forehead against Nadia's. Our lips hover an inch away, and she closes her eyes as the scream tears through the air again.

"I have to leave," she whispers.

I don't move to let her go. Instead, I lean closer and kiss her.

She melts into me and wraps her arms tighter around my neck. Her soft lips caress mine with an intense craving, a hunger, and she kisses me deeper. I'd let her devour me if it were possible. Our tongues meet, stirring desire more intense than her hunger. She tastes amazing, like cinnamon and sugar and of everything sweet I miss from reality. I imagine it's what the dream tastes like to her.

Pulling back too soon, she cups my face in her hands. "Why can't this be easier?" Her eyes shift away, and she glances at the burning house. "Why can't this be real?"

I flinch. "It is real. I'm real and you're real. It's real."

She shakes her head. "We're part of a dream."

"It doesn't matter," I say.

She half smiles. "It does. We can't stay here forever. And if you get your body back, it'll never work out. We were only meant for dreams."

I want to tell her that she's wrong. That it can work. That we can make it work. I want to tell her that I'm falling in love every time her soul touches mine. I want to tell her how much I need her. Not only to get me out of here, but I need her because she makes the world right. She makes me see clearly. She's shown me balance in a tilted world full of human monsters and beautiful creatures like Nadia, who give my black and white world so much color. I need Nadia, because with her, I can change things. I can make it right for us. I can turn dreams into reality.

"Don't leave, please." I need her to stay. Just a minute longer.

"But I have to go."

NADIA

Another scream echoes through the air, but I can't find the will to turn my back on Hunter. I can still feel the warmth of his lips, the strength of his arms around me, and how his need to be with me was so palpable, I could feel it in my soul.

I kiss him again before pulling back. "It'll only be for a while. I promise I'll be back, and I will save you. I won't let anything stop me."

He sets me down but doesn't let go of my hand. "I miss you already."

I smile and squeeze his hand before gliding away. The hunger in me burns with such intensity that I look forward to tormenting Jacqueline for what she has done to me. I don't turn to gaze at Hunter. I don't want him to see the menace in my eyes. I don't want him to see the monster Jacqueline brought out in me.

I find Jacqueline kneeling on the ground in front of an unconscious boy. She wipes black soot from his face with tears streaming down her cheeks. The boy looks similar to her, like he could be her brother. But it doesn't stop me. I lick my lips and glide closer.

Turning to face me, Jacqueline cries out, blocking the boy. I reach out and touch her shoulder. The sky cracks and rains down smoke and fire as I finish the nightmare. I'm out of her dream as everything begins to burn.

18

OUT OF CONTROL

NADIA

I STAND OVER Jacqueline's sleeping body. I can't just leave here like nothing happened. I can't pretend she didn't set the nightmare catcher, and I can't forget about Hunter. My world collapses around me, and I'm being buried alive by the pieces I can't hold together.

I can't stay here.

I can't leave Jacqueline, either.

I can only do one thing.

The door creaks open, and I jerk to face Alyssa. I catch my reflection in Jacqueline's vanity mirror. My wild, white hair hangs limply on my shoulders, and my glassy, nearly colorless eyes shine even lighter than my skin. I look like the monster I am, a dark, angry expression pinching my usually soft features, stealing away everything good I once held.

"We have ten minutes to get out of here," she says, gripping her fingers on the door.

I dig my nails into my hands. "I'm not leaving Hunter."

Alyssa's eyes glaze over, and she stares past me for a second. "Then we have six minutes."

She rolls Jacqueline over and yanks her into a sitting position. The remnants of the nightmare I created still impact her, and she won't wake up for a few more minutes. We each take an arm and lift her up between us, sharing her weight. My heart races and my knees tremble, but it's already too late to change my mind.

We enter the empty hallway and make it out of the dormitory without anyone seeing us. They're probably heading to the dining hall at this hour. The sun has already set, but it's still light enough that Alyssa leads us straight to the barrier, near the fields, and we stumble forward within the cover of the trees.

Jacqueline's dead weight is a lot heavier than I expected, and in my weakened state, I'm winded easily. Alyssa stops every few feet for me, and I pant. It's hard to catch my breath. I can't even glide. It would make it so much easier without tripping over my own feet.

"We have three minutes to grab the talisman before Daisy comes to retrieve it for the night."

I grimace. I don't think we can make it.

Jacqueline moans.

My heart stops.

"Jacqueline? Jacqueline can you hear me? You need to move your feet. We only have minutes to get out of here. The council knows everything," Alyssa says. She's pretty convincing, and I almost believe Jacqueline is the real fugitive.

We gain speed as Jacqueline stumbles with us. She grunts as we jog but doesn't stop or even question what we're doing. "Be quiet, Hunter. I'm moving as fast as I can," she mumbles.

Hunter. She said his name again. I want to say something to him but don't. We're not off the property yet, and she can still fight us.

"Almost there," Alyssa says, dragging us faster.

We stop at the gate to the forest. Alyssa grabs the small talisman from the tree and tosses it to me. I tug it over my head, walk through the gate, and throw it back to Alyssa. She maneuvers it over Jacqueline's head before pushing her through. Jacqueline falls into my arms, but I'm not strong enough to hold her, and she drops to her knees. I yank the talisman from her neck and throw it to Alyssa. Alyssa runs through the gate, throws it near the tree, and helps me pull Jacqueline back to her feet.

We dash a few feet into the forest, leaves crunching with new footsteps behind us. I gasp and clutch the trunk of a tree. The nightmare catcher weakened me so much that I'm already going to need to feed as soon as I can. I'm out of control.

"Can you make it to the car?" Alyssa asks.

I nod.

We help Jacqueline deeper into the forest until we come to

the small clearing and dirt road. Alyssa yanks off the car cover and throws it into the trunk. I help Jacqueline slide into the backseat, and Alyssa jumps behind the wheel and starts the car.

Jacqueline slumps over, still exhausted, and my stomach burns with a fire so intense, I can't even consider not invading her dream this second. I place my hands on her temples and the world shifts.

Everything turns black. I'm hovering in pitch darkness and have no sense of direction. It's disorienting and freaky and absent of anything to feed on.

"Nadia?"

It's Hunter. I can't see him, but the smoothness of his voice wraps around me, melting my fear away. "Where are you?"

An electrifying sensation crawls over me. A pinprick of light grows in front of me until the darkness turns to pure white. The world shifts. Blinking, I stand on an empty dance floor in the middle of what looks like an old warehouse.

"You're back," Hunter says.

"I couldn't control myself. I'm starving."

"Jacqueline's a lunatic," he blurts. "She's incoherent and emotional. It's hard to tolerate her."

I turn and meet his gaze. His hazel eyes appear brown in the colorful lights blinking from the stage. Grabbing my hands, he brings them to his lips.

"It's worse than I thought," I say. "It's not supposed to be like this."

"She keeps complaining she can't think and forces me into

the void the moment I say anything. I can't live like this."

The void. I was in the void before Jacqueline started dreaming. It's exactly how that place felt, absent of everything. My chest tightens, and I rest my head on Hunter's shoulder. "I wish I could pull you out with me. You're dealing with this because of me. I've come too frequently, and she's losing touch of reality." I knew the consequences of visiting Hunter, but I didn't care. I still don't. *You're a monster.* I shake my thought away. "I need to give her a break."

He sighs. "Please, don't forget about me."

I tilt my head up to look into his eyes. "I won't. I'm going to get you out of here."

I kiss him, tasting sugar on his lips from the dream around us. He makes it nearly impossible to pull myself away with the feeling of his arms around me, our souls mingling, feeling so right together. Jacqueline's dream kicks into action without giving me a choice. People swarm the club, crowding us, exploding into dust as they run into me. I grab a woman in a tight black dress and boots. Dream dust erupts from her, and I gulp in the air, tasting the sweet flavor of the dream.

Hunter still holds my hand, watching me inhale what I need to survive. And for the first time, I'm not ashamed. I'm not embarrassed around him. I'll destroy a million dreams as long as he continues to gaze at me with his intense hazel eyes like I'm his perfect dream girl amid this nightmare.

People scream and run around us as we remain in place. The crowd parts to reveal Jacqueline pressing against the closed door of the exit. She pounds her fists on it and struggles to turn the knob. It breaks off in her hand. She twirls around to face me, her eyes wide, her mouth agape.

I smile.

The world explodes around us, and I reach out and cup Jacqueline's chin, taking satisfaction in destroying her dream. Her lavender eyes bore into mine. I drink in everything I can before the air shifts and I leave her dream.

"We're almost there," Alyssa says.

"Where?" I shake my head to get the image of Hunter from my mind.

"The Haven. It's more than a club. Cian can give us a room. We'll be safe there for now. I saw it."

I squeeze my eyes shut. I'm still so hungry, and if I invade Jacqueline's head again right now, there won't be anything to feed on.

Trepidation washes over me, sinking deep into my bones. It was crazy to kidnap Jacqueline and run away from the compound. My actions are bound to have consequences, and they might even affect my father's future with the council. *She tried to kill you.* No one would believe me. I'm always going to be a monster in the council's eyes.

"Can you think of anywhere else?" I wring my hands together. "I'm out of control."

She glances at me in the rearview mirror. "You have to trust that I'll get you through this."

"I can't. Not with you, Alyssa. Look how I've already affected Jacqueline. Hunter said it's worse than it looks." I lean my head on the cool glass of the window.

"Then I'll find you someone." Alyssa cranes her neck to look at me. "You need to eat."

I blow a puff of air between my lips. I can't argue. I need nourishment, especially if I'm going to help Hunter. I just wish it wasn't so embarrassing. It's much easier when the dreamer isn't aware of what is going to happen.

Alyssa pulls into the parking garage and waves to the security guard. He gives her a pass, and she parks near the top of the garage, away from the regular tenant activity. She gets out first and then leans in and says, "Stay here. I'll be back in a minute."

I'd stay in the car all night if she would let me. It's less tempting to stay hidden amongst empty cars than going into a building full of sleeping people.

Jacqueline moans next to me, and I stiffen when her eyes flutter open. Shifting in the seat, she runs her fingers through her mess of dark, curly hair. She blinks a few times, her lavender eyes shifting to hazel and back, and then she focuses on me.

"Is this real? I'm so confused," she says after a silent minute. "Where are we?"

I rub my hands together. "The Haven. The council knows about your deal with the HPA board, Jacqueline." I lie because if I tell her the truth, I'm afraid I'll strangle her for trying to kill me. I need to be her friend while the rest of the world is her enemy so she'll trust me. "Alyssa's getting us a room so we can figure things out."

I jump at the sudden tap on the window and turn to see Alyssa. She opens the door and helps me out, and then stares at Jacqueline who doesn't move. Alyssa pulls a small necklace from her pocket, tossing it at Jacqueline. "You need to wear this."

My knees quiver, and I stumble. "Is it safe?"

Alyssa nods. "Come on. I managed to get a room."

Jacqueline puts on the necklace, her eyes widening. She waves her hands in front of her face and tears drip onto her cheeks. "What is this?"

Grimacing, Alyssa says, "An action control talisman. I'm sorry, I had to. I don't trust you. Now, get out of the car and walk ahead of us and don't say a word."

Alyssa managed to acquire an elf-spelled talisman that will influence Jacqueline to follow our orders. While it can't force Jacqueline to do bad things, it can make her follow simple commands like no talking, no running, and no fighting.

Sliding her arm around my shoulders, Alyssa helps me walk while Jacqueline quietly shuffles in front of us. We slowly climb the stairs, but before we reach the top, the world shifts.

I'm so dizzy. My vision shadows and black stars swirl in front of me. My knees buckle, forcing me to stumble.

I close my eyes. I can't do this any longer.

HUNTER

"Why are they doing this to me?" Jacqueline thinks. "Please, let me say something, anything. Come on, Jacqueline, open your mouth. You can do it. Say something. Say anything. Open your mouth!"

Jacqueline's emotions run hot and fast around me in a wave of terror, confusion, and fury.

"They know you made a deal with the board. Of course they don't trust you," I say.

"But I haven't done anything to them! I wasn't going to go through with it." Her voice rings so loud around me, I almost jump into the void myself to get away from it.

"Calm down, Jackie. I'm sure this will all get figured out." I want to tell her what I really mean when I say it'll get figured out, but I don't. I still have to share her head with her, and I'm sure I'll be permanently put in the void when she finds out she's here because of me.

"How do you know, Hunter? I need to leave, now!"

I laugh. *"How does it feel being trapped? Not good, hopefully."* Jacqueline screams in her mind.

"Nadia? Nadia?" I can hear Alyssa, but I can't see what's going on because Jacqueline stares at the ground.

Turning her head, she peers to look at the commotion, but she stops and glares at the wall. "I can't look," Jacqueline thinks. "The charm won't let me."

I'm slightly annoyed, because if Jacqueline can't look, then it means I don't get to see, either. And I want to see. I need to see. The thought of something happening to Nadia summons a cloud of tangible anxiety around me. I haven't felt this anxious since losing my body.

"Stay with me, Nadia. I'm going to find a volunteer. Jacqueline?"

Jacqueline finally glances at Alyssa, tears blurring Nadia's best friend's eyes. Next to her, Nadia lies on the floor with her knees curled to her chest with an expression of unrelenting agony marring her beautiful features. It hurts just to see her like this.

Alyssa motions Jacqueline closer. "Help me get her inside and watch her until I come back."

Jacqueline and Alyssa help Nadia into the spacious apartment. They carry her to a worn couch behind a coffee table. A few book shelves furnish the room, but I can't see much more.

"Don't touch or talk to her," Alyssa says to Jacqueline. "Don't even move. It'll teach you to mess with my best friend and give you a taste of your own power. It's wrong to hold the souls of humans hostage."

"I haven't done anything to Nadia. What is she talking about? I thought this was about the council." Jacqueline's panicked thoughts send tears clouding our vision. She blinks, but it doesn't help. She silently cries as she shuffles to the couch and sits down. "How does she even know about you?"

I don't answer her question. She deserves this. She deserves to have her lies unraveled, to be discovered for whom she really is. To suffer the consequences of her decisions, even if she did it for self-preservation. It's what I'm doing now. I'm not going to sit back and hope for the best. I'm fighting to get my body back—my life back.

Alyssa props Nadia's head on a pillow and glares at Jacqueline. "Tears aren't going to make me feel sorry for you. If Nadia dies because of that horrible nightmare catcher you set, your life is going to turn into a real nightmare."

"What? What is she talking about? I didn't set a nightmare catcher. I'd never intentionally hurt Nadia." Her racing thoughts freak me out a little.

"*Technically, you did,*" I say. "*You knocked over the gift from*

Ryder, and I guess it wasn't some fake little trinket."

"Oh, no! No. No. No. This isn't happening. This can't be happening, Hunter. They're going to kill me. I know it."

Her emotions cloud my own thoughts. *"What happens to me if you die?"* I need to know. It's very possible if Nadia doesn't recover, Alyssa won't give Jacqueline the opportunity to explain herself.

"We die together."

19

FOREVER CHANGED

NADIA

"HUNTER?" I CALL.

I stand in the middle of a dark parking lot filled to capacity with hundreds of vehicles. The night sky sparkles with millions of stars, and a low murmur of hushed voices swirl on a warm breeze. My hair tickles my cheeks as it blows in my face, and I tuck it behind my ears.

"Hunter, are you here?"

Something's different about this dream. The atmosphere feels unfamiliar. I don't sense Hunter at all.

It clicks in my head. I'm not invading Jacqueline's dream. I've never inflicted nightmares on this person before.

"Come on, Jamie, it'll be fun. You know it."

The unfamiliar dreamer's voice triggers a hunger so overwhelming, so intense, that I reach out and smack the side of the truck next to me. It explodes like a bomb, a boom loud enough to shake the ground. Fire and metal shrapnel crash around me.

Chaos erupts in the parking lot, and shadows shoot past me. Car alarms ring out in unison, people scream, metal rains from the sky and scrapes the asphalt. I saunter forward, gliding to the cacophonous symphony of the delicious nightmare.

I smack the hood of another car, and it bursts into glorious red and orange flames that light the night. Breathing deeply, I coat my tongue with the taste of spicy chili powder and tangy mango. It's quite a change from Jacqueline's ever sweet nightmares.

"We have to get out of here!" a man yells. I spot him in between cars the next row over. His muscular arms wrap around a woman's shoulders, and she stares in horror in my direction.

Her short brown hair blows in the wind. "We'll never make it, Eric."

The woman darts away from Eric. His eyes widen as she runs straight in my direction. I grin at the imaginary woman's sacrifice to protect the dreamer. I brace myself for the inevitable, holding my arms wide for her. She screams and rushes me. When she's within reach, I wrap my arms around her. She disintegrates in my hug. Her dream essence tastes citrusy, sending life and energy flowing through my veins.

"Jamie, no!" Eric races in my direction. There are two types of dreamers—the ones who will run from their worst nightmares and ones who face them head on. Eric's footsteps echo as his feet pound the ground.

He tackles me.

Smiling, I glimpse the fear in his eyes before the world around us begins to crack. I suck in as much of the dream as I can. Eric's wild eyes disappear as I consume the rest of his nightmare. The world shifts, leaving me confused and disoriented, but the burning in my soul eases and I can feel my legs again.

I lean over and grip my knees, my vision still blurry. "What happened? Where am I?" My voice comes out a whisper, my dry mouth making it hard to speak.

Alyssa hugs me. "It's okay. You're going to be okay."

I want to believe Alyssa's words, but the huge pit in my stomach is incredibly hard to ignore. I don't know if I'll ever be okay. At least I'm alive. I'm so relieved to be alive.

HUNTER

Muffled voices come from the front door as Alyssa half carries Nadia back into the apartment. Relief floods through my mind, my own and Jacqueline's. I desperately needed Nadia to be okay. I would trade my soul for hers to guarantee it. Every time I see her, my feelings grow stronger and stronger. I'm falling in love with her, and I can't stop it.

It's strange. I've only spent a short amount of time with her, but I know her. I know the real her, and no one will ever know her as the beautiful nightmare inflictor she is.

Alyssa guides Nadia down a short hallway and disappears into a bedroom. Jacqueline shifts her feet and keeps her eyes trained on the door until Alyssa emerges alone.

"Nadia will be okay," Alyssa says. She strolls to the couch and plops down next to Jacqueline. "As long as you don't scream or try to run, you're free to talk and move."

"What should I do, Hunter?" It's unlike Jacqueline to rely on me to make decisions. She's like a scared kid, and I feel sort of bad for her. Just a little bit.

"Maybe you should start by telling her that you didn't plan on killing Nadia," I say.

Jacqueline clears her throat. "I didn't try to kill Nadia, I swear." She wrings her hands together. "The nightmare catcher was a gift from the boy I met yesterday, Alyssa. I didn't even know what it was. You have to believe me."

"How am I supposed to believe someone who has told nothing but lies?" Alyssa asks.

"I had to lie. I didn't have a choice." Jacqueline sits straighter and thinks, "Please believe me, Alyssa, please. Please. Please. Please." She chants the words over and over again.

I stay silent.

"Don't say that. You had a choice and you chose to lie. You chose to pretend to be something you weren't," Alyssa says. "Why? Why risk it?"

"They'll never understand. How could they?" Jacqueline thinks to herself. She untwines her fingers and rests her hands on her knees, staring at the carpet. Turning to Alyssa, she says, "I had nothing to lose. I admit I've made some bad choices, but I wasn't ready to die. The council would've never considered me as a candidate. I had to lie."

Alyssa clucks her tongue. "If you want the ability to talk, stop skipping around the subject."

"What am I supposed to say?" Jacqueline's voice rises, and she digs her nails into the skin on her knees. "You already know about Hunter and what I am. I have nothing else to say."

Jacqueline's fear turns into anger, and I say, *I think she's expecting you to tell her why you're holding me hostage.*

"Oh, shut up, Hunter! You don't know anything. Do you expect they'll help you or something? You do realize that you're the enemy, right?" Jacqueline's shrill voice echoes through the room. She jerks her head up and stares at Alyssa. Panic rushes around me, and Jacqueline's voice echoes when she thinks, "Not again! Why do I keep doing that? What's wrong with me?"

Alyssa twists her lips to the side and lowers her eyebrows. "Actually, that is exactly why you're here, Jacqueline, because of Hunter."

"His mother is on the board of the HPA. You don't want anything to do with him. He's terrible. He'll kill you if you free him," Jacqueline sputters.

"Nadia doesn't think so." Alyssa runs her hand through her hair. "And I'm not stupid. I know about sin-eaters. I have a lot of free time. I study. I see things."

Jacqueline groans. "Just because he's pure now, doesn't mean he won't change."

"But he already has. Nadia wouldn't risk her world otherwise."

"I don't know what you expect."

"All we want is for you to put him back into his body. If you do, we'll forget about everything."

Jacqueline shakes her head and gets to her feet. "I can't go back to the HPA. The only way I'd come out alive is if I give them the information they want about the council. I don't have it yet. Would you really want me to do that? I'm only safe at the compound. I'd rather die than face the horrors the HPA will inflict on me."

NADIA

I sit on the edge of the bed. The last few hours flood my mind, and it's a lot to take in. I'm drowning in an abyss of questions and what ifs and uncertainty. I should regret kidnapping Jacqueline and for dragging her away from the compound, but I don't. I can't. Hunter deserves to have someone fight for him. I'd hope he'd do the same for me.

And now my life is forever changed. I'm forever changed.

Closing my eyes, I lean back. I imagine the heart-wrenching pain of being pulled into Jacqueline's room by the nightmare catcher. I remember the vile taste of the black fog and how empty I felt. My skin crawls, and I jolt upright. For a split second, I don't see anything except the life sucking fog.

I scream.

The door bangs against the wall. Snapping my eyes open, I peer around the room, nothing out of the ordinary now. I was hallucinating. My heart hammers, trying to calm itself, and it takes me a second to catch my breath.

Alyssa runs to my side and grabs my hand. "You screamed."

I wipe my eyes. "I was imagining the nightmare catcher again. I can't get the fear out of my head. I'm scared to face Jacqueline, Lys."

Her face falls, her mouth pouting. "I wish you never had to go through that. I should've seen it, but Jacqueline didn't set the trap. It was an accident."

I rub my arms. "What do you mean?" My eyes flick from Alyssa's to the open door behind her.

Alyssa bobs her head. "The nightmare catcher was a gift from a boy she met at the club. She had no idea of its effects."

I frown. Why was it set up on her floor? Why didn't Hunter say anything? It takes everything in me not to confront Jacqueline and accuse her of lying. I bet lying is so natural for her that even she believes her own lies.

I heave a shuddering sigh. "It doesn't matter now."

"You're absolutely sure?" she asks.

I nod. "I have to help Hunter."

Biting her lower lip, she drops her gaze to the carpet. "I have a bad feeling about this."

"What have you seen?" I ask, my chest tightening.

Alyssa's emerald eyes sparkle in the light. "A grave."

"Whose?"

"I don't know." She rubs her arms. "I could be wrong and things could change. You know how that is."

I stand up and hug myself. The heavy silence between us makes withdrawing into my own morbid thoughts easy. Reaching out, I touch Alyssa's shoulder. "You don't have to help me if you're afraid."

She wraps her arms around me. "You're my best friend. I'm not going to let you go on this crazy adventure without me."

I laugh and pull away. "I'm glad, because I don't think I can do it without you."

HUNTER

Nadia steps into the living room. "I need to talk to you." Folding her arms across her chest, she glares in our direction. She looks human again, her white hair now back to pale blond. Her indigo eyes sparkle in the soft lighting.

Jacqueline leans forward, clutching her knees. "I want to apologize for what you went through. I didn't know what Ryder gave me was meant to hurt you."

Nadia fidgets. "You have bigger problems on your hands."

Jacqueline looks at the floor and fear sweeps over me. She knows exactly what Nadia wants, and Jacqueline won't give me up easily.

"Why can't you just work something out? I doubt they want to see you dead," I say.

Jacqueline sighs in her mind. "It doesn't matter, Hunter. Just because they don't want me to die doesn't mean anything to the board. You remember what I have to give them if I return, right?"

"You could always lie about the council. It'll take them a while to figure it out," I say.

"Jacqueline? Hello? You need to focus." Nadia shakes Jacqueline's shoulders, and she looks up to meet her gaze. "What's Hunter saying? I see him in your eyes."

Jacqueline rubs her hand across her forehead.

"Tell her," I say.

"I give up. Why don't you ask him yourself? You have five minutes. It's not like I can convince you to be on my side."

What? Suddenly, I feel the pinch of Nadia's fingers and how warm the room is. I'm no longer just hanging out in Jacqueline's head. I have all my senses.

I look down.

I'm in control of her body. "How is this possible?" I say. When I speak, I sound like Jacqueline.

"Haven't you ever heard of possession? I've given you my body to use, but don't enjoy it for too long." Her powerful presence overwhelms me, and it takes me a minute to realize I can move her lips, blink her eyes, and even talk. It's the strangest thing having control over a body that isn't mine. She's smaller framed, less muscular, and is, well, a girl. It's kind of weirdly awesome.

"Four minutes."

I smile and look at Nadia. "Nadia? It's me, Hunter. Before you ask me a million questions to make sure it's really me, just remember I kissed you outside of a burning house, okay?"

Nadia's eyes widen, and she lets go of my shoulders. "Tell me how to help you."

"You need to find my body and make Jacqueline put it back," I say.

"You both lied to me about Nadia invading my dreams, Hunter. I'm not going to help you."

I grimace. I can't force her. "I'm not apologizing for that, Jacqueline. It's your own fault for taking my soul. It's the only reason she did it," I say out loud. I grip my knees and focus on Nadia. "You need to find a way to get me out of her without her cooperation. She's kind of mad about the nightmare stuff."

Nadia presses her lips together. "Okay, I'll figure something out, but where is your body?"

I don't know the answer to that. The HPA has affiliations at several hospitals all over the country and multiple labs, too. "You'll have to call my brother, Mason. He'll tell you."

"And what if he doesn't?" Nadia's eyes line with worry, and she touches my knee—Jacqueline's knee.

Alyssa hands me a notebook and a pen from the cluttered shelf near the window. "Tell him that my mom, Dr. Sullivan, offered my life force to a super and that she's been lying about everything all this time. Also, tell him to wait for me to wake up with my car keys, my wallet, and a bag of clothes." I scribble down his cell phone number. "Don't call from here though. It might not be safe."

"Time's up."

Jacqueline takes back control, my whole soul heaving like she crushed the wind from me. Disappointment swirls through my being. I had a thousand things I wanted to say, to ask, to do, but now I'm back in my mind prison.

It sucks.

"Hunter?" Nadia asks.

"Sorry, it's me," Jacqueline says.

Nadia frowns and tucks her hair behind her ear. "So, are you sure you're not going to cooperate? It'll be so much easier."

Jacqueline turns away and leans back on the couch. "I—I

can't. I'm sorry."

"I'm sorry, too."

NADIA

I look at Alyssa and shrug. "Any ideas?"

Her lips twist to the side. "Sin-eaters aren't the only soul manipulators out there. You can go up to The Haven and see if one will talk to you."

"Now's a perfect time, too," I say. All the night owls will be starting their days, which means the chances of finding someone who deals with souls might be there. I lean closer to Alyssa and add, "See if you can get her to sleep. I need to talk to Hunter when I get back."

She nods. "I'll see what I can do. Just be careful when you're there. The night patrons are an interesting bunch."

20

WE'RE ONLY TWO PEOPLE

NADIA

CIAN RAISES HIS eyebrows, seeing me enter the hall. I wave, sauntering forward to meet the troll. I forgot he's friends with my father. I don't know how much he knows, or if he even knows, what my father asked of me. I wonder if he heard about our sudden escape from the compound. Word travels in the creature community.

I regret coming up here.

"Nadia, my doll, you're looking lovely. I'm surprised to see you." He takes my hand and kisses it. "Are you here with Alyssa?"

I smile. "Yeah, it's a spur of the moment kind of thing."

He grins. "I see. Well, if you need anything, you know where I am." He opens the door and a rush of music pulses around me.

I lean down and say, "Actually, if you could keep quiet about me being here, I'd appreciate it."

His brows knit together. "Are you in trouble?"

"If the council doesn't know, then no."

He nods. "I'll keep my eye out, then. Tonight feels like an invite only night anyway. Whatever I can do to help Dmitri Petrov's daughter."

Gliding through the door, I spin on my feet the second I hit the dance floor. It's much more crowded tonight, but there's an invisible wall around me, like the other creatures don't want to get too close. It would usually bother me but not tonight. I don't think they're doing it out of fear but respect. They're all monsters like me after all.

The atmosphere of The Haven has changed dramatically since the last time I was here, which isn't exactly strange, but it still makes me uneasy. I scan the crowd for anyone who could be a threat to me while also keeping my eye out for a creature that deals with souls.

I'm uncomfortable dancing by myself, so I dance through the crowd toward an empty booth in the far corner next to the door that leads to the kitchen. I sit with my back to the wall and watch bodies sway to the hypnotizing music.

A woman emerges from the crowd and dances seductively a few feet away. Her eyes meet mine, and I refuse to break eye contact. Her coppery hair, pulled into a top knot, sparkles under the rainbow lights. A silver and white beaded headband and dangling silver earrings glint with her movements. Her golden skin shimmers against her white, eyelet lace shift dress that's cinched at the waist. Her nude wedged heels make her a good five inches taller, so that she's over six feet tall in them.

My hands tremble in my lap. She's gorgeous but dangerous, and just the creature I've been looking for. She's a succubus, an energy feeder, and she has her eyes set on me.

I stiffen, watching her dance around. If only it were to get my attention, but I recognize the moves of a predator. I'm one, too. Slowly stalking me, she gauges to see if I could possibly be an easy target. It'd be a better fate than Hunter's, though. At least she wouldn't keep a soul hostage.

The woman stops dancing and tilts her head to the side. I narrow my eyes, knowing she's not going to back off. It's what I want, though. I need her to come closer. This may be my only chance to find out if I can help Hunter without Jacqueline.

My chest tightens. The woman saunters closer, a wave of dizziness rushing over me, and I cover my eyes. It's gone as quickly as it came. I look back up, and the woman stands at my booth with her hands pressed flat on the table.

She leans over. "Your energy...it's mesmerizing."

I lick my lips. "Join me."

The succubus slides in across from me. Her silver jewelry shimmers in the colorful lights. She looks me up and down and smiles. "You're very brave."

I sit straighter. "I could say the same thing about you."

She blinks, taken aback. "I'm sorry, I thought you were..."

Her voice trails off.

I glare. "An easy target?"

She starts to slide from the booth, and I reach across the table and grab her arm. Her eyes shift to the dance floor and then back to me. She freezes. "I was confused by your human half. I could've sworn you were pure a minute ago, but I see it now. This is all just a misunderstanding."

I'm the most human after I've fed on a nightmare, but I'm still irritated that this energy eating succubus thought it would be okay to drain my essence in the middle of a crowded club. No wonder the council is picky about who they accept.

"It's okay," I say. "We all make mistakes. But just so you know, Cian frowns upon stalking patrons in his club. He'll be upset about this." I don't know if it's true, but I'll say anything to intimidate her. I doubt she'll help me out of the goodness of her heart. She thought I was food a second ago.

"Please, I can't lose this place," she says, her eyes widening.

I let go of her arm and touch her hand. "I won't mention it if you let me ask you something."

Her eyebrows knit together. "Go on."

"I heard your kind can take over human bodies."

She nods.

"Has a soul ever managed to escape?"

She taps her fingers on the table. "Not with me. I consume them."

My stomach flips. That wasn't the answer I was looking for. "But is it possible?"

She stands up. "You're asking too many questions."

I push to my feet and block her from walking past me. "Please, I need to know."

She sighs. "It's called projection. It's rare, but what I heard about it, a soul can project away from their body to avoid being consumed by my kind. But they have to come back. The body is the anchor to this world. Without one, the soul will die."

The succubus pushes past me and disappears into the crowd. I blow a puff of air through my lips. I've never heard of projection before, but it may be a way to help Hunter. If he could free himself from Jacqueline, he could go back to his body.

The only problem is that his body isn't here, and it'd be the only thing that would anchor him to life. He'll die without it.

HUNTER

"You need sleep," Alyssa says.

Jacqueline shakes her head. "I'm fine."

"You look terrible, and you're rambling incoherently. You need sleep." Alyssa walks across the room and flicks off the light switch. "I want you to lie down."

Jacqueline groans but is forced to do what Alyssa says because of the charm. "You can't make me sleep."

Alyssa's silhouette crosses the room and stands over Jacqueline. "No, but you'll get bored soon enough. Now, close your eyes and get some rest. No more talking for now."

Jacqueline stares at the backs of her eyelids. Her annoyance and fear close around me. She's terrified of not being in control of her body. I find it satisfying, though. It's the perfect punishment for her.

"You're enjoying this," Jacqueline thinks.

I don't answer. If I do, it'll keep her entertained enough to stay awake. Sleep is the only reprieve I get from her. I'll take it where I can get it.

After a few minutes, Jacqueline drifts off to sleep. I don't think she could resist even if she tried because of how exhausted Nadia's nightmare inflicting makes her.

The door creaks, and I hear hushed voices.

"Did you find anything out?" Alyssa asks. Excitement swells around me. It's Nadia. I can sense her presence.

"She's asleep," Nadia says, not answering Alyssa's question.

The world shifts, and Nadia intrudes Jacqueline's head. I didn't know how much I missed her until I see her standing before me, her gray eyes boring into my soul, her white hair blowing behind her in a dream breeze.

She looks incredible in a sky blue sundress, swaying against her alabaster legs, revealing her thighs with her motion. Her bare feet don't make a sound as she steps forward, offering her hand out for me to take.

"You're beautiful," I say. I should ask her if she has a plan or how she's going to get me back to my body, but I don't. I just want to be near her.

She slides her arms around my sides, hugging me. I wrap my own arms around her and breathe in the sugary scent of her hair. I brush my lips to her forehead. We stand silently together without moving, and I imagine this is what it would be like to be with her in the real world.

I lean down and kiss her softly. I'm afraid it could be my last opportunity. Something sharp bites at my essence, stronger than usual. I can feel her goodbye without her even saying the words. "Why is this only a dream?"

"I'm trying to fix it." She smiles an inch from my mouth before shifting to glance at the empty street in the middle of a rundown neighborhood. The place looks abandoned, like something bad happened, and everyone had to leave in a hurry. Trash spews over the weed covered lawns and cracked street, and many of the houses have open doors and broken windows. It's really creepy.

"I know," I say. "You have no idea how grateful I am. You're the best thing to ever happen to me, Nadia, and not because you're trying to help me."

A smile pulls at the corners of her mouth, but it's not full of happiness, of the light I see radiate from her. It's a sad smile. "I will help you, but—"

I cut off her words with a kiss. "Don't say it."

"This is just a dream, Hunter. I can't stay. I can't ever come back. This is my last visit." She sniffles, turning away from me to peer over her shoulder again. "I have to stop before Jacqueline is too far gone. Something about you and me here goes against things. It makes it worse for her."

It's hard to keep my face indifferent. Her words physically hurt, ripping at my soul, my very being and all my emotions. "It doesn't have to be forever. When I'm back in my body, I can find you."

She tucks her hair behind her ear. "I'm afraid that'll only

get one of us killed. You know the board will murder me if they knew I existed. I don't know what the council would do if they find out how much I care about you."

Twining our fingers together, she leads me to the stoop of the closest house. I kick the trash off the steps and sit next to her. She gazes at me with tear-rimmed eyes, and I slide my arm around her waist, pulling her closer. I rub my hand on her side, holding her as she hides her face against my chest.

As much as it kills me to admit it, she's right. Even if I abandon my family and friends, the board will always be hiding in the shadows. Always. They're willing to kill their own to keep their secrets. They stalk, brainwash, force bystanders to join them, and murder all in the sake of saving humanity from so-called monsters.

"There has to be a way," I say.

NADIA

My heart breaks, fissuring and splitting with every painful beat. I knew this moment would come. I knew I couldn't stay in a dream with Hunter forever. But it doesn't hurt any less. I've never been so sad in a dream before. I can't stop my tears from flowing.

To save Hunter, I have to give him up. This sort of half-life, trapped in Jacqueline, isn't a way to live even if it's the only way I can ever see him. He deserves so much more. My mind is set on helping Hunter get back to his body. I'm willing to die trying because I can't live with the thought of Jacqueline holding his soul forever. I can't bear it. He's destined for more than this, more than visits from a dream girl to keep him company.

I stare off into the distance. "I don't see one. We're only two people, Hunter. It's impossible for us to change things."

"I promise I'll find a way. You know, you've given me so much hope. I'm not going to lose it or you. I'm not."

I tilt my head up until my lips linger an inch from his. He closes the space, caressing his lips to mine until I kiss him hungrily, desperately, like he's the one thing I crave and need to survive. He runs his hands in my hair, and I press against him, kissing him deeper, pushing him back on the ground. My hands lace around his neck, and I feel the heat of his skin on my fingers. His hand trails down my back to run along my bare leg.

Our breathing comes heavily, rhythmic, and his lips wander from mine. They trail to my jaw and then to my neck, and I bury my face into his shoulder.

"Hunter," I whisper. Lifting my head, I gaze into his hazel eyes. He stares at me so intently that I'm afraid to move, afraid to shatter everything amazing I feel in this moment. "We should stop."

He leans on his elbows. "We'll figure this out. We're going to be okay."

I want to believe him. I'd give anything to believe him. But, here we are, in a dream.

HUNTER

Nadia sits up and stares at the abandoned neighborhood. Doubt flashes in her eyes, her disbelief in the chance for us to be together poking at me and my will to give up hope for the possibility. A tear rolls down her cheek, and I smear it away with my finger.

She turns her head to face me. "We have to save our hope for you to get your body back to be whole again. You deserve a life and some normalcy, Hunter."

"It won't be the same. You've already changed things. I can't go back home and live like I did. I'm not going to train to be an agent anymore. I want nothing to do with the board."

She closes her eyes for a second. "I have to go."

I kiss her temple. "Please, stay."

She smiles. "You know I can't, Hunter. Look at who I am. You'll realize it when you're whole again."

I hug her, knowing she's only holding hope for one thing. Not herself. Not us. Just for me. "I'll never forget about you, Nadia. I'll do whatever I can to make the world right for you."

"I hope you do," she whispers.

"I'll miss you until the day I die, you know."

She cups my chin. "You'll miss me until you forget about me. I'll fade from your memory soon enough. Remember, this is just a dream. It can't survive reality."

Dropping her hands to her sides, she turns her back on me. Cold emptiness remains where she touched me, and a hard pit forms in my stomach as I watch her walk away.

I kick a trash can, and it clatters against the stucco wall of the abandoned house. The world ripples and splits apart around me. Utter blackness seeps through like oil and covers everything in its path.

Within minutes, Nadia is gone and Jacqueline's dream world shatters into a million pieces.

NADIA

I cover my eyes with my hands.

I can't let Alyssa see the pain gripping me, leaving tears blurring my vision. It was harder than I expected to visit Hunter, knowing it would be the last time I'd ever see him again. But, I had to do it. It would've been more painful if I'd left hope for us when I feel so hopeless.

Dropping to the carpet, I pull my knees to my chest. I need a few minutes to think things through.

"What did you talk about?" Alyssa asks, plopping down next to me. She touches my knee, and I lean on her.

"I was telling him goodbye," I whisper. "I can't go into Jacqueline's dreams again. Her sanity is at its breaking point."

Alyssa hugs me. "Her fate could be worse, Nadia. Jacqueline's lucky you don't drop her off on the board's doorstep." She looks over my shoulder at Jacqueline asleep on the couch.

I frown. "Actually, I may have to do that. I found out from a succubus that the only way for Hunter to free himself and survive is if we have his body to anchor him."

"So, we still need Jacqueline," she says. "But I see she's not going to help."

I nod. It's hard to believe we can't save Hunter without Jacqueline's cooperation. I didn't go through all this to just give up. I gave up my life on the compound for this—everything. Reconciliation with the council after breaking a dozen rules will be impossible. There are consequences. My father's going to be furious.

I steel myself, mentally putting up a giant wall around me with barbed wire and moats. "Then she'll die by their hands," I say. I tilt my head up and peer at Jacqueline asleep on the couch. "I'm sorry, Hunter. I'm so, so sorry. You deserve better than this, but it has to be done. I'm going to hand Jacqueline over to the board and at least you'll be home. Maybe they'll figure things out."

Deathly quiet settles over the room, even my own heart is afraid to beat after hearing my words out loud. I'll be responsible for not only one death but possibly two. But in the end, Hunter will be out of Jacqueline's head.

He will be free.

21

IN OVER MY HEAD

HUNTER

IT'S THE LONGEST night I've ever experienced with Jacqueline. Nadia is really forcing her to catch up on her beauty sleep, and it's so boring.

It also doesn't help there's a huge possibility that today will be my last day alive. I'm going home, but that doesn't mean anything. It's going to be bad for Jacqueline either way, but she's ridiculous enough to take me down with her so she doesn't have to go alone.

I'm. Going. To. Die.

Well, crap.

Well, damn.

Well—

"There's an old payphone a block away at the Sunset Diner. It's mostly for show, but it still works. We can call Hunter's brother from there," Alyssa says.

I want Jacqueline to open her eyes so I can be more involved in the conversation. I hate only being able to hear what's going on.

"Jacqueline?" I ask. *"Can you hear me?"*

Silence.

"Jacqueline!" I yell.

"What Hunter?"

"Open your eyes, please."

"I can't. I can't do anything. I'm in the void."

"How can you hear me?"

"I can always hear you when you talk to me."

"Oh."

"What are they saying?"

"That today is the end. Nadia is going to hand you over to the board if you don't cooperate."

"Oh."

"I don't get it, Jackie. Why are you so stubborn? Why can't you just put me back in my body?"

"I'm sure the board is keeping tabs on your body, and I have to make a physical connection to put you back. I don't have the information they desire so what would be the point? They'll kill me."

"They won't really care. They've killed their own for much less. I'm not valuable to them, either."

"Then I guess we're going to die together."

"I guess so."

NADIA

"Do you want to talk about it?" Alyssa strolls next to me, swinging her arms at her sides. We left Jacqueline asleep back at the apartment. I'm hoping it will help with her sanity. The last thing I need is for her to lose control of herself when I still want her to see reason.

I glance behind us for the millionth time. "I have nothing to say." With the way I search our surroundings, I probably look overly paranoid. It's not like we're walking the streets after dark or lurking in the shadows of an alley, but I'm not letting my guard down for a second. The way to survive in the real world is to trust no one and notice everything. Even the mother of two jogging with a stroller and an iced coffee in the cup holder could be after me.

"Oh, come on. I see how sad you are." We cross the street at a crosswalk.

I stop at the corner and turn to look at her. "I'm in over my head, Lys. I don't want to lose Hunter, but the life he has right now sucks. Don't you think it'd be better—" I tug the ends of my hair and stare up at the gray sky. "What else am I supposed to do?"

She hugs me. "I don't have all the answers."

I kick a rock off the sidewalk and into the street. "Am I doing the right thing?"

"If you think you are, then yes. It's the right thing if your intent is good," she answers.

"Can you live with knowing I'm going to possibly be the reason for someone's death?" I ask.

"Can you?"

I'd love to say I'd be perfectly fine with having blood on my hands, but the truth is that I'll be haunted until the day I die or the day I decide to stop caring, whichever comes first. This is a situation I can hope and beg for the best, but I really have to accept the absolute worst thing that can happen. With my luck, we'll all die and then it will have been such a waste to give up everything for.

I can't do it.

I can't.

"There's the payphone," Alyssa says, dragging me from my thoughts.

I pull the phone number from my jacket pocket. "Let's get it over with."

I practically run to the front of the small diner where an old phone hangs from the wall. It looks as old as the battered booths I see through the glass window. Popping some change in, I pound the numbers to call Hunter's brother.

I feel like I'm going to die here on the sidewalk. My heart races and my palms sweat as the phone rings in my ear. I beg for it to keep ringing. I don't really want to talk to Mason. Maybe if I never get a hold of him, I can just forget about everything and say at least I tried.

"Who's this?" A male voice echoes in my ear.

My fingers fumble as I adjust the phone. "Mason?" I ask. "Is this Mason?"

He breathes loudly into the line. "Hold on."

A bout of static buzzes through the phone and then it goes silent. I press the receiver harder to my ear, afraid that I lost him.

"Who gave you this number? It's a private line." His voice hums deeper than Hunter's.

I close my eyes for a second. "Hunter said I could reach you this way, but I only have a few minutes. I'm taking a huge risk contacting you."

"You're wasting your time. My brother is on life support. Everyone is just waiting for my mom to make a decision."

I puff air through my lips. "That's why I'm calling. You can't trust your mother. I met Hunter, well, I met his soul, and he asked me to help him. I need to know where to find his body."

"You're crazy," he says.

My heart falls. "Please, it's true. He told me to tell you that Dr. Sullivan gave his soul to a sin-eater and that she's lying about everything. He wants you to wait by his body with clothes, his wallet, and his car keys," I spit out. "You can't trust anyone either, so don't tell anybody."

"I guess now is a good time to visit him. My mom did just ask me if I was planning on ever doing so."

The phone beeps, and I know it's going to cut off soon. "Okay, so where is he?"

He clears his throat. "He's been transferred to Northern Trin—" The line clicks and goes dead.

I slam the phone down and cover my eyes. "I didn't get the

hospital name!"

Alyssa's eyes widen. She grabs my hand, pulling me in the opposite direction than we came. I'm so angry and defeated that I yank my hand away. I stomp behind her, tears rimming my eyes, and then finally give up and lean my back against the brick wall of a building.

"You did what you could, Nadia," Alyssa says.

"It wasn't enough. All I have to show is part of a hospital name. It's Northern Trin-something."

She smiles before reaching out to grab my shoulders. She gently shakes them with excitement. "That's more than enough."

"You're right." I relax, and she steps back. I was so upset with losing connection that I didn't really think about it. I bet Hunter can confirm where it is. He has to know about the hospitals and facilities run by the HPA. *But you swore you wouldn't seek him out again...*

I shake the thought from my head. Knowing the location of his body won't do us any good if I can't convince Jacqueline to just let him go. Visiting Hunter again will probably guarantee she won't cooperate. I have to show her I have good intentions. I don't want to see anyone die.

I cover my face with my hands. I know exactly what I have to do to help Hunter, but it's riskier than dropping Jacqueline off in front of an HPA facility somewhere.

Dropping my hands to my sides, I look at Alyssa. She stares off into the distance, her eyes glassy. She stiffens, her eyes shifting back and forth, watching something I can't see, and then she blinks and looks at me.

"You've made a decision." She rubs her face. "You have to change your mind."

Tears fall from my eyes, and I shake my head. "Don't tell me. I don't want to know."

"Please, Nadia. It's the wrong decision."

I turn away from her and stroll a few feet away. Alyssa has seen something horrible. I don't want to hear it, though. I can't. "You know as well as I do that nothing is set in stone. You could be wrong."

Alyssa comes up next to me and clutches my arm. "You don't understand. I saw the name on the grave."

"It's mine, isn't it?"

She nods. "You're going to die so Hunter can live. Is he really worth it? You don't even know him." She grimaces and smacks the side of a car parked near the curb. "I'm not letting you do this. I'm not. Not for this boy you've only met in dreams."

I press my lips together. Her words sting. "You can't stop me."

She covers her face with her hands. "Please."

"You don't have to help me."

She looks at me through her fingers. "Yes, I do. You know why? Because I can't live with myself if I sit back and hope for the best. If you're this set on doing something you know will kill you, then I'm determined to save you. I'm not letting this vision come true. I'll stop it."

I smile and hug her. "Things will work out how they're

supposed to."

She pulls away and glares at me. "Only I can say that."

We both laugh through tears and head in the direction of the apartment. Even with the idea of death hanging over my head, I don't feel guilty about my decision. I know I'm making the right one, and not just for Hunter. This is the right decision for me. I can feel it.

22

SAVING YOURSELF

HUNTER

"RELEASE JACQUELINE." I'M so happy to hear Nadia's voice.

Waiting in the dark with Jacqueline is pure torture, depressing me out, since she's pretty much given up on life. No matter how much I've argued and reasoned with her, she won't give in. She's the most selfish, apathetic person I've ever met.

Yes, there have been times I thought I understood her. And at times, I would've done what she had done in her situation. The fact is that she put herself in this mess and now refuses to accept her decisions now come back around with consequences. Despite what I thought, she's not a powerful monster. She's a coward—weak and alone and scared. She has lived a life without meaning, and it kills me she might end mine the same. I never had a chance to make something of myself—to be somebody, to do some good.

Jacqueline opens her eyes, sitting up. She blinks and stretches and turns to face Nadia. "What could she possibly want now?" Jacqueline thinks to me.

"I don't know," I say.

Nadia glides closer and kneels in front of Jacqueline. Resting her hands on Jacqueline's knees, she stares into her eyes. It feels like she's looking past Jacqueline and to me, more calm and put together than I've ever seen her.

Her indigo eyes shine in the light. "I don't want you to die," Nadia says. "That's not me. I don't think I could live with myself if you or Hunter dies. I'm not a monster. I'm not. And I don't think you're one either." It sounds like she's trying to convince herself. "You may not think so, but I do understand where you're coming from."

"So, what now? Can I go back to the compound and pretend none of this happened?" Jacqueline swipes a curl from her eyes.

This is crazy. I'm not going to spend the rest of my life trapped in here. I'm not. *"You're the devil, Jackie!"* I yell.

She ignores me.

Nadia blinks. "Well, no. I can't live with myself knowing you're holding Hunter hostage, either."

Jacqueline looks down at the floor. "I don't get it."

Nadia glances at Alyssa standing near the door before meeting Jacqueline's gaze again. "I want to help you. I'll go with you to Hunter's body, and we can protect each other. I'll risk my own life to help you both. You don't really want to live with Hunter forever do you?"

"Of course I don't. Why are you willing to risk your life for him?" Jacqueline asks. "I need to understand."

Her gaze drops to the floor. "You wouldn't understand."

"Try to make me."

"In your dreams, well, I know him on a level that should've never been possible. He's so—it's hard to explain. He doesn't make me feel like a monster."

"Nadia, you don't realize his—"

Nadia shakes her head, her pale hair hitting her cheeks. "I'm falling in love with him."

The room falls dead silent. I'm not even sure anyone is breathing.

And seeing Nadia, the blush blooming on her fair skin, a beautiful blend between the girl of my dreams and the girl I want to be my reality—sends my mind whirling. I wish I could pull her into my arms and kiss her. I want to feel the weight of her against me, inhale the fragrance of her hair, taste her lips. I want to tell her I'm falling in love with her, too. I regret not telling her before she told me goodbye. I crave to be with her in the real world so badly.

"Jacqueline, I can't let her sacrifice herself for me. You have to tell her."

"You love her, too." It's not a question but a realization.

"Tell her I'd rather be stuck in your head than have her die. I

wanted her help, but not like this."

"She won't believe me."

"Please, Jacqueline. I don't want to lose her even if I can never truly have her."

NADIA

Jacqueline's eyes shift from lavender to hazel. My heartbeat resonates in my ears, the thumps like a chaotic war drum as I admit the truth out loud. Jacqueline's eyes revert to normal with a few blinks, and she leans back on the couch, staring at her hands.

Jacqueline finally meets my gaze again. "I'm sorry, Nadia. This is all so crazy. It's still too dangerous. I have to make physical contact with Hunter's body to put him back. Even with your help, I don't think we'd succeed."

"What if you didn't have to touch him?" I ask.

Jacqueline fidgets. "That's different, but what does it matter? I don't know how to make that happen."

A light shines in Nadia's indigo eyes. "I think it's possible Hunter could project himself out of your body and into his."

Jacqueline sits straighter and rests her hands on her knees. "I guess it's possible. He's using my body as an anchor now. He'd just need to let go. But, that usually means death."

"It doesn't have to be," I say. "From what I understand, when a person projects, they are tethered to the anchor, which is you. I think it's possible you can hold onto his tether long enough for him to make it back to his body."

Jacqueline frowns. "I'd have to be close to do that."

"But you wouldn't have to touch him, right?"

Jacqueline's eyes change colors and then she shrugs. "Hunter says he's willing to try."

HUNTER

I can't believe it. Nadia somehow got through to Jacqueline, and she's going to help me. Every time I think it's over, it turns out it's not, and that gives me hope for my future. I'm not sure if it's because a new option is available, that she really does want to get rid of me, or if maybe she wants to make it up to me, but I'll accept the chance. I'd like to think it's the latter, but I doubt it. It doesn't matter anyway.

"We should probably practice, Hunter."

Fear swells around me. I thought I would wing it. What if I'm not successful and just die? Would I disappear and become nothing? What happens next? I thought I'd have more time to prepare myself.

"I think I'll just wait until I'm closer to my body, thanks," I say.

"I promise I'll keep you tethered to me. I'll only release you when you want to be released. I can't just kill you, remember?"

It's hard to trust her, but I know she's right. If she could kill me, she'd have done it the moment she decided to stay at the compound. I'm her punishment for stealing a pure soul. *"Can you walk me through it?"*

"I'm not exactly sure, Hunter. I've never been a soul without a body. All I know is when I redeem someone, I can push them out. I think you have to want to do it."

What I want is to be in the real world with Nadia. I don't want Jacqueline relaying my thoughts to her. I don't want to wait until Jacqueline's sleeping to touch her. I want to be with her so much I can imagine I'm standing in front of her.

A popping noise sounds out and the world shifts. It's like when I manifest into Jacqueline's dreams, but this is different. Everything looks exactly the same but not. I feel different. I feel like a weight has been lifted from me, and I can finally move again. I'm free.

"It worked," Jacqueline says out loud.

I stare into Jacqueline's lavender eyes. I stand in front of her instead of viewing everything through her eyes. Looking down, I imagine this is what it'd be like if I were a ghost. My translucent body looks exactly like me. It's really like I'm just a projection.

"I can't see him."

I turn and look at Nadia. She squints her eyes, staring intently in my general direction. She's close enough to touch, so I reach out and run my hand along her cheek. Electricity tingles through me, and her eyes widen. She touches the spot on her cheek where my energy brushed against her.

"You have to come back, Hunter. I'm losing you." I turn back to Jacqueline and notice a light blue strand of translucent energy connecting us together. It's so faint I can barely see it, but I know it's there. I can feel Jacqueline's presence like a shadow hanging over me.

"Hold onto me for one more minute."

NADIA

"Are you okay, Jacqueline?" I ask.

She doesn't respond.

"Jacqueline?"

Nothing.

She stares straight ahead, lost in concentration. Her lavender eyes suddenly dart to mine, and she points at nothing. She doesn't talk or try to move but just sits there pointing next to me. It's like she's terrified to look away.

A wave of heat washes over me, and I wipe invisible sweat off my forehead. "That's strange."

"Nadia, it's me." Hunter's voice rings loud in my ears, sudden pressure filling my head. *"I think it's going to work."*

"I know it will," I think to him.

"I wanted to thank you. You're my angel, you know. You've saved me."

I smile to myself. "You're saving yourself."

"I'll make things right in the world for us," he says.

A pure and good feeling, one I never want to leave me rushes from Hunter to me. "I know you will."

"I love you, Nadia."

The warmth disappears before I can say anything else, and I'm alone with my thoughts again. It reminds me of what it's like to be with him in the dream world. His love for me is tangible. It still resonates within me even though he's gone. He will always be a part of me. My soul mate.

HUNTER

Jacqueline pulls me back into her mind. Agony washes through my soul, the pain as horrible as the first time she ripped me from my body. It doesn't help that I got to feel what it was like to be in Nadia's head. It was so full of love and happiness. It was nothing like this prison.

"If we're going to do this, we need to leave soon. The council will be searching for us," Alyssa says.

Jacqueline glances from Nadia to the fiery redhead. She wrings her fingers together to keep them from trembling. "We still have to get pretty close for Hunter to make it. What if he's at one of their facilities? We'll never get close enough."

"He's at a hospital that's called Northern Trin-something his brother said. The call dropped before I could get the entire name." Nadia moves from the floor to the couch to sit next to Jacqueline. "I don't think it's like what you experienced before."

Northern Trin? I search my mind for the hospital she mentioned. It has to be Northern Trinity Hope. It's where my mom worked before she got involved with the board.

"Jacqueline, she's talking about Northern Trinity Hope Hospital. A few of the HPA people work there. It's easier to get things done when they're immersed in human communities."

"So, it's public?" she thinks.

"Yes, anyone can go there. It's not even highly monitored because the staff only treats humans there." The HPA is a fairly large organization and goes under a few different guises. To the human population, they're a scientific research organization that covers everything from cancer, genetics, pharmaceuticals, and other random science-y things I've never been interested in. They're privately funded and could take over the world if they wanted to, but it'd never happen. They're not a bunch of mad scientists. They want what everyone does—to live a life free from fear and harm. That's their mission—to destroy creatures

before the creatures destroy them. Funny, right?

"I hope you're not lying. I trust you, Hunter."

"Why would I lie? Nadia's going with you."

Jacqueline looks up at Alyssa and then turns to Nadia. "Hunter says you're right. Northern Trinity Hope Hospital only caters to humans."

23

A FIGHTING CHANCE

NADIA

"WE HAVE TO believe we're going to be fine," Alyssa says. Her vision of my grave hasn't changed, but we're both still holding out hope I'll survive. "As long as we stay out of sight, everything is going to work out."

She reaches into her pocket and hands me a necklace before walking to the couch to put one around Jacqueline's neck. I roll the cracked marble between my fingers. It's another talisman, one created by an elf, and I know exactly what it does. My father has a pair just like it.

"This is just a precaution, Jacqueline. I don't want to risk you leaving us, and with this talisman, you can't."

251

I look in Jacqueline's direction. "As soon as Hunter is out of your body, you'll be free to go."

Alyssa clears her throat. "I suggest not going back to the compound, though. The council doesn't take kindly to liars. We can't keep your secret. They'll punish us, too."

She grimaces. "What am I supposed to do?"

I grab a notepad and scribble an address on it. Ripping the page out, I hand it Jacqueline. She reads it over, twisting her lips to the side before shoving the paper in her pocket.

"Tell the truth, and the Enchantress Sisterhood will take you in," I say.

Jacqueline nods. "Let's get this over with." Standing up, she walks to the door and freezes in place. "Are you coming? I can't leave without you."

I sigh. I should be more nervous than I am but knowing this is really happening keeps me calm and in control. I stare into Jacqueline's eyes. "Are you ready, Hunter?"

Her eyes change to hazel. "He's ready."

Alyssa picks up a small backpack with a few necessities just in case we can't come back here. Slipping it onto her shoulders, she smiles at me before following Jacqueline.

It's hard to believe this is happening. I hope I survive.

HUNTER

Jacqueline watches Nadia tap her fingers on her knee. No one has said a word since we left. Even though I'm just watching everyone, I'm uncomfortable by the awkwardness of the situation. It doesn't help how tense everyone is, either. I don't know how they feel. I'm not afraid of the board like they are.

"You better not make me regret this." Jacqueline's threat throws me off guard. I don't know what I was to expect, but I thought we've come to terms with the situation.

"You'll regret it if you don't do it," I say. I've grown so used to Jacqueline that it'll be weird actually having to do things for myself. But I'd rather have to re-teach myself the basics of owning a body than be stuck forever. Man, I can't wait to taste food again.

Jacqueline looks from Nadia's hand to the window. She leans back in the seat and rests her head on the glass. "You know I did what I had to. I expect that you'd do the same. Maybe one day you'll forgive me and see I'm not a bad person." Her voice whispers to me as she thinks it.

As much as I hate to admit it, Jacqueline isn't a horrible person. She did what was right for her in a tough situation to survive. Force someone into a corner, and they'll fight even harder than if they could just run. There is more to the world than good and evil. Jacqueline and I are alike in a way. We were cultivated and raised to believe that different is bad, but really, different is just different. We all have dark sides.

"I don't think you're bad. I think you're annoying and selfish, and not to mention stubborn, but you're not bad. This situation sucked for both of us, and it was neither of our faults. It was the board and my mom's fault, and they'll get what's coming to them. I promise you that."

"Don't waste your time on revenge."

"Do you have a better idea what I should do with my time since I'm not going to dedicate my future to the HPA?"

"But Hunter, that's exactly what you should do."

I'm quiet for a minute. Why is it that Jacqueline has chosen the time before I'm about to be free to have rational, meaningful conversations with me? I never expected to figure out my life with the person who imprisoned it.

"You make it sound easy."

"I hope it is for you."

"It would be nice."

Jacqueline peers at her own reflection in the window, and I watch my soul peek through. Her eyes blur from the tears she holds back. "While I would do this all over again, I'm sorry you were the one I took."

I never thought Jacqueline would ever apologize, and I don't know what to say. Her emotions swirl around me, a mixture of sadness, fear, relief, and grief, but I know she is being honest. *"Look on the bright side of things. If you hadn't, I never would've met Nadia."*

"I hope you two can figure things out. I really do."

"Me too."

Jacqueline's quiet for a moment, but I can feel she has a lot of things to say. Finally, after another minute, she thinks, "You know, they're going to interrogate you. Are you ready for that? What will you say?"

"I'll make up something. Being around you turned me into a pretty good liar. Are you ready to be on your own again?" Our shared life is almost over, and I'm getting antsy. I shouldn't care what happens to her, but a small part of me hopes she's okay in the end.

"I'll manage. Don't worry about me."

Shifting in her seat, Nadia draws Jacqueline's attention away from the window and to her. Nadia sucks in her bottom lip, hiding her pout, though worry still furrows her brows. I want to hug her and comfort her, tell her we'll make it through.

She bats her eyelashes, blinking tears away, before she says, "This is almost over."

A building in the distance catches my attention. Northern Trinity Hope Hospital stands nine stories high with concrete block walls up to the third story and then all glass windows to the top. It brings back vague memories from when I visited my mom there. She was a medical oncologist with an office on the fourth floor before getting a seat on the board. Now, I don't even know what she does. I don't care, either.

I'm done with her.

Nadia turns to gaze out the front window. She flips down her visor and looks at Jacqueline in the mirror. "We're almost there."

Jacqueline swipes her hair from her face and doesn't respond to Nadia. Instead, she thinks, "Should we wait to say our goodbyes, Hunter? Even if you don't want to hear it, I will miss you."

NADIA

I feel sick to my stomach with anxiety. Rolling down the window, I stick my face into the wind. It only helps a bit with the dread I can't shake, making me want to throw up.

"I'm going to circle around," Alyssa says, driving past the hospital. I consider begging her to keep going, so I have more time. She glances at me in her peripheral vision. "As long as you don't do anything unnatural, no one will notice you're not human."

"Wish you could say the same about me," Jacqueline says from the backseat.

"We're all going to be okay," she says. I think she says it more to convince herself because she doesn't sound very hopeful.

I fidget in my seat and adjust the seatbelt on my shoulder. "All we need to do is get in and out without being noticed."

"Sounds easy enough," she says.

Jacqueline clears her throat. "Hunter says the HPA manages the basement, and that's where his body will be." She leans forward until her face is near mine. "We only need an access card to get down there."

That makes things more difficult. "Can you tether Hunter there from the lobby?"

Jacqueline is quiet for a minute. "The same floor would be better."

My heart sinks. How am I supposed to get my hands on an access card? I doubt someone will hand one over. I wanted to avoid confrontation, but that's not going to happen. *You can figure it out.*

"We'll have to steal one," Alyssa says.

"From where? Who? It'd be easier to rob a store than to get our hands on an access card." My voice rises, and I wince at its squeakiness.

"Hunter says the HPA doctors and scientists are not like

their agents. They lack most combat skills and should be easy to take out," Jacqueline says.

Take out? Is he crazy? I don't want the entire board after me. They wouldn't stop until I was dead—until we're all dead. "I'm not killing anyone," I say. I cover my face with my hands and take a deep breath.

Alyssa taps her fingers on the steering wheel. "It's three against one, Nadia. We can handle that without killing anyone."

She pulls into the hospital parking lot and parks in the farthest row away from the entrance and closest to the street. The road is pretty dead, a car speeding past every few minutes, and there's a shopping center across the street with an empty parking lot. It's underwhelming. We may actually get out of this unscathed.

I don't move to get out, and neither does Alyssa. Jacqueline sits with her arms folded across her chest. The only noise comes from my open window and the rumble of the engine.

Jacqueline shifts in her seat, and I watch her in the mirror as she peers around the parking lot. "Hunter says his car is parked a row over. It's the black BMW wagon. His brother is here."

My heart flutters. His brother could easily give us access. I can call him from the payphone across the street, and he can get us in without having to worry about getting caught or hurt or worse. "He can get us in," I blurt. "It really is that simple." I turn back to look at Jacqueline.

She stares out the window for a second longer before meeting my gaze. "He's not sure we can trust his brother. It'd be too easy for him to trap us in the basement and then there would be no way to get out. He agrees with Alyssa. We need to get our own access card."

Alyssa swivels in her seat so she can see both me and Jacqueline. "It's our only choice. Hunter's brother will get caught if he tries."

I rub my eyes. "Where are we going to find someone with an access card? Won't they all be inside already? It is the middle of the day."

"Actually, it looks like someone familiar just pulled up," Jacqueline says. "Hunter says his name is Dr. Bradley. If we can get to him before he gets to the lobby, we may have a fighting chance."

24

YOU CAN'T SAVE THEM ALL

HUNTER

WHY ISN'T ANYONE moving? Dr. Bradley is getting away. It's not like he's some six foot something, broad shouldered, scary dude—he's scrawny, barely five and a half feet, and not to mention old. He's in his late sixties and uses a cane, but I doubt he could beat anyone to death with it. He's more likely to let you borrow the thing than use it as a weapon. He's harmless.

"Any day now!" I yell.

"Maybe try being empathetic and see if you're the first to move," Jacqueline snaps.

Alyssa turns off the car and the doors unlock. Nadia opens hers first, and then Alyssa gets out and opens the door for

Jacqueline, but she doesn't move. She's purposely wasting time.

"Seriously, Jackie? You're going to be the reason you guys get in trouble. You're not changing your mind are you? This is the best solution to save both our asses."

"Not everyone can be as brave as you, Hunter."

Nadia grabs Jacqueline's arm. She pulls her out, causing her to stumble. Jacqueline slaps her hands on the window of the car next to us to catch herself. Turning to Nadia, she glares.

Nadia raises her hands. "We're running out of time. I think we should get him to come over here."

Alyssa nods and plays with her braid. "I have an idea. You two wait here and be ready to tackle him."

"What a terrible idea," Jacqueline thinks.

"Will you help, Jacqueline?" Nadia asks. "I need to know I can count on you, and you won't leave me to fight alone." I don't blame her for not trusting Jacqueline.

Jacqueline bobs her head. "I just want to get this over with and get out of here."

Alyssa grins at Nadia. "We fought an agent remember? This man will be easy."

Nadia grimaces. "Just be quick."

NADIA

What if Alyssa's plan doesn't work? So many bad things could happen. I don't like not being able to see her through the parking lot. She's not invincible even if she can predict the future. A million horrible thoughts zoom through my mind. This could be it for us.

"One of us should hide," Jacqueline says.

"I'll do it," I say.

She frowns. "Don't go far."

I stroll to the front of the car, making sure to touch my feet to the ground with each step, and hide out of sight. I wish Alyssa would've parked elsewhere. The street does nothing to cover behind me.

"I should call a field agent. I'm not equipped for this kind of situation," a male voice says.

Alyssa's head, with her neatly styled braid, bobs past a shiny, red sports car parked a few spaces over. "It's tied up in my car. We're both safe."

"What made you bring it here?"

"Mason said to," Alyssa responds. She sounds so natural. I'd have stuttered my way through it, making it obvious I was lying.

"Mason Sullivan?" the doctor asks.

"Yes, sir."

Alyssa and the doctor reach the corner of the truck, and I rush around to come up behind them. The doctor freezes, seeing Jacqueline, and raises his black cane.

He stumbles back and closer to me, reaching into his coat pocket. "What is this? Who are you?"

I lunge, jumping on his back. His legs buckle under him, sending us both to the asphalt. He yells out, but I grab his head and press my hand over his mouth. He struggles against me, but I'm stronger than him and squeeze tighter.

Jacqueline grabs his cane and holds it like a baseball bat while Alyssa hoists the doctor off me while restraining his hands. I rise to my feet with them, still holding my hand over his mouth. I'm surprised he hasn't bitten me. He's probably overly cautious with my creature germs and all.

"No one will get hurt if you cooperate." I almost sound like my father. Straightening my back, I channel him the best I can. Lifting my hand a few centimeters, I test to see if he'll scream.

"I ca—"

I slap my hand back down on his mouth. "Don't speak."

Jacqueline stands frozen in fear, facing the doctor. I snap my fingers at her, drawing her attention, and she shakes her head. "It should be on a retractable tether attached to the inside of his coat," she says. "Hunter says to grab his wallet, too. Inside a small zipper there should be a syringe with a tranquilizer."

The man's eyes widen.

Unbuttoning the two top buttons of his coat, I feel the small plastic spool with the card attached to it. I yank it hard enough to tear a hole in the fabric and rip the access card free. "Do you have any weapons on you?" I ask, reaching into his back pocket for his wallet.

He shakes his head.

"Check his ankle," Jacqueline says.

I lift up each leg of his black trousers and only see a pair of mismatched socks. "Anywhere else?"

"Hunter says not that he knows of, but you'll need his pass code," Jacqueline says.

I stare at the doctor and then pull my hand away. Tears line in his eyes, his cheeks red. He glares at me with undeniable hatred. Conditioned hatred. But can I blame him? Attacking him in the parking lot probably solidified whatever the HPA instilled in him.

Blinking a few times, he licks his lips. "Please, don't hurt me. I have a family."

Jacqueline marches closer and touches his face. "I had a family, too, before your board murdered them."

He cringes. "Please, it wasn't me. I only heal people, not kill them. Just leave me alone."

I study the doctor for a minute. "But how can you work for them? How do you live with yourself?"

A tear drips on his cheek. "The good I do makes up for it. I am an honest man. Please leave, and I won't call the board."

Alyssa stares at me. "Tell us your pass code."

He shakes his head. "If I do, they'll kill me. Please, just let me go."

I shake his coat. "We'll kill you if you don't."

The doctor hangs his head in defeat. Might as well use his fear of creatures to our advantage. "It's seven, two, two, two, zero, one, two."

Alyssa clears her throat. "Sedate him, Nadia. We're running out of time."

HUNTER

Things would go smoother if I could talk to Nadia myself. It's like Jacqueline purposefully relays my messages in an untimely manner. I also feel bad for Dr. Bradley. I'm sure Jacqueline would've killed the poor guy if she had the chance. She has a lot of hate toward the board and it shows.

Jacqueline spins away as Nadia injects Dr. Bradley with the

tranquilizer from his wallet. She glances at the empty road and then at the looming hospital. "How long does that stuff work for?" she asks me.

"Not long. It's just enough to knock someone out to restrain them," I say. It's definitely not enough to keep Dr. Bradley down while we go inside and body jump.

Swiveling on her feet, she glances back at Alyssa and Nadia as they lay Dr. Bradley on the ground. "Hunter says the tranquilizer only lasts a few minutes."

"I'll take her," Alyssa says to Nadia. "You can stay with the doctor."

Nadia shakes her head. "Do you know what they could do with you if they caught you? I'm coming with you. We'll put him in the trunk."

Alyssa groans. "You're right. I can't go at all with the future I just saw. It'll end badly for everyone with all of us. You'll sacrifice yourself for me."

At least she didn't say Nadia will sacrifice her life for Jacqueline.

"It'll be okay, Lys. I won't be alone. Jacqueline is here," Nadia says. "We'll get in and out."

Jacqueline clears her throat, her anxiety and determination palpable. "You can trust me. I promise." Thinking to me, she says. "You ready, Hunter?"

"You bet," I say.

NADIA

Alyssa leans closer and whispers, "Careful, Nadia. She'll risk your life to save herself."

"Have you seen it?"

She shakes her head. "I just know it."

I'll be fine." I turn to Jacqueline. "Ready?"

Grabbing my arm, Alyssa stops me in place. "You need to hurry. If you can't get out within fifteen minutes, you'll get caught."

I hug Alyssa. "I'll get out."

Locking my arm with Jacqueline's, we dash away from Alyssa. If I only have fifteen minutes, I have no time to waste psyching myself up to go into the building. When we reach the aisle of cars nearest to the entrance, we slow down to stroll the rest of the way.

An elderly man sits in a small quad area away from the door, smoking. His heavily wrinkled skin hangs loosely on his face, and he looks like death incarnate. A cane props against the bench next to his leg, and a standard poodle with a working dog vest rests at his feet.

His milky white, glassy eyes meet mine. Like a bad omen, a chill runs down my spine. His head turns, making his gaze follow us, and I wonder if he is the grim reaper waiting to gather our souls.

"We're being watched," I whisper.

"He can't actually see us," Jacqueline says.

The old man grabs his cane and stands up. He points it in our direction and yells, "I've been a bad man!"

Jacqueline's arm stiffens, and she tugs me faster. "He's close to death. Some souls just know."

"You're going to leave me to die with a guilty conscience?"

the man asks. "Please, save me."

Jacqueline looks over her shoulder and whispers, "Only you can save yourself."

The glass doors to the hospital automatically open and freezing cold air rushes around me. Fake potted trees sit sporadically around a seating area. Off to the right, a gift shop entices a few people with all sorts of figurines, stuffed animals, balloons, flowers, and random stuff people don't need.

A man in a blue security uniform stretches at a podium and greets us with suspicious eyes. His thick brows lower on his head as he presses his lips together. I'm terrified he's an HPA agent, but Hunter said they don't even have security at this hospital.

"We're here to visit our mother," Jacqueline says. It surprises me how confident she sounds. "She's in room 4G."

The guard looks each of us over. We can't pass as biological sisters, but I doubt he'll say anything even if I can see he's thinking it. He nods slowly before pulling a marker from his chest pocket and scribbles something onto two guest passes. He hands them to us. "Visiting hours are over at seven."

I smile and stick my pass to the front of my shirt. Tucking my hands in my pocket, I nudge Jacqueline to move with my elbow. We head straight for the elevator and call for it. The doors slide open, and when we get on, my heart sinks. I don't see a button for the basement.

"You can't access the basement from here," Jacqueline says, hitting the button for the fourth floor.

I wish I could speak with Hunter directly. It would be so

much easier if it weren't filtered through Jacqueline. Who knows how much she's leaving out? "I don't know why I'm surprised."

She shrugs. "Because you have no idea what really goes on in the real world. You've been so sheltered. I'm surprised you're actually here with me, and we're going through with it."

"I didn't want to die with a guilty conscience," I say, remembering the old man's words from the parking lot.

She spins toward me. "You can't save them all."

I'm not sure if she's referring to me or herself—maybe the both of us. "But you should try to save who you can."

She turns away as the elevator door slides open. I hesitate for a second, letting Jacqueline exit first, and then stay close on her heels as she marches down the pristine white hallway. It smells like disinfectant, and loud whispers come from the nurse's station twenty feet away.

Jacqueline's hand flies out and smacks me in the chest, stopping me in place. I reel backwards and hit my shoulder on the wall next to me. Fear slices through me like a blazing knife, and I press my back to the wall for support.

Rushing to me, Jacqueline bows her head to lean closer to my ear. "We have a problem. Security measures must've changed since Hunter has been here. An agent is heading our way. Hunter says this particular agent is different. He can see auras, and he can tell when someone isn't human."

I blow a puff of air through my lips. There aren't any doors close enough to run into to hide, and we won't make it back to the elevator, either. I straighten my back and clench my fists to prepare for a fight. While I'm not trained in combat, I'm fast. I also have the sheer will to live on my side. I will not go down without a fight.

Jacqueline wraps her arms around my neck. "I'm letting Hunter take control. His aura should mask mine. Because you're half human, you should be fine."

That doesn't give me much hope. Sweat beads on my forehead, anxiety gripping my chest, making it hard to breathe. This could be the end for me. Jacqueline is safe, but no one is here to hide me.

"I won't let anything happen to you, Nadia." It's Hunter speaking through Jacqueline.

I heave a breath, sobbing into Jacqueline's shoulder. I can't help it. I'm so scared that I can't be strong. It's funny how after everything I've gone through to get Hunter back to his body and away from Jacqueline, I'm the one who loses in the end. *You knew the risk. Alyssa predicted your future.*

Hunter shushes me, hugging me tighter, pressing my back harder into the wall. I wish it were really him and not Jacqueline's body. It's not the same. I can't help that I despise her.

"I'm scared," I sputter.

"He's coming," Hunter whispers.

I hate that the last thing I'm going to do in my life is cry.

25

CHANGE OF PLANS

HUNTER

"MOM'S GOING TO be okay. Please, don't cry." I say it loud enough for the agent to hear. His footsteps slow, and I can feel his gaze on my back, but he doesn't stop.

If the agent from the Special Ability Task Force notices Jacqueline's life essence with mine, he'll make it known. He's highly trained and deadly, and also scientifically gifted with strength and some serious fighting skills. He's the result of the board's many experiments, and one of their most successful. It's his job to investigate and destroy supers.

"*It's working,*" Jacqueline thinks.

I nod. "You're a quick thinker."

"What?" Nadia whispers through her tears.

"Sorry, nothing."

Nadia relaxes, and I turn my head to peek behind me. The agent rushes past without a second glance and to the elevator. I pull away and meet Nadia's eyes. She wipes the back of her hand over her cheek and blinks.

"Time's up, Hunter."

"I'm really going to miss you," I say to Nadia.

Jacqueline forces me back into her mind.

NADIA

I almost can't believe I'm alive. The agent walked by like we weren't even here. My uncontrollable sobs were pretty obvious, and I'm mortified I couldn't stay calm in the face of danger. I'd be the first one to die in a horror movie. For being a monster, I'm not as tough as people think.

"The elevator is after the nurse's station," Jacqueline says.

I lock my arm through hers, and we stroll along with our heads bowed. I don't look up as we pass the station, even though I sense a pair of eyes on me, and then we turn right when Jacqueline nudges me in that direction.

The elevator lies ten feet away. For going to an authorized-only part of the hospital, there's nothing special about it. It doesn't say Employees Only or require the access card, so I push the button and wait. We stand a few feet back in case someone is on the elevator, but it's empty when the door slides open.

Jacqueline enters first. I rush to follow, afraid to be in the corridor, and immediately press the close door button a few times instead of waiting for it to slide shut automatically. My chest tightens in both fear and relief at the sight of a button marked B. It takes me a few seconds to gather my courage to press it.

I keep my face away from the camera blinking in the corner and lean against the side wall of the elevator just in case someone waits on the other side of the door when we reach the basement.

"I can't do it," Jacqueline says.

I jerk my head to look at her. "What?"

My palms sweat, and for the first time ever, I'm feeling claustrophobic. The thick air sparks panic in the back of my mind. Hunter can't go back to his body if Jacqueline won't help and then all our efforts have been wasted.

Jacqueline twists the ends of her curly hair. She leans closer and whispers, "I'm scared."

Out of all the times to pick to change her mind, now is possibly the worst moment in the world. Alyssa was right. She'll be the reason I fail. She's basically engraving my name on the headstone Alyssa saw in her vision.

"You don't think I am? We're here, Jacqueline. We can't go back. Don't make me drag you to his body. That'll get us both caught with no way to escape," I say, anger raising my voice. "We don't have long."

The elevator dings, and the door slides open.

I hold my breath and peek out.

An empty hallway leads to a set of double doors with the words 'Employees Only' painted across them. On the wall next to the doors, a keypad and access card reader blinks at me. As long as no one comes out, we're safe in the hallway for now.

I grab Jacqueline's arm, but she plants her feet and doesn't budge.

"Come on, Jacqueline," I say.

She shakes her head. "No. You don't understand. They'll kill us. Someone will catch us. I can try to let him go here."

"But you said he had to be closer. You sure he will make it?"

She looks at the floor, her eyebrows pinched together. She doesn't know. I'm not putting my faith in her getting him safely back to his body from a distance she's not sure of, not when we can go a little farther still.

Tucking my hair behind my ear to get it out of my face, I glance at the double doors once more and start walking toward them. Jacqueline cries out, and I turn and watch as she trips and slides across the tiles behind me. With the talismans we're wearing, she has to go where I go whether she wants to or not.

"Please, Nadia, I need a minute. I'll do it. I swear. Please, just stop. I need a second."

I freeze. I'm running out of seconds. "Fine, but we're going through the doors first. I don't like being so open in this hallway."

"But you don't know what's on the other side of the door," she argues.

I stroll back to her and tug her to her feet. "I'm sure Hunter does. Just ask him."

HUNTER

"You'll find a bathroom to the left side of the hallway when you

enter," I say, answering Nadia's question without being prompted by Jacqueline. It would be a lot easier if Jacqueline would give me control again, but she's already told me no about six dozen times since running into the agent in the hallway.

"I don't care. I don't want to go through the doors yet," Jacqueline thinks.

"It's a single stall with a lock," I say.

"People tend to use the bathroom. Someone will discover us."

"It's not the only bathroom on the floor."

"Shut up, Hunter. You're not the one who has to worry about getting out alive."

Yet, I kind of do.

Nadia tugs Jacqueline's hand, straightening her on her feet. She looks paler than she did a few minutes ago, and her hair appears lighter, too. She wasn't lying when she said they were running out of time. A deep, unmistakable hunger shines in her eyes as her patience with Jacqueline grows weary.

"I'm not going to shut up, Jackie. Look at Nadia. Don't you see what's happening?" I ask.

"What are you talking about?"

She's playing oblivious, and it pisses me off. She knows exactly what's happening. *"Don't act clueless. Nadia's getting weaker, and the longer you take, the more likely she's going to lose control. People will notice."*

"That's not my—"

Nadia squeezes Jacqueline's hand. "We are getting out of here alive. You have to trust me. We're strong and powerful.

These people, they're afraid of us, too. Pull yourself together. I believe in us."

Jacqueline forces her feet to move. "We are powerful. We're getting out of here alive." She repeats the words to herself, and I can feel her fear ease. She's clinging onto Nadia's faith and using it to gather her courage. She closes her eyes for a moment and then meets Nadia's gaze. "Let's get Hunter home."

NADIA

Jacqueline picks up her pace and walks next to me.

"I can sense Hunter's body," she says.

A lightness eases the pain in my chest at her words. We're so close I can feel it. I was worried Jacqueline would put up a fight and make a scene and then push me at the doctors to make her escape. She has no regard toward others, and it shows in how she acts. She's the type to make a deal with the devil and then beg for mercy when it's time to pay her dues.

"Where do we need to go?" I ask.

We reach the double doors, and she peeks through the small window. "We have to make it past the clerical counter. It's at the end of the corridor when we enter. That should be close enough." She crosses her arms, rubbing her hands on them like she's cold. "We only have a few seconds to get back out. The secretary is bound to see us."

I nod. I'm strangely confident we'll get in and out quickly without having to face any of the HPA members. If they're anything like the doctor from the parking lot, then they won't want to confront us either.

"We can do this," I say. "You'll be really relieved once it's over."

Jacqueline twists her lips to the side. "I hope so."

I slide the access card and the screen asks for the pass code. Jacqueline punches it in. We stand off to the side as the doors automatically open inward. The corridor looks identical to the rest of the hospital with white walls and tiles, except a few framed posters of people I've never heard of hang on the walls. I look at each one we pass and realize it's a memoriam of people the HPA has lost. I smirk when I see one of our council members, Veronica Sanders, on the wall. I guess she never told the board she quit. If only they knew.

I try not to panic at the sound of voices. They echo from the end of the corridor, where the clerical counter is. A woman laughs and then a phone rings, and the voices turn into quiet murmurs.

"When we get to the end of the corridor, bend down," Jacqueline whispers, her hands trembling.

I reach over and twine my arm through hers. Her lips curve up in the corner, but it's nowhere near a smile, and I don't blame her. Someone could come around the corner at any second and see us, and there's only one way out that we know of. The odds are against us. I should be angrier with Jacqueline since she's the reason I'm in this mess, but I feel bad for her. I pity her. She truly is alone in this world.

"Now," Jacqueline whispers.

I hunch over, dropping my arm from hers. It'd be easier to get down on my knees, but I'm not risking it. I'm too worried about not getting to my feet fast enough to escape.

We sneak past the counter and turn into the first hallway on the right. A doctor strolls down the corridor, reading over her clipboard. She enters a room, too busy to notice us or care. I let out my breath.

"Goodbye, Nadia." Hunter's voice echoes in my head and then slips away as quickly as it came. I turn to look at Jacqueline, and she nods, confirming Hunter is gone. I blink tears from my eyes, relieved that it's finally over. Hunter can live his life again.

But I already miss him.

"Let's go," I mouth to Jacqueline.

HUNTER

The air changes. It's like I'm watching things happen from a different perspective. Reaching out, I touch Nadia and my hand passes through her. I'm a ghost until I reconnect with my body, only tethered to this world through Jacqueline. And since I left her at my own freewill, I could accidentally snap the tether and die if I don't hurry.

I bound down the hallway and to the last room on the left. I can sense my body behind the door. It's strange, like I'm stuck in a magnetic pull, and it wants me back. It needs me back.

Without a body, I'm much faster, freer, not restricted by flesh and bone and the heaviness of it all. I hesitate before going through the door. All I've wanted the last few weeks was to be back in my body—to be me again—and now that I'm standing so close, I don't think I can go through with it.

I can't live the life that was given to me. I can't pretend like everything is going to be okay and that somehow I will miraculously change the world. I can't pretend I'll change the thoughts of the board and make a place where Nadia is free from fear—make a place where we can be together. I can't pretend it's okay if my mom is a delusional doctor trying to save humanity. It doesn't even need to be saved in the first place. What will happen to me now if I go back? How will I live my life feeling this way?

"You have to do it or you'll die." The words whisper faintly, but they resonate within me. It's Jacqueline's thoughts coming through our tether. I look over and see her staring in my direction. She's the only one who can see me like this.

"Maybe that's how it's supposed to be," I say. I don't know if I believe in fate or karma or divine intervention, but given all the signs and all that I've been through—not to mention what Nadia has been through—maybe I should really think about what I'm going to do. What if it's not what is supposed to happen?

Hot energy zips through me, like a shock of electricity. "It's why we're here. It's why we went through all this trouble to get you here. You can now make a difference. You'll have a voice we don't have."

"With no one who will listen," I say.

"Then you'll have to yell and force them to listen."

I glance from Jacqueline to Nadia and see the fear puckering her eyebrows. She looks so fragile and beautiful with her shimmering, white hair and light gray eyes. She looks like the girl I first met in Jacqueline's dream. I can't give up. Nadia would hate me. I would hate me, too.

Lifting my hand, I wave. Before I enter through the door, the agent from the Special Abilities Task Force waltzes up and stands on the opposite side of the counter, just feet away from Nadia and Jacqueline. All he'd have to do is move to the other side to see them.

I'm not going to let that happen.

NADIA

Jacqueline shoves me against the wall, stopping me from moving forward, sending my heart racing. Voices echo around the corner. This is the only way for a person to go. We have nowhere to hide if they come this way. Jacqueline points at a door about ten feet away, and I glide toward it.

"Anyone new come through here, Lacey?" a masculine voice asks.

Jacqueline rushes in the room behind me and partially closes the door.

"Can I help you?"

I swivel to see a woman sitting at a desk, holding a mug halfway to her mouth. Charging her before she has a chance to do anything, I slap my hand over her mouth, sloshing coffee over her desk.

"Don't do anything," I whisper, leaning down. "We're not here to hurt anyone. We were just leaving."

"He's coming," Jacqueline says, searching the room. She picks up a metal folding chair and holds it up to protect herself.

I don't move. I don't breathe. I just hold my hand over the startled doctor's mouth and wait for the agent to storm in.

But nothing happens. The world comes to a standstill.

HUNTER

Gasping, I sit up.

I rip the breathing tube out and cough and spit. Wires stick to my bare chest, and an IV drips clear liquid into my arm. I'm disoriented and dazed and feel like I was hit by a bus. I curl and uncurl my fingers and wiggle my toes, and then my ears pop as the tether anchoring me to Jacqueline snaps.

My body is really mine, and I don't have to share it with anyone anymore. It's awesome and crazy and not to mention a relief to be myself again. I wasn't sure if it would ever happen, but here I am.

I rub my hand over my scruffy face. I need a serious shave and a few showers. I smell pretty bad. I wouldn't normally care, but I'm not exactly at home. The last time I was in a body, it was Jacqueline's and she smelled nice, feminine, but nice. I hold up the blanket to look at the rest of my body and grin. It's good to be back.

The door swings open, and my brother walks in. "Hunter?"

I drop the blanket. "Shut the door, Mason."

"You're awake."

I raise an eyebrow. "I was never sleeping."

He sits down on the edge of my bed. "So, it's true?"

"Yeah, and I have a lot to tell you, but I need you to yell for help first," I say.

"I brought what you asked," he says.

"There has been a change of plans."

26

SAVE WHO YOU CAN

NADIA

"HELP!"

Voices murmur in the hall as people start gathering to see what's going on. Dread knots in my stomach. The more people around, the harder it's going to be to escape. Someone will see us.

"Where's Dr. Agatha? Someone get Dr. Agatha! Hunter Sullivan is awake."

Jacqueline's face falls. She points at the desk, and I curse under my breath. The woman I'm holding is Dr. Agatha. We need to leave now. It would be worse for someone to come in here than risk being seen in the hallway. Here, we're trapped.

I swallow the lump in my throat. "Get up and go to the door. If you mention us, I'll kill you. You don't even know what I'm capable of. We just want to leave, all right? You can ask Hunter about us if you have any questions."

The doctor nods, and I pull her to her feet and guide her to the door. She waltzes into the hallway where a dozen people loiter. My heart pounds so hard, I bet anyone can hear it. I expect Dr. Agatha to give us up, but instead she rushes away and out of sight.

Jacqueline drops the chair, and it clatters on the floor. "Let's go." She holds up her fingers, counts to three, and bolts out. I glide on her heels, pushing her to move faster. We race past the clerical counter and down the empty corridor to the double doors.

It requires the access card to open, and I fumble in my pocket to pull the card out. My hand shakes as I slide it, and then Jacqueline punches in a few numbers. Instead of opening, the lock blinks red and displays the words 'Access Denied' across the screen.

"Try again," I say. "You hit the wrong number."

"Hey!" A feminine voice rises above the resonating murmurs of the crowd around the corner. Wearing a familiar black uniform, a young woman with her hair pulled in a severe bun waves at us from nearby. "Stop! Don't move."

Jacqueline punches the buttons again. The keypad beeps as the double doors swoosh open. I shove her forward, and we run to the elevator and press the button to take us up. The agent runs down the corridor, her combat boots echoing with each thud. She's going to reach us before the elevator arrives.

It's over.

Reaching up, I grab the talisman and yank it from Jacqueline's neck. She cries out but doesn't resist. "I'll hold her off. Tell Alyssa that I'm sorry."

And I am.

But I regret nothing.

HUNTER

Thrashing on the bed, I yank all the wires off and rip the IV out. I pick up the metal stand and swing it at the wall. Mason stands in the doorway, glancing at me and then to the hallway. My weak body trembles, nearly sending me to the floor, but I gather strength from my determination to make a scene.

"Get me out of here!" I yell. I have to make enough commotion to get the attention of everyone. If they're all distracted by me, Nadia and Jacqueline will have a chance. If they can't get out of here, there won't be anything I can do to save them. I'd do anything to protect Nadia, even die for her, but that's exactly what will happen if she gets caught. I want us both to live. We need to live.

"Help!" Mason yells again. "He's confused and in shock."

I pick up the metal stand again and charge at my brother. He steps out of the way, and I lunge into the hall. People gasp at the sight of me. I spit and cuss and swing the IV rod at anyone too close. I hit a guy I've never seen before on the shoulder, and he reflexively grabs the pole from me and yanks it away.

"Hunter," a familiar voice says.

I jerk my head and meet Dr. Agatha's eyes. She was my

mother's mentor and the doctor who recruited her to join the HPA in the first place. She looks me up and down, and my jaw twitches as I hold back my embarrassment. I didn't even bother to grab a robe or anything.

She reaches out her hand to me. "It's okay, Hunter. Everything's going to be okay."

"Is it? Is it really, Dr. Agatha?" My voice lowers in pitch, and I narrow my eyes. "Are you going to continue to drug me? I'm not an experiment!"

The hallway goes silent, and everyone stares between me and Dr. Agatha. She steps closer. "You're confused, dear. Please, calm down and we can talk about it."

"Talk about how this is all a lie or how you're okay with turning against your own kind?" It's not really a lie. My mom was the one who willingly offered my life force to Jacqueline, but unfortunately she's not here to take the fall, so Dr. Agatha will do.

"This about the girls, isn't it?" she says, her voice lowered. "You're protecting them?"

Blinding, red rage slashes through me. How does she know about Nadia and Jacqueline? This isn't right. They were counting on me, and I've let them down. Clenching my hands into fists, I race toward Dr. Agatha. I slam into her, and we tumble to the tile before I roll on top of her.

I tilt my head down and breathe into her ear. "If anything happens to her, I will kill you."

"I gave them a head start," she whispers. "Now get off me and let's talk like rational people."

I push off her and glare at our audience. "What? You'd better get out of here if you know what's good for you," I say to no one in particular.

Dr. Agatha stands, holding her hands up. "It's under control. I have it under control. Go back to what you were doing." She turns to me. "You have a lot of explaining to do."

I nod. I'm not promising to say anything true.

NADIA

Jacqueline shakes her head. "I'm not leaving you. We'll fight together."

The elevator door slides open. Grabbing her arm, I yank her in and hit the button for the ground floor even though I have no idea where it will let us out. I should go back the way we came, but I'm sure the agents will have locked down the hospital by then.

My heartbeat slows down as the door starts to close, but then the agent's arm darts through, and it slides back open. The agent rushes in and yanks a knife from her belt, aiming it at me and then to Jacqueline and back to me. "Put your hands where I can see them," she says.

The elevator door slides shut behind her, and she glances over her shoulder with furrowed brows. I guess she wasn't prepared for that to happen, because her back stiffens and she grips the knife tighter.

I fist my hands. "We won't hurt you if you let us go. We don't want to cause any trouble."

She glares at me. "I can't do that. You're under arrest under the authority of the Human Preservation Agency. If you resist,

I'm ordered to euthanize you."

She says it like we're animals, like killing us isn't murder. To her, maybe we are and ending our lives isn't.

"What are you talking about?"

"You cannot deny you're a super," she quips. "Now, let's make this easy."

I grimace at her the catch-all phrase the HPA uses to define people of the non-human variety. "Make what easy? I didn't do anything wrong. I'm not—super? Please, I'm human."

"Don't play stupid, monster. I saw the way you ran. Your feet weren't even touching the floor."

I should've listened to Alyssa when she told me to be aware of how I move. Fear took control, and my will to survive was my driving force. I'm faster when I float. All I was thinking about was getting away.

"I'm not a monster," I say. It's all I can manage.

The elevator shakes, coming to a halt. The agent hits the close door button, stopping us from trying to leave. She raises her finger to drop the elevator back to the basement, and I charge the agent. I can't go back down. Not when I'm so close to escaping. It's two against one, and the only way to escape is to fight her.

She thrusts her knife out, realizing her own odds against us. I swivel sideways out of the way, and she catches the blade on my jacket, ripping it. I knock her into the wall, the force sending me stumbling back into the opposite wall.

The agent growls and dashes at me again, knife up, but Jacqueline rams into her to get her away. They spin and hit the wall together. Jacqueline's cry echoes through the small space. The agent pulls the blood-covered knife back, watching Jacqueline slide to the floor, clutching her stomach.

I scream.

Rage engulfs me, tears blinding my eyes, and I swing my arm out and hit the agent in the face with my fist. Her free hand flies up to protect herself, and then I knee her as hard as I can in the stomach. But it's not hard enough. She doesn't flinch or move. Instead, she rams her knife into my shoulder blade.

Pain bursts in my arm and another scream rips from my mouth. The knife sticks in my back in such a way that I can't reach it to pull it out. The agent rushes at me again, and I duck before her hands wrap around me. Gripping her legs, I pull them out from under her and she hits the floor. I roll on top of her and pin her down with one hand and use my other one to sucker punch her in the nose.

Blood runs from her nostrils, and she groans through gritted teeth. I slide my hands around her head and slam it into the elevator floor as hard as I can until her eyes roll back in her head.

I pull myself to my feet and trip over the agent's body to get to Jacqueline. She's slumped over, covered in blood, and unconscious. I hit the open door button, and the elevator door slides open to reveal an empty lobby with a glass sliding door leading to a well-manicured courtyard. It's a private entrance to the hospital.

"Jacqueline, come on, wake up."

"It's too late."

My blood runs cold when I hear the voice. It's the agent. She lies propped on her elbows but doesn't move. Strands of black hair hang over her face, pulled from her bun, and her eyes stare at Jacqueline's body.

I stumble back and out of the elevator. Tears burn my cheeks, and I'm so angry and sad and scared, I just want to run back in and kill the agent. I want her to feel the pain I feel. I want her to regret ever coming after us. I want her to regret signing up with the HPA in the first place. I want revenge. But, I don't move.

I can't bring Jacqueline back. She's dead.

She died saving my life.

I bring my hand to my mouth and whisper, "I'm so sorry, Jacqueline. You weren't supposed to die. I'm so, so sorry. It's all my fault."

Jacqueline wasn't an honest person, and she was selfish and stubborn, but she didn't deserve this. No one deserves to bleed out and die on the floor of a rickety elevator with no one there to hold them while they go. She shouldn't have died at all. If she had just left like I told her to, she'd still be alive. She could've lived her life in a safe place away from the danger of the board and the influence of the council. She could've had a normal life.

But her life ended so tragically and I'll have to live with the guilt that it should've been me. I was the one willing to risk everything to save Hunter, but that didn't mean killing someone else even though Jacqueline was the one who put me in that situation in the first place. I should hate her and be glad it was her, but I can't. The ache in my chest is so painful I'm not sure it will ever go away.

"Don't cry, Nadia. It was just a body."

I blink my tears away, my mouth hanging open, and I step forward. "Jacqueline?"

"This isn't ideal, but it is what it is."

"How?" My voice cracks as I ask the question. I stare into the agents dark eyes and then they suddenly shift to a lighter color. Jacqueline's eyes look different against the fair complexion of the agent's skin, almost human.

"The same way we taught Hunter to do it. I didn't know I was capable, but here I am, and since this agent wasn't pure, I get her body and memories as a token. She had a lot of blood on her hands. She kidnapped, tortured, and murdered dozens of people. She's lucky I saved her. She was lucky to move on without a guilty conscience. She's been redeemed."

My eyes widen. "That makes you scary invincible."

She smirks. "I'm guessing if I didn't touch the agent, I would have died. I still had to make physical contact. Instead of pulling her soul into me, I pushed mine into her body."

This entire situation is crazy, but I don't have time to think about it. I offer out my hand and help Jacqueline get to her feet. "We need to hurry."

"Help me with my body. I need you to take it with you so the HPA doesn't get their hands on it. Give it a nice resting place."

My mouth dries. "You're not coming with me?"

She shakes her head. "I'm tired of running. I don't want to

spend the rest of my life hiding. I can make them believe I'm still one of them. I can help Hunter figure things out."

I hug Jacqueline. "I won't forget you. You saved my life."

"You have to save who you can, remember?" she says.

I smile, hearing my own words come from her. "Thank you."

HUNTER

"You knew about this, Mason?" Dr. Agatha asks.

He shakes his head.

"But you haven't visited your brother once since he was transferred here," she says.

He shrugs. "It was luck."

She turns to me. "How are you alive?"

"What do you mean?" I ask. They were the ones keeping me alive. She should know that answer.

"You were brain dead," she says.

"No, I wasn't," I say.

"We haven't seen any brain activity for weeks," she says.

"Then why all the hassle?" I wave my arms around the room. Dr. Agatha doesn't know about the deal my mom made with Jacqueline. The board was keeping it a secret. I'm not going to be the one to tell her, though—not yet.

"Your mother had plans for your body."

I turn to Mason, and he looks away. "Are you kidding me? After everything she did to me, she was going to experiment on me?"

"You were unresponsive, basically dead."

I stand up and lace my fingers together on the back of my

head. "She knew I wasn't, though. I'm through talking to you. Call my mom. Call the board. I'm done. I've had enough, and I want out."

Dr. Agatha smiles. "Sure, Hunter, whatever you want. Just know, dear, nothing is that simple."

NADIA

I wrap my fingers around Jacqueline's body's ankles and Jacqueline grabs its arms and together we drag it out of the elevator, leaving behind a bloody trail. The glass doors automatically slide open and warm air swirls around me. Birds chirp and the sun shines, and if my shoulder wasn't stinging so bad, or if I wasn't struggling to get Jacqueline's body out of here, I'd think it was a nice day. *A beautiful day to die.*

"I can't go far. Can you manage?"

My eyes burn in the bright light of the sun. It feels warmer than it actually is, but I don't say anything. My energy fades fast, and soon it'll hurt to stand in the sun.

"Yeah, just help me pull it up."

Jacqueline helps tug her old body up, and I wrap my arms under hers so I'm half dragging it and half carrying it.

Jacqueline touches my shoulder. "Take care of yourself, Nadia."

Before I have a chance to respond, she dashes away and back into the hospital. My head throbs, the warmth of the sun washing over me, my shoulder aching. It takes everything in me to glide forward through the small courtyard. I've exited from the side of the hospital with the parking lot to the right. It's a straight shot down the path to it. I hope I can make it.

The body's blood soaks into my shirt, and if anyone saw me, they'd force me back inside. I take one step at a time, my body lagging and fighting to stay up with my determination. Heat runs over my skin as I walk out from the shadow of the building and into the sunlight.

The fight and my injuries have worn me down. I've lost almost all my energy, and if I don't take cover soon, I'll get a horrible sunburn.

"You can do this." I don't know why I say the words out loud, but I do. It helps me focus.

I hobble my way to the wall and slide to the ground, half landing on Jacqueline's body. Sitting it up, I kneel next to it, pressing my bloody hands to the wall. I bow my head and gulp in a few deep breaths. I can't go on any farther. I don't have the strength or energy. I have to leave the body behind if I want to make it out of here. I don't have a choice.

Closing my eyes, I listen to the sound of the cars in the parking lot. I need to pull myself together. I need to keep moving. I shift, my body aching, and then I slump on my knees. I'm so exhausted.

I hear footsteps, but I can't open my eyes to see who's coming.

Tears blur my eyes, distorting the silhouette that appears over me. I cringe and cower against the building when hands grab my arms and tug me to my feet.

I moan. "I don't want to die."

"Stay with me, Nadia. I'm here. Stay with me, okay?" Alyssa's soft voice wraps around me, and I lean my head against her shoulder as she helps me walk to the car.

I can't believe we did it. I can't believe we survived.

I'm alive.

I'm really alive.

27

HOPE FOR CHANGE

HUNTER

MASON SITS NEXT to my bed. I'm not allowed to leave the hospital until I'm granted clearance. If I'm granted it at all. I'm starting to believe I have a destiny, and it's to be incarcerated for the rest of my life—whether in someone's mind or locked in a room without access to the outside world. I know too much, and if anyone finds out how much I actually know, I'll be a dead man.

"You want to talk about it?" Mason asks.

"No."

"I can help you."

"Just keep your mouth shut. Play stupid or they'll kill us

both, Mason."

"Mom won't let that happen."

"She's the reason I'm in this mess. Now, just forget everything and trust no one."

Mason stands up and crosses his arms, his brown hair, longer than I remember, hanging over his forehead while also sticking up in the back. He wears a wrinkled blue T-shirt and dirty jeans in need of a serious wash. He's usually better kept than this, but I don't mention it. I just want to be alone.

"What do you want me to do with your stuff?" he asks. He motions to a small rolling suitcase and pulls out my car keys from his pocket.

"Hide it somewhere. Not at home, though. If I find the opportunity to leave, I'm taking it, and I don't want to have to stop at home first," I say, swinging my legs off the bed to sit on the edge. "It'd be too easy for them to find me."

He lifts an eyebrow. "Who?"

I press my lips together. "Doesn't matter."

Mason glances at the floor and back to me. "I'll leave your car behind Billy's. Will you tell me before you go?"

I shrug. "I honestly don't know."

NADIA

I hover in the middle of a rainbow. The vibrant colors shimmer around me and glimmer against my porcelain skin. I run my hand through the misty air, and it swirls and moves like it's alive. The dream world is a magical place, unlike any nightmare I've seen, and I expect it to abruptly shatter at any second.

But it doesn't.

It's my dream.

It's the first one I've ever had.

"Nadia?"

Spinning on my feet, I peer through the rainbow mist. I can hear Hunter, but I can't see him. I just want him to hold me. It feels like it's been days since I've seen him, but it also feels like I've only been asleep for minutes. I'm disoriented and confused by what is happening to me. Dreamers aren't supposed to be aware that they are dreaming, but I am. I feel almost stuck in my own head.

"I'm here, Hunter," I say.

"Open your eyes."

The world shakes, and I stumble and fall. Instead of hitting solid ground, the air rushes around me, my stomach crashing to my chest. I've lost control of my dream, and I can't stop free falling. I scream a long, loud wail and flail my hands out searching for anything to grab on to.

I scream again.

A hand grips my arm, and the world freezes.

Opening my eyes, I gasp. I'm awake and still in the front seat of the car. A familiar cityscape looms in front of us, so close yet so far. It feels like home, but I'm not sure where my next home will be.

My shoulder burns with agony, and I struggle to touch the spot it hurts the most.

"Don't, Nadia. A knife is in your shoulder blade. I was too scared to pull it out. It's bleeding enough as it is," Alyssa says. "Thank God you're more resilient than a human."

I frown and swivel in my seat. "Jacqueline?" I ask.

My memories come rushing back to me, and I remember the agent stabbing her and her sliding to the ground covered in blood. I remember the grief I felt—the intense, heart-wrenching, utterly hopeless feeling when I thought she was dead. And I remember the surprise and relief when I discovered she body jumped. I remember she chose to stay. She's not running from her fears anymore. She's facing them head on, and I know she won't be a victim anymore. Jacqueline is stronger than that.

Alyssa squeezes my leg. "She's gone, Nadia. I don't understand how, but it wasn't supposed to happen. You were the one who was supposed to die by the hand of a black-haired agent. I saw it minutes before I found you. I was running to help Jacqueline and found you instead. What happened?"

My chest tightens, and I climb between the seats until I'm in the back with Jacqueline's body. I know she's not there, but I can't help kneeling on the floor next to her. I brush her hair from her face and sling an arm around her neck to pull her against me. Tears spill from my eyes with my sob, my chest heaving, making it impossible to breathe.

It hits me hard. Jacqueline and Hunter are gone, and I probably won't ever see them again. My heart aches, because things can't be different. I wish I could've waited at Hunter's bedside to watch him wake up, to see him in the real world, to know what it's like outside a dream.

"Jacqueline's decision to save me changed the outcome of your vision, but she's not dead. She took over the agent's body who attempted to kill her. It all happened so fast, and I didn't have time to talk to her about it. She decided to stay."

Alyssa taps her fingers on the steering wheel. "Why did you bring her body?"

"Jacqueline asked me to."

"What are we going to tell the council?"

"That she died. I don't think she wants anyone to know what she has done."

Alyssa glances at me in the rearview mirror. "Okay. Her secret is safe with us. I know we'll never tell."

I'll be forever grateful for what Jacqueline did. I will not remember her as being the girl who held Hunter captive. I'll remember her as the girl who saved me—the girl who was willing to die so I could live.

HUNTER

A knock resonates on the door, but I don't get up to answer it, and I don't say it's okay for them to bother me. Instead, I sit at the edge of my bed and stare at the white tile floor. Mason left an hour ago, and I'm not sure if I'll see him again.

The door creaks open, and my mom saunters in. Her black heels tap the tiles as she shuts the door behind her. She looks exactly the same as the last time I saw her, wearing her usual white lab coat over dress clothes. Pushing her gold-framed glasses up like a headband, she keeps her straight, shoulder-length hair from her face.

Her eyes, the same hazel color as mine, shine with tears. She holds her arms open to me. "I'm so relieved to see you."

I shift my legs and turn to face the wall. "Are you, Dr. Sullivan?" She never liked being called anything but Mom, but I refuse to give her that joy. No mother should be okay with giving their kid to some soul eater in exchange for a little information. This woman, who may have given birth to me and took care of me, is not my mother anymore. She's no one to me.

"You're upset," she says.

Tensing, I stand up and turn to her. "I'm pissed!" I step closer and glare down at her, digging my fingernails into the palms of my hand, imagining what it would feel like to punch the fake concern off her face.

"You have to understand, Hunter. I did it for the greater good. Sacrifices had to be made. You'll understand one day. You'll see and then you'll forgive me." She wraps her arms around me despite my glower.

I shrug away, stepping back. "You're delusional and twisted. This isn't the greater good, you know. I've seen what good is and it's not this."

She gasps and swings out her hand, slapping me across the face. I touch my stinging cheek. I can't reason with her. I can't reason with anyone here. They really believe they are doing good in the world. What they don't see is that they're ruining the lives of people just because they don't understand. Supers aren't innately evil. But I'm starting to think my mom is.

Her eyes widen, and she brings her hand to her mouth. "I'm so sorry, baby. I didn't mean that. You've been through some traumatic things. You need rest. It'll all make sense soon enough."

Nothing I say can change her view of the world, but I

won't stop trying. I'm not going to waste my second chance just going with the flow of things. I'm going to make a difference, and I will be heard and taken seriously. I refuse to stand here and accept that I can't change anything because I can. And I will.

Another knock sounds out on the door, and an agent peeks in. Her jet black hair tangles loosely from what should be a bun and blood smears across her bruising face. "Dr. Agatha said I should let you know that I injured one of the intruders."

I swallow and fist my hands. I meet the agent's violet eyes. "What did she look like?"

My mom turns toward the agent. "Don't answer that, Agent Camille."

The agent presses her lips together. "Would you mind signing off on the report? I can't leave until you do."

My mom nods and steps into the hall. The agent hovers in the doorway and watches my mom walk away. I can hear her heels tap down the corridor. The agent slips in my room and shuts the door behind her.

I raise my eyebrows. "I'm not up for company. Forget about my question. I don't want to know."

She smiles. "Oh, shut up, Hunter. You know you want to know."

I frown. "Do I know you?"

Strutting forward, she bends down to whisper into my ear. "Forget me already? It's only been a few hours."

I can't believe it. A chill runs down my spine, and I jump to my feet and put distance between us. Jacqueline somehow managed to body jump into an agent. My chest tightens, my palms sweating. I really didn't plan on seeing Jacqueline again, even if it's not in the body I've become so familiar with.

She crosses her arms, her smile faltering. "I'm not going to hurt you, Hunter. Some new opportunities came up, and I took them. Can I trust you to keep my secret? You know as well as I do that there needs to be some changes around here."

"What happened to the soul?"

"She's gone. She fatally wounded my body. I did what I had to."

I nod. I understand how Jacqueline works and thinks. Arguing with her won't amount to anything and the past can't be changed, but the future can, and she can help.

"Nadia?" The sound of her name as I say it brings back all my memories of the girl who fought for me, who made sure I'd get to be whole again. I'm anxious about what Jacqueline is about to say. What if she was hurt? I couldn't stand knowing it and not being with her.

"She made it out of here."

I release a breath. "We have to change the world. We have to do it for all of us."

I will do it for every person I saw through Jacqueline's eyes. I'll do it so Jacqueline won't have to steal another body. I'll do it so Nadia can live without fear. I'll do it for myself, so I can be with the one I'll always dream of. We can't only be destined for dreams.

Being taken from my body has changed me. It made me see that the world isn't black and white or good and evil. It's full of color and life and dreams. Through meeting Nadia, I now have hope. Hope for a future. Hope for change. And through my beautiful nightmare inflictor, hope for me.

NADIA

The elf slides the knife from my shoulder, causing me to flinch. He hands it to Alyssa, and she wraps it in a dark blue hand towel. The elf presses a wet towel to my wound before coating some sort of magical salve over it.

I stare at the blood under my fingernails. "Jacqueline deserves a proper burial. I don't want the council to touch her body. People should know she existed. They should remember her," I say.

Alyssa and I agreed to tell no one about Jacqueline. Anyone who knew her will think she's dead. She really does get a fresh start—a second chance. She won't have to worry about the consequences from the council.

Alyssa sets the bloody towel down. "Your dad can make the arrangements. Cian said the council notified him we were missing, and Cian was the first person your dad called."

I cringe when the elf starts stitching my wound.

"Can we stay here until he comes home?" Tears blur my vision when I imagine the disappointment I'll see in my father's face. He won't understand.

"I'm sure he'll want us to. It's better if he's here before we go in front of the council."

I don't even know how I'm going to explain myself to the council. I'll have to tell them about Hunter. They won't understand. They'll think Jacqueline died because I wanted to save a human with ties to the HPA. I'm a traitor, and they don't take kindly to traitors.

"It's bad, isn't it?"

Alyssa touches my blood soaked jeans. "It'll be okay. They don't have to know everything. Hunter was an innocent human. They'll see that."

The elf hands me a shirt and quietly gets up and leaves the apartment. I slip the shirt over my head the best I can. It hurts to lift my arm, but I do it anyway without asking for help. It makes me feel better, alive, because I can feel pain.

I wipe my eyes again. "They're going to make me feel like a monster. She should've come with us." Thinking about Jacqueline makes me think about Hunter. I hope he's happy to be back in his body. I hope he can move on and live again. I hope he gets the best of what life has to offer.

Alyssa leans over and hugs me. "We won't forget her. Don't feel guilty. Everything happens how it's supposed to."

I pull away and tuck my hair behind my ear. "I know, Lys, and I'm sure I'll be okay. Guilt is good for me. It keeps me human."

"Acceptance and love and bravery also make you human. Knowing how you impact others, too. Life is complicated and mysterious like that. It keeps you grounded."

Alyssa's right about that. Hunter and Jacqueline changed my life. I'm no longer afraid of who I am. It's okay for me to be different, and it's okay for me to embrace even my darkest side as long as I know how it affects my life and those around me.

I'll never forget the girl with the dark, curly hair and lavender eyes. She showed me how lonely life is when you shut eve-ryone out like I was doing. I'll be forever grateful to Jacqueline for saving my life and for bringing Hunter to me.

I'll always think about the boy who taught me to be brave. He showed me how strong I am and how I can live in this scary world. He showed me that it's okay to be who I am and that I'm strong enough to live outside of dreams. He will always be a part of me.

I lift my gaze to look at my best friend. "I don't know what I'd have done without you."

"You'll never have to know, because we're in this together." Everything feels so normal despite the throb in my shoulder and Jacqueline's body in the car. Not to mention I'll have to face the council about everything.

Maybe this is my normal.

After all, I am a nightmare inflictor.

But more than that, I am a good person, a good friend, and in the end, nothing else really matters to me.

EPILOGUE

— ❧ —

WORTH THE FIGHT

— ❧ —

HUNTER

I STARE AT the ceiling of my new bedroom and imagine what it would be like to project myself out of it. I've been trying to do it for the last hour, but nothing has come from it. I did fall asleep for a minute, but the annoying neighbor mowing his lawn before the sun has risen startled me awake.

Sitting up, I swing my legs off my bed. It's been two weeks and I still haven't bothered to unpack my boxes. I decided to move in with my aunt the moment I stepped in my old bedroom and realized I didn't want to be under the same roof as the woman who thought it was acceptable to trade my soul. I don't think I can ever forgive Dr. Sullivan. I can't even think about calling her Mom without it getting under my skin.

Someone knocks on my window, and I sit up. I pull the blinds open, meeting Jacqueline's smiling face. It's hard to get over the weirdness of her being in a different body, but I'm getting used to it.

I open the window.

"Guess who has been assigned to keep tabs on you? Your mother thinks you're keeping secrets from her." Jacqueline pops the screen off. She wears a standard agent uniform—black boots, pants, a shirt, and a weaponry belt with a knife, taser, and tranquilizer gun. Her eyes look more blue than purple, and she's maybe twenty years old. The board starts young.

Camille, the original agent, was part of the Special Abilities Task Force, and that's why Jacqueline's been assigned to me. She can determine if I'm hanging with supers behind the board's back. She is also the only agent who saw the girls who got away.

I cross my arms. "Are you kidding me? I think you just can't stay away from me."

"Oh, shut up, Hunter. Would you rather I call someone else?"

I grin. "You're making me nostalgic, Jac—Camille. I wonder what—" I snap my mouth shut.

Everything and everyone reminds me of Nadia. I dream of her sometimes. I wake up hoping she's sitting on the edge of my bed, like she's been searching for me and finally found me. But I'm always alone. I'm always without her.

Jacqueline blinks back a few tears. "I have an idea. Come

on, let's go for a drive."

NADIA

I shade my eyes from the blinding sunlight. It warms my bare legs, and I run my toes over the thick green grass. I watch my father and Alyssa smile at each other through the bay window of the kitchen.

It's strange having such privacy, but I wouldn't trade it for anything now. Our large backyard is protected by tall cement block walls and spelled talismans created by the craftiest elf my father knows.

I can hear the phone ring from out here. It's hard getting used to how quiet it is being away from the compound, but I'm not complaining. I like it—prefer it.

"Nadi?"

My father waves at me through the window, and I pad across the grass and to the back door leading to the kitchen. The scent of citrus and sugar wafts through the air, and Alyssa holds up a frosting covered spatula in my direction.

"What's up?" I ask.

My father shifts away from the counter and meets my gaze. "That was Mr. Soto. The council has made a decision."

My heart drops. It's taken them weeks to decide what my punishment would be for forcing Jacqueline to release Hunter. As far as they know, Hunter was an ordinary human and Jacqueline's death resulted from unforeseen circumstances, but I also have to answer for breaking about ten other rules. I could be in serious trouble.

I blow a puff of air through my lips. "It's bad, isn't it?"

His expression doesn't give anything away. "You can say that."

"Just tell me."

My father touches my shoulder. "You've been marked an outcast and exiled from the council and its community. You will no longer get protection, funding, or help from anyone in relation to them. You are technically on your own and cannot access any of their safe havens or resources."

My mouth drops open. "And Alyssa?"

Alyssa's eyes glaze over, and she drops the spatula she's holding. "That's not fair. I helped Nadia do this. I deserve the same punishment."

My father shrugs. "They believe you wouldn't have done anything if Nadia hadn't influenced you."

"But—"

I wave my hand and cut Alyssa off. "I'm okay, Lys. It's okay." I turn back to my father and meet his gaze. "What about you?"

He hugs me. "I'm indebted to serve them, Nadia."

I frown. "I don't understand. How can they banish me and make you work for them?"

"It was part of the deal. They wanted your freedom so I traded it for mine." He kisses my head. "It doesn't change anything between us. I'm still your father, and I'll still look after you."

"Unless they send you away," I say. "What if something happens to you? I can't live with that."

"Yes, they can send me away, but they already do now," he

says.

"Dmitri can take care of himself, Nadia," Alyssa says. "And we can take care of ourselves. Look at us. Look at this place. We're safe here and don't need the council. They're the ones who need us. They'll see."

She's right. I have everything I need and don't have to rely on people who are afraid of me and who make me feel like a monster. I just wish they didn't trap my father into doing their dirty work. He deserves freedom as much as I do.

"You can both laugh in their faces when they do," my father says.

The doorbell rings, startling me. It'll take time getting used to everything—the new house, my new freedom, my new life. My father smiles and nudges me to answer it. I stroll through the kitchen door to our quaint living room. Living away from the sanctuary of the compound has made me more courageous. I'm no longer terrified of who I'll bump into or who will come knocking on my door. My fear was my worst enemy, and it doesn't have the same hold on me that it used to.

I peer through the peep hole and smile at a delivery man from The Haven as I open the door. He hands me a small envelope. I thank him and close the door, leaning my back against it. I tear it open to find a small piece of paper and another envelope with my name on it.

I read the note.

This was left with our security guard. -Cian

A pot clatters in the kitchen, and I turn toward the kitchen door. Alyssa flies out and snatches her car keys from the front table. She grabs my arm and pulls me to the front door. "Come on, we have to hurry."

I let her tug me onto the porch. "Where are we going?"

"You'll see, but we need to go now. You can open the letter in the car."

HUNTER

I'm nervous. After dropping off a note in the city in hopes that it would find Nadia, Jacqueline insisted we hang out at a small park in the suburbs. She needed a break from the board, and I need a break from my room, so here we are.

The heat of the afternoon makes me sweat. Jacqueline sits on the park bench next to me, and we watch the ducks swim on the man-made lake. She tosses a handful of duck feed she purchased from a small machine and the ducks waddle to the shore.

I dry my hands on my jeans. "Are you sure this place is safe? You don't want anyone catching us hanging out."

"Maybe that's what needs to happen for them to trust you again." Jacqueline pushes her sunglasses on her head. "It'll show your mother you believe in their cause."

I lower my brows. I don't think I can fake it. Thinking about the board's hatred toward supers makes me sick. "I want to show Dr. Sullivan what I really think of their cause."

Jacqueline bumps my shoulder and grins. "We will. Give it time."

"I just want to make it safe for Nadia, you know?"

I stand up and go to the edge of the water, startling the ducks. I pick up a rock and throw it into the lake and turn to look at Jacqueline. I blink a few times and then rub my eyes. I can't believe it. Maybe I fell asleep, and I'm dreaming.

Nadia stands at the edge of the parking lot. Her long, blond hair blows behind her as she tilts her head toward the sky, laughing at something Alyssa says. Her ivory halter dress stops just above her knees and glittery gold sandals sparkle on her feet. She looks just like I remember her—beautiful, ethereal, angelic—not the monster she thought she was.

I'm overwhelmed with so many emotions that I don't move. It feels like I'm meeting her for the first time, but I know I love her. This is real. She is real.

Seeing Nadia gives me hope for a better future, a future with her, and a future without the board or the council. A future where we only have to worry about ourselves.

Jacqueline stands up next to me. "Then make it safe for her. I'm with you, Hunter, and I bet others will be, too."

I grin. "I plan on it, but, I'm not going to do it just for her. I'm going to do it because it's the right thing to do. I plan on changing the world."

It needs to be changed.

I know I can change it.

NADIA

"You didn't tell my father?" I say as I get out of Alyssa's car.

She shakes her head and follows me out. "Nope."

"We're going to be grounded for a week."

She cringes. "Actually, make it two."

I sigh, and we both laugh. I'd follow Alyssa again even if it meant I'd be grounded for the rest of my life. It'd be worth it.

I turn away from Alyssa to look toward the small man-made lake. My breath catches, and I bring my hand up to my lips. Hunter's still here. I was so afraid he'd be gone by now. Slamming the car door, I glide through the field in the direction of the lake. It feels like I've been waiting forever for this moment, one I never thought would come.

Hunter's hazel eyes meet mine. He runs his hand through his dark hair, shining with golden streaks in a messy mass of curls around his head. He adjusts his blue-plaid shirt under his tan jacket and steps away from Jacqueline. She's in the body of the agent I'll never forget. The one who almost killed us both.

"You found me," he says.

"I got your letter. Alyssa had a vision of you coming here."

He opens his arms, and I fall into them. "You're real. This is real."

Tilting my head up, I meet him for a kiss. Electricity zings through my lips like my soul recognizes his familiarity—it does. His soft lips brush mine, kissing me deeper, tasting of mint and orange. I want to stay in his arms forever. It takes everything in me to pull away.

He tucks my hair behind my ear and smiles. "I'm glad you found me. I was afraid you wouldn't want to, but I can't picture not being with you. I hated being away."

I kiss him again before meeting his hazel eyes. "It's going to be hard."

"I don't care. I'll fight to stay with you."

And I know he will.

From Hunter, I've learned that life isn't supposed to be easy. It should be messy and out of control sometimes. It should be unpredictable, full of love and hope and promise. It should be worth the fight.

And now, as I stand here with the people I care about, I know it is.

Love Nadia and Hunter's story so far? Read on for a sneak peek at *Nightmare Reality*, book two in the *Destined for Dreams* series.

1

OUTSIDE OF OUR DREAM WORLD

NADIA

MY HANDS TREMBLE.

Hunter sits next to me on the park bench, clasping my hands. "It's not that bad." A tendril of dark brown, curly hair peeks from beneath his beanie. His hazel eyes shine, reflecting the overcast clouds. A storm brews in the distance, matching the dread swirling in my heart.

I lean into him. "It's awful. People will notice I'm not—like them." I want to say *not human*, but Hunter doesn't need the reminder. It's been five tough months since I discovered Hunter in Jacqueline Matthews' dream when she first arrived at the Creature Council's compound.

Jacqueline is a sin-eater, who took Hunter's soul as collateral in a deal she made with the Human Preservation Agency, an organization who hunts creatures like me on the notion that they're saving humanity from monsters. The worst part of it is Hunter's mother is a prominent member of their board and because of that, Hunter and I will never experience a normal relationship.

I sometimes believe that's just the life a nightmare inflictor must live. My father and mother's relationship was complicated, and eventually my father drove my mother crazy by inflicting so many nightmares, which led to her being murdered by an HPA agent.

I'm determined to not follow their fate.

I push the thought away. It doesn't matter if Hunter and I could never have a normal relationship, because what we've fought for is extraordinary. We know each other unlike anyone could ever know us since we met in Jacqueline's dream. Our souls connected instantly. Hunter is the only person to ever see me in a dream world as a nightmare inflictor. He's seen me turn dreams into horrifying nightmares, and yet he still accepts me for who I am and loves me regardless. He's my soul mate.

Hunter kisses my temple, drawing my attention away from my thoughts. "They won't."

I sigh, staring at the muddy snow. "They might." Winter arrived like everything else in my life— hard and fast, cold and unavoidable. My entire world changed the moment I met Hunter. I lost the safety of the compound when I forced Jacqueline to return him to his body, but I wouldn't change anything. I'd risk my life all over again so he could have his life back, and I could experience my love for Hunter outside of our dream world.

He laughs and touches my chin, running his fingers up my jaw to tuck my light blond hair behind my ears. "Alyssa will be there with you. It's only until you graduate in a few months."

I glare at him and pull away. "That's what my father said."

I still can't believe my father is making me go through with it. He casually left the student handbook for Northern Bell High School on my vanity table for me to find. I thought the tutor had been working out fine, but since I've been shunned by the Creature Council, it's cheaper to get a public education—in the real world, amid humans. *You're half human...*

The council believes my actions of saving Hunter, who they think was an ordinary human, resulted in Jacqueline's death. Unbeknownst to them, Jacqueline's body died, but she lives on in the agent who tried to kill her. Because I'm an outcast, I can't use any of the council's resources, and since my father traded his freedom for mine, he's been forced to work for the council on a reduced income so our luxuries are limited.

I wish I could tell my father the truth about Hunter, but he'd never trust Hunter with his ties to the HPA. He'd forbid me to see him because the HPA ruined our lives when they killed my mother.

Hunter puffs air through his lips, and I see his breath. "Everything will be okay. You're strong—" He pauses and kisses me before adding, "You're powerful. You're fearless."

I smile into his lips. "I'm a wimp."

"Your boyfriend is an HPA agent."

I pull away and narrow my eyes. "Not really."

He smirks. "I'm still dangerous."

I raise my eyebrows. "So am I."

I tilt my head toward the sky and laugh. He grabs my hand, pulls it to his lips, and kisses my bare knuckles. Warmth blossoms against my skin, and I lean into him until he puts his arms around me. I could stay with him forever if the world would just stop. I sometimes miss our dream world, where it was the two of us.

This empty park will have to do for now.

A car horn blares, drawing my attention over my shoulder. Alyssa parks her silver Corolla and honks twice more, flashing her high beams. I groan and lean my head on Hunter's shoulder. I hate saying goodbye.

"I have to go," I say.

"Please, stay. Just a few more minutes." Hunter kisses the top of my head.

I bury my nose in his coat, breathing in his warm sandalwood scent. "You know I can't." Tilting my face up, I meet his gold-flecked eyes. He kisses my nose, making me smile. "I'll call you as soon as I can."

I get to my feet, and Hunter reaches out and takes my hand. "Stay safe."

I smile again before I turn away and walk to the parking lot. I don't look over my shoulder, because it's hard to leave without knowing if I'll ever see him again. I'm terrified of the day we'll get caught by the HPA or the council. Either one can force us to end our relationship.

Alyssa motions for me to hurry, so I glide the rest of the way to the car. Opening the door, I slide into the front seat. The hot air from the vents warms my frozen hands, and I lean my head on the headrest.

I tap my finger on my knee. "What's up, Lys?"

Alyssa's red braid shines in the warm rays of sunshine peeking through the cloudy sky as the sun sets. "I had a vision Dmitri was on his way home early."

Alyssa, my best friend, is a seer. Two years ago, she found my father while he was on a job for the Creature Council, and he took her back to the compound where I lived at the time. After I was exiled from the compound, Alyssa left with me, and my father takes care of us both. He considers her a daughter as much as I consider her a sister.

My chest tightens. "Will we make it?"

"Maybe with seconds to spare."

HUNTER

I should be used to Nadia leaving me by now, but I'm not. Her pale blond hair sways as she glides toward the parking lot. She only wears a gray sweatshirt and light denim jeans despite the slushy snow, and her boots don't leave a single footprint.

She never looks back when she leaves me, but I always watch her go. I can't help it. I want to follow her so badly. I want to know where she lives now outside the compound. I don't ask, though. It'd be dangerous to have that information. If the Human Preservation Agency's board were to find out about our relationship, we'd both be dead.

My cell phone rings in my jacket pocket, and I slip it out and hold it to my ear. "Something wrong?"

"Are you on your way back?" It's Jacqueline, the sin-eater who held my soul captive in a failed attempt to gain amnesty from the HPA. If it weren't for Nadia persuading Jacqueline to return me to my body, I'd still be stuck in Jacqueline's head or worse. We have the world's most awkward relationship, but Jacqueline's grown on me over the last few months. Kind of was unavoidable after sharing the same body.

I stand up, surprised she's calling me now since my shift with the HPA ended over two hours ago. She usually doesn't bother me when she knows I'm meeting Nadia. "Leaving now, why?"

Jacqueline breathes into the phone, creating static. Her silence speaks a thousand words and without her even having to say anything, I can sense she has a lot on her mind—and it can't be good if she's calling me.

I hate to admit it, but spending so much time imprisoned in Jacqueline's mind has given me a sixth sense in recognizing her emotions. While I can't always pinpoint what she's actually thinking or planning, I know when something's off.

"Your mom is looking for you. She has a new assignment."

"What is it?"

I press the phone harder to my ear, expecting Jacqueline to explain, but I'm greeted with silence. I'd think Jacqueline hated talking to me with how cold and steely she is, but that's just her personality. Her ability to redeem bad souls exposes her to the evils people are capable of doing. She takes a person's wrongdoings onto herself and releases the soul to die in peace.

She doesn't talk much about her past, but from what I know, it haunts her in ways I couldn't ever imagine. I think it's why I'm not afraid of her like I was when she first took my soul. I understand her, so I've forgiven her. We're on the same side now as we infiltrate the HPA in hopes to change things for the better by getting people to realize humanity isn't in danger from creatures. In the end, creatures and humans want the same thing—to live life without fear.

I check my cell phone to make sure Jacqueline's still on the line. "Ja—Camille? You there?" It takes a lot of getting used to calling her Camille even though she's in the body of the former Agent Camille. After saving Nadia from being killed by the HPA agent who had trapped them in the elevator at Northern Trinity Hope Hospital while freeing me, Jacqueline body jumped into Camille to save herself. Jacqueline told me she saved Camille's soul by killing her, but I think no matter how often she tells herself that she saves people by setting their souls free, she still feels bad about it. It's why I know Jacqueline isn't some horrible person. The guilt she carries is almost palpable— even if she wouldn't do anything different.

"Yeah, sorry. I'll let you find out for yourself, but I wanted to warn you that you won't like it."

I shake the thoughts from my head. "I don't like most of the assignments."

"You really won't like this one, though. Just hurry up and get here."

"See you in thirty."

I hang up the phone, a heavy pit settling in my stomach. I've been pretty lucky in my agent training, only having to push paperwork and follow around a few field agents, but so far nothing has made me regret staying with the HPA. Something in Jacqueline's voice tells me my luck has run out.

NADIA

I fly behind Alyssa into the house. She jumps on the couch, her red braid smacking her cheek, and I slide into the chair across from her. I breathe through my nose to calm my heart, grinning at Alyssa when the front door's knob turns. She really was right about only having seconds to spare.

My father struts in and drops his keys on the small table by the door. His inky black hair veils his face, and he pushes it out of his eyes. His pale skin, a shade lighter than mine, contrasts his black jacket.

I smile. "You're home early."

He leans over and kisses the top of my head. "There's trouble in the city, and everyone is on alert. I came to check on you. I'm glad you girls are safe."

I knit my eyebrows together. "Is everything okay?"

He shakes his head. "The HPA is relentless. An influx of agent activity is scaring the city dwellers."

I lick my lips, swallowing the knot in my throat. It takes everything in me not to rush out the door to call Hunter. He could find out what's going on. "Does this mean no school tomorrow?" It's worth a shot. If the situation is as serious as it sounds, maybe he won't want us to leave the safety of our house.

Alyssa shifts on the couch, her eyes glassing over. "We'll be fine," she says before my father can answer my question.

My father moves away and sits on the couch next to Alyssa. He leans forward, rests his elbows on his knees, and twines his fingers together. His dark eyes shine in the lamp light as he gazes at the rug. "I don't want you to live in fear, Nadi. I was wrong for sheltering you for so long. The board doesn't control our life." He lifts his head to stare at me. "School's going to be fine. I've picked a good one. You'll be with a good friend of mine, Sandy Augustine. He was your mother's best friend growing up. I promise it's safe."

I twist my lips to the side. The name sounds familiar, but I can't find any memories of the man in my mind. "That's not what I'm worried about." While the HPA makes me nervous, I'm nowhere as afraid of them as I used to be. It helps that my boyfriend has an in with them, but I'm more afraid of putting myself in a position where I have to pretend to be human. I look at my pale fingers. "What if someone discovers what I am?"

"We'll figure it out if it happens," my father says. "There are protocols the Creature Council follows that we can, too."

Alyssa stands up. "Dmitri's right. Everything's going to be fine tomorrow."

"Until it's not."

Alyssa laughs and walks toward the kitchen, leaving me alone with my father. I get up from the chair and pad to the couch, plopping down next to him. He slings his arm over my shoulders, and I lean into him. I hardly see him anymore because the council keeps him occupied.

"I know you don't like to talk about this, but I think you need to see a volunteer tonight. You're starting to lose your color." He squeezes my arm. "I can call around if you'd like."

I meet his gaze. I hate this conversation the most. I'm aware I'm going to need to inflict a nightmare soon, and I don't need to be reminded. I raise my hand. "Dad, please, no. I can handle it. I'm not a child anymore."

He sighs. "You're waiting too long, Nadi. It's harder to find volunteers outside the compound."

I don't tell him the reason I suppress my nightmare inflictor side for as long as I can. I'm afraid of losing control again like I did with Jacqueline. I was dreams away from causing permanent damage to her sanity. I barely survived saving Hunter. I can't put myself in that situation again.

"I'll call Cian now." Cian is a longtime friend of my father. He runs The Haven, a club for supernatural creatures, within an apartment building that serves as a refuge for people with special abilities. Since I've been exiled from the compound, he gives me the addresses of people in my suburban community who want to experience what it's like for me to inflict a nightmare on them. It's easier than night stalking humans — and safer.

"Okay," he says. "Would you like me to join you?"

I grimace. "Some other time."

"You want to take my truck?"

"No, I'll walk. I could use some fresh air." Even though I finally got my license, I still don't like driving. I only drive when I have to. I prefer to move by foot.

"All right then but be careful."

I sigh. My father is being more paranoid than usual. I thought he'd gotten over his protective streak months ago when we first left the compound, but I guess nothing's really changed after all. If he didn't still have to work for the council, I bet he'd have found another sanctuary with more protection than what we have at the house.

"I'll be fine. Stop worrying. You've done a great job teaching me how to protect myself." I walk to the door and snag the spelled charm bracelet from the front table. "And I'll wear my protection bracelet."

He glides to me and kisses the top of my head. "I sometimes forget you're not a child anymore."

I hug him. "I haven't been for a while."

He looks down at me and I see how hard it is for him to let me go so I can grow as a person. I just hope he sees past the fact that I'm his daughter. I'm more than that. I'm strong and independent—and I'm not scared anymore.

"I know, Nadi. And that's why I know you'll do great in a public high school. It'll teach you what I couldn't while hiding you away at the compound."

I frown. "So, this whole thing is a test?"

"It's more of a learning opportunity."

"And if I fail?"

He chuckles. "You won't. It'll be no different than visiting The Haven or going to the store with Alyssa."

"Yeah, you're right." Except The Haven is full of people

with special abilities like me and if I mess up at the store or somewhere else in public, I could avoid returning. It's different to me.

I turn away to stop from arguing because it won't matter. I'll just take it one day at a time like I've been doing and hope for the best. Until things change with the HPA, this is life—hiding and playing human. I can't wait for the day it can be something more.

Soon.

I know Hunter and Jacqueline will make it happen.

HUNTER

I jog into the reception area of the HPA's termination facility. I haven't been here since my soul imprisonment, and I contemplate turning around and walking out. Jacqueline leans against the reception counter, whispering to Phillip, the office manager.

Her black hair twines in a bun on the back of her neck, and she wears the same black uniform I do. Her purple eyes look blue in the fluorescent lighting as she draws her eyes to me and smiles. She saunters from Phillip and nods toward the double doors that lead to the elevator.

She touches my arm, tilting her head toward mine to whisper in my ear. "Your mom has lost it."

I grin. "We already knew that."

"No, Hunter. This is different."

Dread pools in my chest. "What do you mean?"

"You'll see."

The double doors swing in, and the elevator door slides open before we can call for it. Dr. Sullivan, the woman who thinks she deserves to be called my mom, pushes her gold-framed glasses on top of her head, pushing back her short, dark brown hair. Her gray slacks and light pink blouse peek from under the white lab coat over it, which I swear she sleeps in.

She used to be a decent person—an oncologist who dedicated her life to saving people—but after the board recruited her to join the HPA, her whole personality shifted. She went from a loving mom to a workaholic, and then she let the power of becoming a board member go to her head. The HPA exposed her to all the bad things of the supernatural world—the destruction and death of humans caused by creatures. But more so, they brainwashed her into believing humanity was on the brink of devastation. She doesn't even think her trading my soul to Jacqueline was wrong. She claims she did it for the greater good.

I force myself to smile. It's necessary to fake a cordial relationship with her. I need her to trust me.

"I tried to call you, Hunter."

Rolling my shoulders, I step onto the elevator with Jacqueline on my heels. "I left my cell phone in my car while I was patrolling the perimeter."

My mom huffs. "You'll never graduate to being a field agent unless you step up."

"It won't happen again, Dr. Sullivan." I won't give her the satisfaction of calling her Mom.

I actually left the HPA issued cell phone in a lockbox I've hidden in the empty field where I usually park my car when I'm on perimeter patrol. While I doubt the board will track me because I've given them no reason to be suspicious, I don't like to carry my work phone unless I have to. I also use a prepaid phone for personal use to make it harder for the board. It's not perfect, but Nadia and I are willing to risk it to stay in contact with one another.

"It better not. We have a reputation to maintain."

Jacqueline doesn't say anything through our conversation, and when the door slides open, she exits first. I follow Dr. Sullivan out, and she leads the way to a restricted area I've never had access to. She stops in front of the door and enters a pass code before it opens.

Cold air hits my face, the temperature vastly cooler in this section. The plain cement corridor greets me with bare, recessed lighting running along the ceiling. Dr. Sullivan's black stilettos echo as she struts in front of us, and I glance at Jacqueline who stares straight ahead, stone-faced. She's not giving anything away.

I clear my throat. "What zone is this?"

Dr. Sullivan glances over her shoulder. "It's the green zone."

I scrunch my brows, trying to remember what that means.

"It's the holding area of non-threatening supers," Jacqueline whispers.

I stiffen my shoulders. Dr. Sullivan stops in front of a door with a small window. I shove my hands in my pockets and press my lips together, feigning a bored expression to mask my curiosity.

"What are we doing here?" I ask.

Dr. Sullivan touches my shoulder. "Congratulations,

Hunter. You've been promoted to caretaker of the green zone with Agent Camille. The board sees great potential with you two as partners. The green zone will give you experience for field work." She adjusts her glasses from her head to her nose, and they reflect blinding light in my eyes.

I drop my gaze to the floor, the corners of my mouth twitching up. "Awesome." My voice sounds flat, but I haven't exactly been enthusiastic since reuniting with my body.

Tugging me closer to the door, she points through the window cutout before tapping her nail on the plexiglass. "The green zone is practically empty for now, so it won't be overwhelming. This specimen was caught assisting a shape shifter. He beat up an agent before being tranquilized."

I peek in the window, blinking to hide my surprise. "What is he? He looks human."

Dr. Sullivan chortles. "That's what his DNA says."

"Why are we keeping him?"

"Because I'm not fully convinced he is. He's unaffected by Serum-A127," she says.

I rub my hand across my forehead. Serum-A127 is an amnesia-inducing drug that allows the HPA scientist and doctors to manipulate the memories of humans. It's their way of cutting a human's ties to the supernatural world without having to hurt humans. "Interesting."

"He fought fiercely to protect a shifter, so we think he's working with the Creature Council. He'll be detained until we get answers."

"And then what?" I catch Jacqueline's eyes, and she shakes

her head. "Never mind." I know what the answer is. We're at the termination facility after all. It's where they bring supers to murder them.

I watch the guy shift on the bed to glance at the window. He meets my stare, and I think about how one of these days it could be Nadia imprisoned, or even me, for going against the board. I stayed to protect her. But what about everyone else? I want to make a difference, and this might be my chance.

The guy's blond hair shines in the harsh lighting, his bluish-green eyes creasing in the corners from frowning. He wears plain white scrubs that are the standard attire provided by the board and looks miserable. Seeing him locked in this room reminds me of my time imprisoned in Jacqueline's mind with no one to help me until Nadia came along, and I remember how hopeless I felt. No one deserves that kind of fate. I'm going to have to figure out how to save him.

ACKNOWLEDGEMENTS

I'D LIKE TO thank first and foremost, Jamie Hall, who was the very first reader for *Lost in Dreams*. She saw my novel at its roughest and still loved the story enough to read every draft I sent her way. She spent many late nights talking me through characters and plot points, and I don't know what I'd do without her. Secondly, I'd like to thank both Bev Katz Rosenbaum and Marlene Engle for their editorial insight. Your knowledge and expertise was invaluable.

I'd also like to thank Jan Moran, my mother-in-law, for helping me make *Lost in Dreams* possible. It would've never made it into my readers' hands if it weren't for her knowledge, passion, persistence, and the faith she has for me and all my endeavors.

I owe so much to my husband, Eric, for all the hours I spend sitting at my desk, lost in my head, and for thinking I'm only a little bit quirky for conversing with imaginary people. Thanks to my daughter, Zoë, for sharing my love of books at such an early age.

Thanks to my mother, Elaine, for encouraging me to continue writing when I want to give up, for introducing me to creative writing through her own stories, and for all her unconditional love. Thanks to my father, Gary, for sharing my love of all things fantasy and supernatural. No one I know is more enthusiastic about supernatural creatures than he is. Thanks to my step-dad, Eddie, for his love, kindness, and guidance over the years. I know my teenage years weren't always easy. Also, thanks to my step-mom, Sue, for her love and support.

More thanks is owed to my family and friends for their support through the years—thanks to Jazmin Garcia for reading my novels and loving my characters as much as I do, and for letting me talk about them as if they're real people. Thanks to Renee Behrens for sharing the same love of fantasy and art. Thanks to Malory for rekindling my love of reading many years ago after I took a year hiatus from opening a book. It wasn't until then that I wanted to write novels.

And lastly, a special thanks to the rest of my family and friends, without your support, I might still be lost in my dreams.

ABOUT GINNA MORAN

GINNA MORAN IS a writer from sunny Southern California. She started writing poetry as a teenager in a spiral notebook that she still has tucked away on her desk today. Her love of writing grew after she graduated high school, and she completed her first unpublished manuscript at age eighteen.

When she realized her love of writing was her life's passion, she studied literature at Mira Costa College in Northern San Diego. Besides writing novels, she was senior editor, content manager, and image coordinator for Crescent House Publishing Inc. for four years.

Aside from Ginna's professional life, she enjoys binge watching television shows, playing pretend with her daughter, and cuddling with her dogs. Some of her favorite things include chocolate, anything that glitters, cheesy jokes, and organizing her bookshelf.

Ginna Moran loves to hear from her readers so visit her online at www.GinnaMoran.com. You can also find her on Facebook, Twitter, Instagram, and Snapchat (@GinnaMoran). To stay up-to-date on new releases, sign up to her newsletter. You'll not only get a FREE story, but you'll be able to participate in monthly giveaways!

Ginna Moran is currently hard at work on her next novel.

www.ingramcontent.com/pod-product-compliance
Lightning Source LLC
Chambersburg PA
CBHW051634180726
48284CB00006B/1728